GOODBYE, PARIS

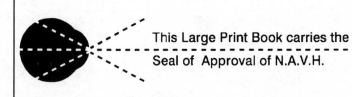

This Large Print Book carries the
Seal of Approval of N.A.V.H.

GOODBYE, PARIS

ANSTEY HARRIS

THORNDIKE PRESS
A part of Gale, a Cengage Company

GALE
A Cengage Company

Farmington Hills, Mich • San Francisco • New York • Waterville, Maine
Meriden, Conn • Mason, Ohio • Chicago

LIBRARY OF CONGRESS CIP DATA ON FILE.
CATALOGUING IN PUBLICATION FOR THIS BOOK
IS AVAILABLE FROM THE LIBRARY OF CONGRESS

ISBN-13: 978-1-4328-5953-4 (hardcover)

Published in 2018 by arrangement with Touchstone, an imprint of Simon & Schuster, Inc.

Printed in Mexico
1 2 3 4 5 6 7 22 21 20 19 18

For Colin

CHAPTER ONE

We were staying at David's apartment in Paris the night the woman fell onto the Metro tracks.

It was late July, one of those sweating, angry evenings when the heartbeat of the city quickens as it reaches a breaking point, where it readies itself for the rushed exit of August. Shopkeepers hurry their customers through with the same urgency that they will use to take to the motorways any day now. Children bubble with excitement and young people shout across the summer air. They will all be leaving in less than a week and they can't wait. I've never been in Paris long enough to feel like that about it.

That night, David and I had been to the conservatoire for a concert. It was a surprise gift, a romantic gesture.

"These are for you," he said, and slid the envelope across the breakfast table towards me. It said *For Grace* in his neat handwriting, the sloping letters drawn with the black fountain pen he always uses. "You've been working too hard. And I" — he stood up and came to my side of the table, curling his arms around me and kissing my face — "have been a lousy boyfriend."

"As if."

David is never a lousy boyfriend. He thinks of everything and leaves nothing to chance; it's part of his charm.

I opened the envelope, gasped at the program, the appropriateness of it. David can bring things to my life that I don't even know are missing.

"What did I do to deserve this?"

"I'll think of something," David said. "Maybe coming all the way here when you've been working nonstop for weeks? Maybe for being so patient and forgiving me for missing my last two trips over to you? Maybe just for being beautiful." He pushed my side plate out of the way, leaving a thin trail of apricot jam across the table. He pulled me to my feet. "You want to earn those concert tickets, both of them?"

We went back to bed, laughing.

In the ornate concert hall of the Paris Conservatoire, I sat openmouthed and barely breathing as that year's finest students gave their end-of-year recital. A young cellist, not even out of his teens, did such justice to Corelli's "La Follia" that it brought tears to my eyes. When I was his age, even when I practiced for six hours a day, I could not play like that. I lacked the right kind of soul.

David had a perfectly ironed white handkerchief in his jacket pocket and he handed it to me, gesturing towards the fat, quiet tears about to tip onto my face. He smiled as he did it.

We only have three days together: two nights and three precious days in Paris before I take the two-hour train journey back to the UK and he heads off home to Strasbourg. We try not to pack these short trips full of activities. We spend our time cooking or trailing our fingers along the edges of market stalls, wondering which vegetables to get, how best to dress salad: mundane and comforting domesticity.

We get up late and go to bed early, cocooned. We mostly stay in the apartment, drinking coffee on the iron balcony, or we drape ourselves across the deep sofas and listen to music. We don't go out to restaurants and we don't have friends here; it would dilute our tiny amount of time together, time made precious by its scarcity.

So it is unusual for us to be standing at the Metro station, to be traveling home with those people itching to leave the city. The Porte de Pantin foyer is crowded; we knew it would be. We could have waited at a bar nearby, sat outside and watched the swallows dive for the evening gnats above us in the open air, but we want to be back. I will be leaving tomorrow afternoon; our time is so brief, so funneled in, that even the blissful moments at the concert seemed like a tiny treachery.

David takes my hand and we squash between the other passengers. We walk along the white-tiled corridors, down into the belly of the packed station.

On the platform, a fug of hot engine grease hangs in the air like the ghost of a train. The old-fashioned box sign clicks through its announcements; the next train is only moments away. We get ready to jostle our way through the crowd, the girls with impossibly slim legs in bright-colored trousers, boys in suit jackets with their sleeves rolled back, just once, to reveal knobbly wrists, old women in gabardine raincoats who must be stifling in the heat.

Directly in front of us, her feet almost touching the platform edge, is a woman. She wears some kind of salwar kameez in black and a shimmering head scarf threaded through with gold across her hair and shoulders.

Everything happens too fast. I can't register the order of events, let alone the consequences. One moment she is there, her feet parallel with mine, her shoulders the same width, her head the same height, and then she vanishes. She crumples to the floor like a conjuror's trick. I see how her knees buckle and I get ready for her head to hit the ground, although I am not swift enough to catch it. My getting ready takes the form of a split second's anticipation rather than any action.

But there is no ground for her to hit. She is standing at the very edge of the platform.

Someone screams and I hear the rumble of the train.

I look at my own feet, at the rail down below where the mice scuttle, at the lump of her, unconscious and curled in the black sump of the railway track.

Next to her is David.

More screams. Not mine, but all around me people are screaming. They are shouting words I don't understand. I am — utterly — frozen.

"*A l'aide bon Dieu! Au secours!*" David shouts up at the platform. He is half standing, one leg bent and his foot under the rail, bracing. The other leg is straight, deep in the pit of the track. He has the woman in his arms, cupped like a baby, her head lolling downwards and her shawl trailing onto the rail.

The rumble of the dragon in the tunnel gets louder. A blaring noise startles everyone. In hindsight, I presumed the helpless train driver could see them in his headlights.

Three or four men get onto their knees at the edge of the platform. They drag the woman from David's arms and pass her behind them. Once more she is right in front of me.

They pull David by his arms and shoulder blades, heave him clear a second or two before the train grinds to a screeching stop in front of us, in the spot where his shadow is still warm, where drops of his sweat are left behind on the tracks.

The woman is unconscious and people fuss around her. She is lying on her back and, through the folds of her clothes, I can see that David has saved not one life but two.

I hear myself giving instructions, loudly telling people what to do. "Tip her over. You must put her in the recovery position. She can't lie on her back like that when she's pregnant." But I'm speaking in English and no one reacts. I buy every new pregnancy book that comes out, even now. I am something of a barrack-room expert.

I push past a large man who is crowding over her and start to move her into the recovery position. David shouts in rapid French and I assume he is telling those other hands to let go, that I can manage this.

I can manage; the woman is slight, even smaller than me. I assume in my racing head that she has fainted with the heat and this heavy burden of baby. Her pulse is solid, her breathing clear. I put my ear by her mouth to be sure and can see the tiny black hairs around her upper lip, the rouge on her cheeks.

A man in uniform comes along, wrenching his way through the crowds gathered around. He skitters to a halt by us and I assume he is the train driver.

David shouts across the thick crowd. *"Est-ce qu'il y a un médecin ici? Elle a besoin d'un médecin."*

A woman pushes her way through the crowd and kneels beside me.

"Je suis sage-femme," she says and puts her hand on the woman's face.

"Je suis Anglaise," I say before she can

13

continue talking. Later, David tells me that she said she was a midwife, but she may as well have been a florist. I just wanted someone else to be in charge.

David pulls at my hand. "Come on." He helps me up and out of the way. He turns towards the exit and starts to lead me through the crowd.

"Shouldn't we wait and see if she's all right?"

"We need to get a phone signal, call an ambulance." He is running towards the escalator and, breathless, I trip along behind him. "I'll run up, see you at the top." Even in this rush he turns and smiles at me, makes sure I'm calm and on my way up into the light.

I watch him run up the escalator; a tall man, an inch or two bigger than most other people in a crowd, broad shouldered and fit. His jacket is so elegantly cut that it doesn't really move as his elbows power like pistons and he nears the top of the long staircase. At the top he disappears and I hurry up.

"It's OK, Grace," he says when I get up into the foyer where we started. "The train driver sent up a signal. The ambulance is on its way." He pulls me to him, bends over the top of my head, and buries his face in my hair. I can feel the tension ripple through him, almost smell the adrenaline. "Let's go home."

This humility is so very him. The last thing he would ever ask for is praise. He knows who he is and what his faults are. He plays down his strengths.

He is, in one of my few French phrases, totally *bien dans sa peau:* happy in his skin.

We walk back up to the street and hail a cab. The roads around us are as we left them. The air is thick and exotic, the pavement dry and dirty in spots, the outside seats of cafés full with chatter and the sounds of Paris.

It does not feel like David nearly lost his life or, worse, that I stood with my hands by my sides and almost watched him be smashed by a train, gone forever. Those things will hit us later.

We get into the apartment and lock the door tightly behind us.

In the taxi I had tried to talk about what had happened but David had shaken his head at me, one finger across his lips in a gesture of silence, of secrets. This city, his city, is a small one. It had not occurred to me that the driver might speak English.

At home, he kicks off his shoes, looks

down at the knees of his linen trousers, black with grime. He walks over to the sink and washes his hands methodically, turning them around and around under the running tap, soaping them three separate times.

"Sit down, sweetheart," I say and move behind him, my hands on either side of his waist.

"God, I'm sorry. Are you OK?" He wheels around, looks straight in my face. "You must have been terrified."

I hold him tight and feel his arms slide around me in response, pressing my face into his chest. "Me?" I ask him. "You're nuts. You just came within a whisker of being killed. You're worried about me?"

"I just thought how I would feel if it was you on that track. And then, in another sense, I didn't think at all. It was instinct. Somewhere, someone feels about her like I feel about you. I owed it to that person."

Tears well up in my eyes and I think about how close I came to losing him, that for a few heart-stopping moments I'd been convinced that would be how tonight ended. I can't bring myself to think about the way that would play out, how mourning David would even begin.

I shudder and grip him tighter. David kisses the top of my head and loosens his hold on me. "I think we need a brandy." He is smiling again, color has returned to his face, and his skin looks smooth and soft.

"Drink this, darling," he says, and puts a round goblet into my hands. I realize I am trembling.

I blow into the brandy and feel the fumes flood my face. My cheeks redden. I take a sip.

David holds his glass in one large hand. With the other, he reaches across and pops the catch on the balcony doors. He tucks them back into the walls and the noise of the river, of the city, floats in to join us. It is wonderfully calming.

The apartment has one bedroom, just along the chalk-white corridor, and a bathroom designed for indulgence. David talks about letting clients use the apartment when necessary, but, as far as I know, none of them ever has. Just in case, though, it retains this elegant air, this impersonal but classic Paris *feel,* from the moment you step out of the art deco elevator, all dragging iron doors and colored glass, to the floor-to-ceiling balcony doors with their hazy drapes.

The fifth-floor windows overlook Passy Cemetery on one side and the river Seine on the other. If you could crane your neck around the next corner, the edges of the next-door apartment, you would see the Eiffel Tower; as it is, you have to rely on trust that it is there.

"The concert was something else," David says, and I realize I'd forgotten all about it in the crisis.

"Did you know it would be 'La Follia' when you booked it?" I'm curious; Corelli's version of the little folk tune is in my all-time top ten of music, but I can't remember telling David that.

"Of course I knew." He is on the balcony, leaning with his back against it and looking in through the tall gap at me. "It's almost always in your CD player and, when I came over last time, the dots were on your music stand."

"I'm so grateful. I love it so much."

"That's not why, though." He wrinkles his forehead up and under the dark fringe that almost touches his eyebrows. " 'La Follia,' the madness, that's the song that plays in my head every time I see you walk into a room."

He looks down as he says it. It isn't intended as a boast; he's almost embarrassed at the intimacy, the romance. "Right, make yourself busy, darling. I need to change these filthy trousers. I want to shower, too. Will you be OK? I won't be more than fifteen minutes."

"I've got plenty I need to do," I say. "I haven't checked the shop emails all day." I don't want him to be distracted worrying about me, so I mention these mundane things with a calm I don't really feel.

I open the laptop amid the noise of David's shower, the water playing on the tiled floor in the background. The sounds of having him nearby make me feel content, loved.

When I'm in France, my laptop home screen shows the headlines from Metronews; it's not too highbrow for my feeble French, and translating the stories helps me develop my language skills. I need little translation to understand the front-page story of this evening.

CCTV images capture the grainy shape of a man on the Metro track. It could be anyone. I click through to the story. *L'hommemystère* and *héros du soir* are pretty clear, even to me. I manage to decipher that the young woman is fine, that she fainted in the heat and is eternally grateful to David for saving her.

There is a Paris-wide appeal to find the man and thank him for his bravery. The news has been dark and miserable lately, and what David did seems to have given

Paris an antidote. A banner flashes up across the bottom of the screen: *Qui était-il?*

None of the pictures are clear enough to be certain that it's David. The crowds were heavy, but one can certainly see that the man is unusually tall, and that he has thick dark hair and an elegant light-colored suit. No one would be able to see his smaller, unremarkable girlfriend or pick her out by her ordinary short hair, feathered around the fringe and sides, or her neat, green skirt.

Lower down the page I notice a grainy still with a black square across it and inside the black square, a white arrow. My fingers are tense on the keyboard. It is a video clip from the station's security system.

When I press play, David is bounding up the escalator, unmistakably David for anyone who knows him. Behind him, inelegant, and not nearly as fast, a small woman in a bright-colored skirt scurries to keep up.

Anyone would know it was him, us. You can see by the way he glances back that he has a vested interest in the woman behind him. Anyone could tell we are a couple.

Even his wife.

Even his children.

CHAPTER TWO

My trip home is uneventful. Whenever I return to England and leave David behind I'm sad, but the end to this visit has been unexpected and uncomfortable. The shock of what happened left me anxious and clingier than I would ever normally be; at the same time, it left David wired and touchy.

I had to tell him about the CCTV footage and I could see immediately how affected he was by it. His normal composure was engulfed by a surge of the adrenaline that still buzzed through him. He shut himself in the bedroom, the door slammed against the attention of the media, the world, and, as an innocent victim of that, me.

The high ceilings of the flat bounced an echo of his rapid French. While he shouted into the phone, I could hear him pacing up and down behind the door.

When he came out he was awkward, preoccupied. He went into the kitchen and searched through the kitchen drawer for the stale packet of cigarettes we left there after a Bastille Day carnival last year. He went out onto the balcony to smoke, pulling the tall French window shut behind him to keep the smell off the curtains.

When he came back inside he just needed me to hold him, and we did not speak for some time. Eventually his mobile rang again and the spell was broken.

David is taking his family to Spain for a few days. No doubt the surprise holiday was met with whoops and yells of excitement by his children, less so — I would imagine — by his wife, for whom spontaneity does not come so easily.

Although they still live in the same house, David and his wife rarely talk nowadays. If David has to call her, he is gentle enough to make sure I can't hear him. He takes himself off to another room or stands outside on the balcony or the pavement. He does his best not to hurt me, not to rub it in.

I have learnt, over the years, to avoid thinking about David's home life. To imagine that he and his wife share a bedroom, that they used to talk in the dark like we do, would twist a cruel knife deep into an already livid injury.

For me, suspending my disbelief has become as natural as breathing. I have had eight years to practice. I know that I am doing wrong; I am not a natural mistress, not an accomplished fisher of other women's husbands, but the way that David and I met, the way we began, is very different from most other love stories. Our relationship is not, and never has been, without its reasons.

When I get home, the mail is piled against the inside of the door. There is something so bleak about the little eruption of communication, so impersonal. It reminds me — every time — that the whole world ticks and turns when I'm with David, even though we feel as if we've enchanted ourselves.

I walk around my empty house making an inventory of the silence. Everything is as tidy as I left it: the carpets hoovered, little furrows of tamed fibers not trodden down by anyone; the clean dishes put away in the cupboards; the bedspread neat and flat.

In my en suite there is a spider in the bath. He is round and black and stubborn. He's probably been there for days, absolutely certain that this is his bath and his alone.

I poke him gently with one finger, trying

to get him to walk onto my open palm and to safety. He rears up, furious and ineffectual.

"I'm only trying to help," I whisper at him.

I look around for something soft enough to rescue the spider with. I'm already worried that I might have damaged his fragile little legs when I tried to coax him onto my hand. The nailbrush has soft filaments and he grudgingly takes the lifeline I've offered. I put the brush and its precious cargo on the floor behind the basin. When I look back, after I've unpacked my wash bag, the spider has gone. I'm relieved I didn't hurt him. Not for the first time I am conscious of how much this house could do with a pet.

"Just you and me, I'm afraid," I say to the hiding spider.

It is ten o'clock and a warm, patient day; I have much to be grateful for. David left for Spain at first light this morning and I didn't want to stay in the apartment without him. I was on the train, rushing across English soil, by eight. There is a whole day to fill with whatever I want now; bright, clear hours of quiet. No one is expecting me, no one knows I'm home.

I go downstairs into the sitting room and

open the windows. The smell of sunshine seems to ease the silence and I feel instantly better, positive.

There is still a thrill to knowing I have the time — and the privacy — to play. My cello stands silent in the corner of the sitting room and its pull is hypnotic. Before I met David, I spent every spare minute I had, or could find, playing the cello. With him — for the first time — I didn't resent the diversion; there was room for them both, albeit alternately, in my life. One day, I promise myself, I will bring them together.

I take my cello from its stand. I sit down and turn the tiny fine tuners on the tailpiece until the strings tighten to pitch. I flick the A string with my fingertip and feel the vibration against my cheek. I listen for the note, gauging how close it is to perfect.

Outside, birds call into the warm air and the occasional car rattles past in the street. I am alone and I am ready to play.

I fill my mind with the choices, tunes vie with one another to come to the front, to be the one I pick. It is only ever going to be "La Follia."

I take the bow from its case.

I roll the silver button at the end of the bow between my fingers and the hair shortens and draws into place.

With my eyes closed, I picture the notes, the first bars of "La Follia."

I put my fingers in position across the strings and the previous twenty-four hours run away from me through the neck of the cello and out along its lightning conductor into the floor. The tension runs from my arm into the wood of the bow and I'm gone.

My knees poke out, bony and white, cushioning the pointed lower bouts of the cello, and the scroll rests, where it belongs, against my ear. The cello takes up its rightful place and I become nothing more than a mechanical part of it.

This is what I have always done, how I have always found myself when I've been lost. When I first went to music college, eighteen years old and paralyzingly shy, when ringing my parents from the pay phone in the corridor just made me miss them even more, I would feel the strength in the neck of my cello, flatten the prints of my fingers into the strings, and forget.

I play and play; through thirst, past hunger, making tiredness just a dent in my soul. I play beyond David's marriage, his holiday, even how frightened I was when he disappeared below the platform.

I play on until the world is flat again and the spaces between my heartbeats are as

26

even as the rhythm on the stave in front of me.

There is a tapping on the window. I worry I've been too loud, that my neighbors are trying to nap on this lovely afternoon and think I've turned my stereo up full blast. According to the sitting room clock, I've been playing for almost three hours.

Whoever tapped on the window has moved, sideways, to the front door. The doorbell is a piercing squeal through the notes I left hanging in the air. It draws a definite line under my tune.

It is Nadia.

"Holy fuck, Grace. Was that you?" She has her feet planted firmly on my doormat, her face close to mine.

I'm too slow and it's not convincing. "Was what me?"

"That was you, Grace. That was you playing the cello. I thought it was a CD. Jesus."

A terror inside me threatens to rise out of my mouth. I can feel my skin pulsing scarlet and my forehead beading with sweat.

"Are you all right?" asks Nadia. She looks quite concerned.

I open my mouth but I feel too sick to speak. I put one hand out onto the door frame.

"Fuck's sake, Grace, what is it?" Nadia steps into the hallway. "Maybe you should sit down."

"I'm fine." My mouth is full of dust, my tongue and tonsils too big for the dry space. I try to swallow but I can't. There is a fizz on my skin as every tiny hair raises in defense. Purple blotches of panic manifest themselves across my forearms.

Even the thought of someone hearing me play can leave my head swimming, my lungs tight and choked. I haven't played in front of anyone for over twenty years. I squeeze my sweating palms together.

"Do you want, I dunno, a glass of water or something? Cup of tea?"

Nadia is genuinely worried.

I nod. My shoulders slump against the cool paintwork of the hallway wall. I wipe my palms on my skirt, to rub away the imaginary dirt, the shame of being heard. For other people it is rats or heights or blood, but this is the stuff of my nightmares.

Nadia is in the kitchen, her back to me as she fills the kettle. "Is it too warm for tea? Should we have a cold drink?" She opens the fridge. "No, then. Because there's nothing in here, Grace. Not even milk." She hasn't grasped the seriousness of the situation, hasn't noticed my agitation.

I force myself to speak, hoping I can change the subject, compose myself before she comes back into the hall.

"I was in France." I sound petulant. I don't know why I'm defending myself to my seventeen-year-old Saturday shop assistant, but Nadia often makes me feel like this. I fight for some neutral territory. "How was business while I was away?"

Nadia has been watching the shop for me. She is teenaged, rude and angry, but she is a wonder with the customers. They adore her.

David gets on particularly well with Nadia. Something about the two of them really chimes. I know it's because he's so experienced with teenagers that he can talk without being patronizing, because that's what he does at home, but I fight down those intrusive truths.

Last year David and Nadia cooked up a plan — a surprise for me — between them. The subterfuge and planning that went into it warms my heart. The Cremona Triennale is a violin-making competition that carries the title of Best in the World: to win a gold there is as good as any Olympic medal. There are four categories: violin, viola, cello, and double bass. David decided to enter me for the cello competition and Nadia agreed to give him all the technical information he needed. I've always wanted to enter but, like so many things I yearn for, I was just too afraid. David had absolute faith that I could do it, but, just in case, he made sure my application was in — a done deal — before he told me.

It's not just vanity or fame at stake; the winners of each category are considered the top makers in the world. Collectors from every country desire their work and the price of their instruments skyrockets. Winning would mean I could close my shop and work from home, a home far closer to David.

Talking about the new cello is my way back in, my way to direct the conversation onto solid ground, away from the precipice of my fears. I need to move her attention out of this room. "I finished the varnish on the Cremona cello. Did you see?"

Nadia is more desperate to tell me what she thinks of the cello than I am to hear about it; my blood is only just slowing back down. There is still an uncomfortable thunder in my ears, my skin is still prickling hot, but Nadia has moved on.

While she is talking, I lose concentration. To the left of her, the fridge front is stuck with a montage of photos of David and me.

The one of us in New York is on my eye level; I am face-to-face with David's smile, with the way his arm drapes across my shoulder. I can see the blurred skyscrapers in the background down long straight streets.

Eventually, when we have our own family, this trickle of time will become a torrent. David will move in here; he will bring items of his past, connections, permanent fixtures. We will have spare bedrooms for his older children and they will require pictures of the holidays they had when they were younger; even this trip to Spain will be photographed, will be part of their arsenal of memories.

Perhaps, eventually, when everything is sorted — when the children David and I will have are older, school-aged or even at university — things will be civilized with his ex-wife. Maybe she will move on too, re-marry, build her own new collection of travels and experiences and photographs. When that happens, perhaps the pictures of their lives together will be split between the two homes, the two new families.

"And one of the customers kept looking at my tits while I was playing."

I startle back into Nadia's conversation. "Jesus, who did? What?"

"No one, but you weren't fucking listening and you are now."

I mumble an apology and pour boiling water onto herbal tea bags. It's not what I want and even less likely to be Nadia's first choice, but there's no milk or juice. There's not really anything at all if Nadia were to open the cupboards and look, but luckily she doesn't.

I need to ask Nadia what really happened in my shop while I was away, but before I can speak, she wheels around to look at me. Her eyes are bright as a blackbird's; I swear she has prey in her sights.

"So why didn't I know you play cello like that? Why doesn't anyone?"

I pull a chair out from under the kitchen table and sit down. I don't look at her. "Leave it, Nad. Please."

Maybe an older person might have noticed the need to drop the subject, heard the flat surrender in my voice, but Nadia is only seventeen. "You're amazing. I'm not kidding you. I honestly thought you were a fucking recording. Why haven't you played before?"

The inside of my mouth feels like it will crack. My lips are stuck together as if I have varnished over both of them and the gap between them has disappeared. Only David knows why I won't play in public; can't play, even for him.

I put my elbows on the table, cover my eyes with my fingers and press hard. It loosens my mouth. "I got kicked out of music college."

"No way."

"When I was nineteen. I don't talk about it. I never have." Except, I think to myself, to David — and even when I tell David, I only tell him parts of it.

I stuck out like a sore thumb all my life. Carrying a cello around everywhere you go isn't really something you can hide. I didn't fit in anywhere until I got to music college. There, finally, I was completely normal. More than normal: for once, I was good at something that other people wanted to be good at too. That hadn't happened at school; no one cared about music there — the badges of honor in the sixth form were hockey or tennis or, the ultimate, getting a boyfriend with a car. I didn't excel in any of those. I didn't even compete.

At music school I did, finally, find a boyfriend. A boy as studious as me, as shy and quiet. A boy with black straight hair and white straight teeth. A boy who slept with my best friend on what was already the worst day of my life.

"I was thrown out," I say to Nadia when the memories become too much. "I didn't even do my second year."

I press my fingers down on the kitchen table to try and keep calm. My fingernails glow white from the blotchy pink skin around them.

"So what? You're fucking awesome. Play anyway." Nadia is away with the idea. She is too young to understand that life doesn't always let you have what you want.

"It's not what I'm good at. I'm a restorer and a maker. Not a performer."

She is shaking her head slowly. Nadia wears black eyeliner, thickly painted, across the outside edges of her eyelids. It tapers to tiny flicks and makes her already almond eyes even more striking. Her father is Arabic and she takes her coloring and bone structure directly from his side of the family. Her mother is a tall, thin European with a marked sense of style. Nadia has the best of both parents. "College isn't everything," she decides.

"Isn't it?" I'm short of breath, uncomfortable with the subject. I wish she would just go home.

"It really isn't. They don't know shit." She tries smiling at me. "So you never play in front of anyone else? Not even David?"

I shake my head. I wish it were otherwise.

"Do you want to?" Nadia has a way with the truth that's like an arrow. Sometimes her perception amazes me.

I want to play for David, almost more than I want anything. I've tried counseling; I've tried therapy. I've sat in front of him — motionless behind the cello — trying not to cry, until he finally took the cello from me, held my hands in his, and begged me to just be happy with what we have.

When David finally leaves his wife and we set up a home together, I know — in a fundamental way — that it will all be fine. I will be able to play for him and he will sit, content, and listen.

"So anyway, your secret's out now," says Nadia.

I still have a mental picture of David and I jump, worried that she knows.

"You're a brilliant player. Awesome."

At college, Nikolai Dernov had despaired of me. He was the most eminent professor in our conservatoire, his reputation as a musician and a teacher rippled across the world. In my second month there, I was picked for his personal master class: Nikolai Dernov's famed quintet. I remember trembling as I read the pale orange slip of paper in my pigeonhole, telling my mum on the phone in awed tones. Only the very best played for Nikolai.

We crowded into a small rehearsal room as summoned; the heating was up too high and the air was thick. There were six of us when there should only have been five: one of us was playing for survival from the first draw of the bow across the strings. I probably would have been too frightened to stay at all if it hadn't been for the smile of the dark-haired boy with the viola.

The creased and photocopied sheet music that had been in our pigeonholes with the invitation was Mozart's String Quartet no. 5 in D Major. Even though he'd clearly picked a piece we should be familiar with, Nikolai could not possibly have known that I had spent a three-day workshop that summer, organized by my youth orchestra, playing just that piece. I could almost play it with my eyes shut.

As soon as we started to play, the heat of the room, the claustrophobic shyness, and the weight of what was expected of us disappeared. I swept through the bars and codas, my head moving with the music, my eyes closing in happiness when the other instruments melted into a perfect liquid sound around me.

As I soared into my favorite part of the

piece, Nikolai rapped on my music stand with the side of his hand. The stand wobbled and the air was suddenly silent, the room so quiet that the sheet music made an audible *shh* as it slithered onto the tiled floor.

"Is this a quintet I am building here?" Nikolai roared. "Or is it a solo showcase for one musician who does not know the meaning of 'together'? A player who is too proud to be anything but the star?"

The other players stared at me from around the circle, their bows lifted from the strings, their fingers frozen where they had been when Nikolai had broken the spell.

I didn't care what Nikolai said next as long as he didn't expect me to talk back. No one had ever spoken to me like that in my life and I had nothing to say. My other tutors, conductors, mentors, they had only had praise for me, had only ever talked about my talent.

I clenched my teeth to stop my lips from trembling.

"And the rest of you. While this girl needs to learn to listen, the rest of you need to learn to play like that. I have never seen sight-reading like it."

I looked at my feet, burning with shame. I should have told him that I wasn't sight-reading — that I knew the piece like the back of my hand — but my mouth was frozen, my words numb.

To the right of me, the boy with the dark hair edged the tip of his viola bow towards me. It was a tiny gesture of solidarity, a minuscule proof that he didn't hate me, even if Nikolai was using me to humiliate the others.

And then it wasn't me who Nikolai asked to leave. It was the only other boy in the group, another cellist. We would be a "viola quintet": two girls playing violin, the dark-haired boy and a Scottish girl on viola, and me. The single cellist imposter.

Each rehearsal after that, I fell a little bit more in love with Shota, the boy with dark hair. And each rehearsal, Nikolai became more convinced that he'd picked the wrong cellist.

Nikolai Dernov was the last person I played in front of. He would wholly approve of my terror at playing for an audience, any audience. In my darkest dreams on the loneliest of nights, I still hear the rasp of him clearing his throat in disgust.

CHAPTER THREE

When Nadia has gone, I sit at the kitchen table with my laptop and try to work out how long David will have to be away. Maybe it's all blown over and he can come home.

No such luck. The story has made it to the UK. The same banner headline, this time in English, runs across the screen: *Who was he? Paris Mystery Superhero.* Online news sites are making much of the girl's Islamic clothing, tying the lack of rescue into the rise of neo-fascist groups across Europe. It's nonsense. I would love to be able to call the reporters and say, "You weren't there. You don't know how it felt, how the slow motion played out and how we were all rooted to the spot."

I want to shake the orange-faced news-reader and scream at him that David jumped first because he's that kind of guy. That everyone there wanted to help, just as

I did, but that not everyone there was David.

When I navigate my way to a French website, a bilingual news channel, there are calls for the mystery man to be honored, for his gallantry to be recognized by the government. For the first time, there is a clip from the camera in the front of the train, the same chilling view that the driver had. It is worse even than I remember.

I wonder if David has seen it. He is in Spain trying to avoid exactly that. His teenagers have been unplugged from the internet and the whole family is being distracted from the TV. I wince at the thought of their togetherness and wonder whether it includes the children's mother.

Last year Nadia set up a Twitter account for the shop; she is in charge of it and tweets pictures of interesting instruments or links to music she's found online. The account is permanently logged in on my laptop and I open it up.

David is an actual hashtag. I don't know how I feel about that. I'm certainly surprised and — at first — amused. His reaction to #hérosmystère is going to be very different. This is exactly what he was worried about. And then I see what has happened. There was a silly, made-up day being celebrated on Twitter. It called for everyone to #Be-aSuperhero and, from all over the world, people have put up examples of how they joined in, of what they did. David jumped onto a train track and saved a woman's life. It couldn't be worse timing. I hover the mouse over the words and click on the hashtag. #hérosmystère is trending. It is the main topic of conversation in places as far-flung as Canada, Belgium, and Vietnam. David will be mortified.

The last few days have heaped event on top of event and I am exhausted. My bed-time ritual is the same whenever David and I are apart, but now I carry it out with even more rigor. I check my mobile for messages, in the unlikely event that the sound was turned off. I check the house phone and its answering machine and dial through to the shop and check that one. I tell myself that I'm keeping up with business, making sure I haven't missed anything while I've been out, but even I know that's a lie.

There are no messages from David.

In the morning I drive over to my shop. I could have walked, but the whole incident with Nadia has left me weak, shaken. The car smells of quality leather and its dash-board is softly backlit, subtle. David chose

41

this car, although I insisted on paying for it. We pored over car magazines and websites, for all the world like any other couple, discussing and comparing. We thought of all the things we might need to put in the car: double basses, dusty tools, and cobwebbed wood. We squeezed each other's hands at the page in the catalog that mentioned car seats and dog guards; things that will, one day, decorate our lives together.

Every time we drive this car anywhere, it paints a vivid picture of the normality that will be ours. It helps. Even driving it by myself reminds me of him. This car has far more class than one I would have chosen.

This small town is chocolate-box pretty, its heart is old — surrounding a market square that, when I was a child, still had cattle pens and auctions in it — and it spirals out to green fields and ancient hedges. Nowadays, the town is tidier and more genteel than it was. There are a lot of older people here; partly because it's so quiet and partly because the rising market has priced out younger families. I've been here — on and off — for most of my life and I like the quietness. Most of the people my parents knew have, like them, died by now. People I grew up with who are still here — and there aren't many of them —

don't really bother with me, much as they didn't at school. I spent too much time with my cello and not enough time socializing. I didn't think I needed too many friends, and that has never really changed. Around when I thought I might leave for good I met David, and stayed because it's near the Eurostar terminal.

I love my shop. It is a long way from the direction I had planned to take, the one I worked towards my whole life. But it is all my own work. Every day I open the door with a sense of my own achievement. I inhale the smells of varnish and wood shavings and I am strong and capable.

The shop is quaint. It is essential to my trade that it is like stepping back in time, that customers feel connected to history. The carpet is a nostalgic shade of country-house red and the expensive lighting run was designed, specifically, to give all the benefits of high-tech reproduced daylight.

The shop counter is a long glass cabinet, at least a hundred years old. It must once have stood in a tailor's or a dressmaker's shop. The front and sides are clear glass and the top red leather, complete with the nicks and tears of its story.

Nadia is good at keeping the shop counter

clear. She will, with just a little reminding or — sometimes — cajoling, clean the instruments, dust the shelves. She leaves the backside of the counter, below the glass and behind the bow cases where the customers can't see, absolutely filthy. I pick up a handful of drying orange peels and go to throw them away.

The work computer is on the counter above the bin. I tell myself I am going to check the work emails, look at the accounts.

It takes seconds to check the email and then Twitter distracts me from the accounts I was never really going to open. #hérosmystère is worse than it was; it's #mysterysuperhero now too and the UK is chattering with it. This must be tearing him apart.

I am constantly aware of the burden David carries in order to juggle these lives without hurting anyone, but there is nothing I can do to help. I leave him in Spain, dealing with it methodically and in his own calm way. It takes a lot to spook David.

I relax my eyes and blank out the computer screen; its content goes hazy, harmless when it has no decipherable words. The walls of the shop, lined with violins, come into focus around it. I force my thoughts away from the internet, away from David splashing around the pool at a Spanish villa, laughing and playing with his children.

The parade of violas, hanging by their scrolls, segues without incident into the violins. The violins are mainly full-size. There are forty-three at the moment and they move through an autumn of colors: reds, burnt ochre, gold-toned browns, and dark maroons that make customers think of chestnuts and old polished furniture.

There are eight three-quarter-size violins, just a little smaller than the others. These are for children or very small players but they are antiques, valuable instruments for children too talented to play on something of a lesser quality.

Nadia was once one of these children and that's how we first met. I struck up a surface-level friendship with Nadia's mother back when they started coming into the shop, back when everyone was just beginning to understand the breadth and depth of Nadia's talent.

We chatted, her mother and I; we dug into the unseen parts of each other's lives, at least as much as is polite. I don't think it was long before she began to suspect that my boyfriend might be someone else's husband and that, really, was that.

Nadia's mother and I dance around each

other but nothing ever develops. We exchange Christmas cards and a bottle of wine. The invitations to come for supper dried up long ago. I am not one of those single women whom people seek to heal anymore.

I went on a girls' night out with Nadia's mum and her friends once. I hadn't anticipated the straightness of them, the conformity, the soul-destroying responsibility they felt towards their children's success and the smooth running of their homes. It exhausted me just to talk about it. In response, I had a little too much to drink and was perhaps not as careful as I normally am when I outline the peculiar paradigm that exists between David and me. They didn't invite me again.

I like the children who come in for the tiny, but expensive, instruments. They are bright and able and have parents who tune their own lives out in favor of the needs of their little prodigies. These children are always nicely dressed and, for the most part, faintly eccentric, a little off-the-wall. These are the kind of children I would like to have. My parents and I were so different, almost apologetic, when we went into a music shop. My parents worked hard to get me the lessons and the instrument I wanted, but they never belonged in that world, it was always alien to them. A little bit of that has rubbed off on me. My train of thought slams abruptly back to David, back to the #hérosmystère. Children are the real crux of this matter; his children, our children. If his family are forced into a corner by this publicity, David and I will be denied the civilized space we had dreamed of — a peaceful time where he appears to live alone after leaving their mother and then, after a tasteful pause, meets the English lady, the violin maker. If that can't happen, his children may even hate me. My own overly cosseted childhood hasn't prepared me to deal with angry teenagers, injured children.

I was shy to the point of disability as a child. I wore my cello like armor, hid behind its shield and let it speak for me. I kept myself busy practicing and poured all my anxiety into my music instead of working on human relationships. Not much has changed.

In the shop, the cellos lean against a wall. The display is the same as for the other instruments; they start full-size, the same height and width as mine, and they teeter down to children's instruments.

They come in the same multilayered tones of tilled earth. The cellos go down to tiny sizes, taller sometimes than the children who will play them.

In the workshop behind my beautiful shop front, there is the beginning of a tiny cello, a 32nd size. It is smaller than an instrument a two- or three-year-old might play. This is a cello for an infant.

This is a cello for someone who is born to be a musician, given an instrument to lean on, roll around, pluck at, and explore until it moves into their consciousness and becomes an extension of their own limbs. I didn't start playing until I was eight, too old really. The extra edge I would have had if I'd started before I could talk, learned to read those spidery dots before I learned to read words, that extra edge would have made everything different.

It isn't finished, this little cello. It is still a set of ribs, thin strips of pale wood bent into classic curves around a bending iron. The minuscule scroll, a Fibonacci curve of wood no bigger than a baby's hand, sits on a shelf in my workshop. These pieces are hidden behind dusty cardboard boxes. What is in the boxes isn't important, what's important is that they hide the bits of that tiny instrument.

I started to make the cello eight years ago. I made it for a baby who didn't live, who was never born. I have never had the heart to finish it.

I know that today is going to be busy and that I will jump every time the door goes, imagining the gutter press on the doorstep, paparazzi in my shop. Most of my customers make appointments before they come, although a few drop by on spec. They know that if they want my undivided attention and a good chunk of my time, they have to book ahead.

I have arranged to see Mr. Williams today — he is one of my favorite customers, Nadia's, too. He isn't a great player, although he's a good one, but he's erudite and interesting and there's something delightfully anachronistic about his perfect suits and silk cravats. The other thing that draws me to Mr. Williams is that I know loneliness when I see it.

I am in the workshop at the back when the doorbell rings. It is early. Mr. Williams is never anything but on time.

When I go through to the front it's Nadia who stands, petulantly, with her finger on the bell.

"Stop it," I say, but it's a mock scold. "I heard you the first time."

She doesn't apologize for the racket, just

walks past me into the shop.

"What are you doing here?" I ask her. "It's a school day."

"I'm a big girl, Grace. We keep our own hours in sixth form." She looks at her feet. "A bit, anyway."

I don't comment.

"I'm on my way there and I called in to see you. All right?"

"Yes. Of course it's all right, but I'm working. You'll have to come through to the back."

Nadia stands behind me while I work. She is silent — unusual for her. I can hear her shiftiness behind me.

"What?" I ask.

"Nothing." She moves around the workshop picking up tools and weighing them in her hands. She knows better than to touch the instruments in pieces on the bench.

"Stop it," I say without looking behind me.

"Stop what?"

"Nadia." I turn around and look at her. "What do you want?"

She looks slightly sideways, as if my shoulder is talking to her rather than my face. I peer at her, but she won't make eye contact. "I was thinking about the other day."

I grit my teeth and push my lips together.

I can hear the grating of the knife in my hand as it pushes through the ebony of the cello peg I'm working on. The workshop clock ticks loudly. My cheeks are warm and flushed.

"I was thinking about the other day too. What were you doing at my house when you knew I was in France?"

"Watering the cat?"

"Were you going to have a party?" Nadia has a spare key for my house; I pay her to cut the grass in the summer if I'm going to be away for more than a week.

"Fuck, no. Anything but," she says. She throws her schoolbag on the workshop floor, kicks it out of the way. "Actually, I was going to sit and listen to some music. Maybe watch the telly."

I'm not sure I believe her. "Have you got no home to go to?"

Nadia just looks at me, her nose wrinkled in distaste. "Anyway, about your playing."

The weight settles deep in my stomach, my palms heat up around the handle of the knife and I rest it on the bench. "You can't just let yourself into my house. That's — I don't know — weird. I think it's weird."

She sits down on the workshop stool. "Soz." Her shrug is defensive. "I won't do it

51

again. I just needed to get away."

I put the peg down and look at her. "What from?"

"Shit," she says, and makes it clear that this part of the conversation is over.

"I'm going to coach you," she says. With other people, there might be a gentle warm-up to this. It might be a question rather than a statement or an offer couched and hidden in less controversial things. Nadia is her mother's daughter — although she'd kill me for saying it.

"Nadia, thank you. It's sweet of you. Really it is. But it's been twenty-one years; I don't want to play in public."

Nadia can't see the images that flash into my brain, the number of times I've tried to play for David; the times it's nearly worked. She could never know how much it would mean to me — let alone to him — to share my passion. I attempt to smile at her, to cover my sadness in nonchalance, but my face doesn't obey the command and my mouth twists into a lopsided grimace. I have, as my late mother would have said, got my knickers in a right twist.

"I don't want you to play in public."

I breathe a little more easily.

"I want you to play with me," she says. "I'd be so sad if I couldn't play in a group, with other people. So I've been reading my psychology textbooks. Looking at how things like this work, how they happen."

I steady my hands and remember that this is a kind gesture, an attempt to help. I try to be rational.

"Nadia." I wish she would stop talking about it.

She runs her finger through the fine black sawdust at the edge of my bench. "I can help you."

"Why now, Nad? What do you think is going to make a difference?"

Nadia turns and stares at the stand in the corner of the workshop. I follow her gaze even though I could draw every detail of what she's looking at with my eyes shut.

Nadia points to the cello I've been making, slowly and surely and with a rigid concentration, for the last year and a half.

This cello is special. Its varnish is smooth and flawless; it looks as though it has been dipped in a huge vat of molten barley sugar and come out with a fairy-tale coating of orange glass. It is my entry for the world's most important instrument-making competition.

I am not a naturally competitive person, but I try, really hard, to be the best at everything I do. Being sent away from music college before I'd even finished my first year broke my heart. If I were to win the Triennale in Cremona, Stradivari's own hometown, I know I could lay some of my ghosts to rest. I'd actually feel like a success, like I'd achieved the thing I set out to do, and that would change my life.

"The Triennale cello," Nadia says. "You need to get the sound moving. It can't go to the competition without being played in. We could do it together."

I've stopped working on the cello peg in my hand and I'm concentrating on my breathing, trying to swallow the rising fear, trying to cool the sweats. "Nad, I've tried. I swear. Counseling, therapy. I've tried everything."

She picks up her bag and swings it over her shoulder. She looks back at me as she walks out of the workshop and off to her untroubled school day. "You're already doing it, Grace. All the time."

I look at her.

"In this shop. You tune them up, you pick out little riffs for customers. It's mostly pizzicato, but it's still playing."

And Nadia is gone.

The fire under my skin burns harder than ever.

CHAPTER FOUR

David and I met at a party. I was thirty-two and had just started to find my feet and myself. I'd ridden out a basic apprenticeship working hard for someone else's profit and spent four years in an airless back room of a workshop in London. My days were spent squashed too close together between a sweating Dutch bow repairer and an Israeli double bass maker with an unpredictable temper.

I'd had a few uninspiring relationships with men as gauche or distracted as me, but, since college, I couldn't say I'd ever been in love. My work and my personal life moved forward in lethargic tandem; neither had quite found the spark.

When my parents died within three years of each other and left me their little house to sell, I used it as a springboard to stop working for someone else. My dad had dearly wanted me to start a business.

When I met David, I was just about to open my own shop.

The couple hosting the party were lawyers; Natalie was a whippet-thin high achiever who played first violin in an impressive amateur orchestra. This party would be like everything else Natalie and Jonny had invited me to: a vaguely veiled attempt to set me up with their single friends.

I'd go out with people once or twice, then shrink back into my shell, lock myself in with my cello and a bottle of wine. I screened calls and I practiced Dvořák.

Natalie directed me through the house and out onto the patio. The double doors to the garden were open and venetian blinds clicked against the glass in the faint breeze. The first decade of the twenty-first century was drawing to a close; huge Romanesque planters and enormous concrete troughs were the fashion for gardens, choking with lobelia and hot, rude colors of pelargonium.

Just past the forest of pots, a group of people stood with drinks in their hands. I looked around for someone to make a welcoming face, to smile or offer me a drink.

A tall woman with red hair was making her goodbyes. "I don't feel at all well," she said. "I'm ever so sorry." She smiled at me apologetically. "It's honestly not you. I had already said I was going." She put her hand at the top of her chest in that gesture polite people make when they want to avoid mentioning the fact that they feel sick.

"I hope you feel better soon," I said.

The red-haired woman raised her hand and waved at a man on the other side of the lawn. He nodded towards her in recognition that she was leaving.

He was completely different from everyone else at the party. He was older, possibly the oldest person there; I judged him as late thirties, maybe just past forty. He was unusually tall, distinctly handsome, and he was on his own. He saw me and smiled.

My mouth was dry when I tried a half smile back.

We introduced ourselves: David, Grace. We talked about the wine, the potted plants, the other guests. For the rest of the evening we laughed. Everything he said resonated with me. He made me sound funny; clever.

"There is this idea where I live, in France," David said, "and I didn't believe in it at all until tonight."

I could barely breathe, my face still aching with the ripples of our laughter; it was hard to set my mouth straight and listen.

"They believe in the *coup de foudre*," he said, "the lightning bolt. The French say that it will hit everyone just once in a lifetime. It could be someone you see on the other side of the street, just one time, and never even speak to. It could be when you're a child or just seconds before you die."

I looked around to see if anyone else had noticed the drop in our voices. No one had; we were the last people left in the garden.

He talked calmly, as if he was discussing something rational, a fact. "Your life is never the same again. It is an appointment with destiny. It doesn't matter what's come before or what comes afterwards; it's a moment for fate."

I looked it up a few days later. *An overwhelming passion or a sudden and unexpected life-changing event.*

Just as David had said, the *coup de foudre* took no notice of anything that had come before it. It exploded into our lives, leaving tiny blisters of chaos behind it.

If I heard my story from an acquaintance, if I knew someone who had been sleeping with somebody else's husband, trying for a baby amid the chaos of two lives and two houses and two separate sets of facts, I would think they were stupid. Naive and stupid. I am neither of those things; I never have been. If anything, I am too far the other way. I am prickly and bossy. I learnt the hard way that if you let other people make decisions for you, everything will be lost.

I have spent twenty years working and building, establishing a reputation that is, literally, worldwide. I probably drink too much and I definitely don't eat enough, but I do it when and how I want. I would love to go to France, to be closer to David. Life would be so much easier if we were just miles apart instead of me being stuck here with cultures and sea and tall unshakable cliffs separating us, but I can't leave my business.

That is the *coup de foudre.*

It is eleven o'clock. I have put coffee on for Mr. Williams. I have checked all my messages, kept an eye on the internet news. Eleven o'clock and all's well.

I see Mr. Williams through the glass of the shop door. He is wearing a gray silk cravat and a paisley waistcoat; fabulous in the dull everydayness of our twinset-and-pearls town center. His white hair is swept back into a sparse quiff and dressed with some sort of oil. He has his violin in a smart navy-blue case that I sold him last year. It is one of many and I suspect he changes them to match his outfit.

He smells delicious as he comes in.

"You look fantastic," I say. "Special occasion?"

"I like to make an effort now and again." It is part of our dance; this is Mr. Williams's everyday wear. "Is that coffee machine on?" The coffee machine is always on for Mr. Williams, has been once a week for ten years.

We walk through to the back room and Mr. Williams looks fragile as he takes the one step down from the small dark hallway into the workshop. He holds on to the door frame with his empty hand to steady himself.

The workshop is flooded with light; the windows are wide and tall and my varnish bench sits underneath them so I can see the colors I'm working on in natural daylight.

I know why Mr. Williams likes coming into this wide back room. The shelves and the benches and the cupboards are full of alchemy. Bottles and jars, chisels and knives, powders and potions, line the walls. I have paintbrushes arranged in order of size from thick inch-round dabbers to tiny single-hair retouching brushes, hairs so fine they let me retouch varnish cracks on three-

hundred-year-old wood without anyone seeing the join. There are tangy odors of
chemicals and the smell of wood hangs here
constantly; each morning fresh curls of
shavings fall into a pile beneath my desk
and perfume the room.

"A friend of mine has just kicked the
bucket," Mr. Williams says.

I am emptying biscuits onto a chipped
gray plate and drop two on the floor, taken
aback by his opener. "That's very sad."

"Old as the hills, dear, a jolly good in-
nings. May I?" Mr. Williams gestures to the
high stool at my bench and I nod for him to
sit. "Actually," he says, "he left me a violin."

I look up, definitely interested.

"Not quite what you're thinking," Mr. Williams says and smiles. "He made it himself."

This isn't uncommon. There seems to be
something irresistible to men, and it's
almost always men who dabble in woodwork, having a crack at a violin — like it's
the ultimate test of skill. I suppose I should
be flattered.

"It's a lovely thing." He strokes the violin
case. "Not to play or perhaps even to look
at, but it will be like still having a part of
him."

I touch his arm. "Let's have a look." I un-
clip the silver catches on the front of the

case. The instrument is sitting tightly inside. A red-and-white spotted handkerchief, definitely silk, is laid carefully across the front of it.

"Hold on." Mr. Williams takes something out of the inside pocket of his jacket. "Look at this first. This is Alan." The black-and-white photograph is of three young men, probably no more than twenty-five years old. They are wearing morning suits and it is, presumably, one or other of their weddings. They are all devilishly handsome, with slicked-back movie-star hair and bad-boy grins.

"And is that you?" I point at the beautiful young man on the left of the picture.

"I haven't changed a bit." Mr. Williams winks at me and the gesture makes me laugh.

"I was best man at both of Alan's weddings." He raises his eyebrows a little and, in the language of betrayal, I assume he means the second marriage had a similar start to mine and David's. "He and his second wife, Anne, made my late partner and I godparents to both their daughters. The light that those girls brought to our lives . . ."

"I've seen far worse amateur work than this." I hold the violin up to the window.

"The varnish is really pretty."

"I think so." His skin wrinkles up around his eyes when he smiles. "Do you think you could fix it for me — make it playable? I'd love to use it as my everyday instrument, think of Alan every time I play it."

"I think that's an absolutely beautiful idea." And I do. There's a lot I could do to make this instrument work. Straightaway I can feel that the belly is too thick and the action too high. The whole thing is heavy and dull in my hands. "It won't be particularly cheap, I'm afraid. Shall I do you an estimate for the work and then you can decide which bits you really need and which you don't?"

"No, Grace." He is firm. "It costs what it costs. I know you'll be fair and, frankly, I've got enough money to see me out. There might even be some left after I've expired."

I write Mr. Williams's name on a brown paper label and tie it around one of the violin's pegs. There is one slot left at the end of the rack and I stretch up on my tiptoes to slide the violin's neck into the velvet-lined recess in the shelf.

I put his coffee down on the bench and move the plate of biscuits towards him. Mr. Williams always appreciates buns or biscuits with an almost indecent enthusiasm. I suspect he had a wartime childhood, but I'd never ask him; he is sensitive about his age.

"What a lovely girl you are, Grace." When Mr. Williams smiles, his large ears move upwards into his white hair and the sides of his face crease into deep lines.

"Your violin will have to get in the queue, I'm afraid. I have some bits I need to do on my Cremona cello first and a couple of jobs on the bench. Will it wait?"

"He's already dead, dear girl, and I don't think that situation's going to change much over the next few months. Is this your grand competition cello?"

I nod and I pick the cello up off its stand. I put it on the bench, lying on its side so that we can look at it together.

"It's very beautiful." Mr. Williams dares to touch the edge of the cello.

He's right. Everything has gone just the way it should with the instrument. I didn't experiment with varnishes, wondering whether this or that might give a better shine, testing if a little more red or a little less yellow might mix me the perfect shade. Instead I stuck to the things I know. I concentrated hard on bringing together all the experience of eighteen years of making. Eighteen years of trial and error and lessons, of successes and failures, triumphs and disasters.

"How does it sound?" Mr. Williams asks. "As good as it looks?"

"I haven't tried it." I smile. "Not so much as a ping on the A string."

In my imaginary world, I'm going to cook David a special dinner, dressed up smart, and then have a formal unveiling and first play. In real life, it will just be me — in jeans and a T-shirt — locked away in the inauspicious setting of the workshop, too afraid to play in front of him.

"I can't wait to hear it," says Mr. Williams, because he has no reason whatsoever to suspect that he won't. "How incredibly special."

There is a sudden and loud ring at the front door of the shop. I make a face at Mr. Williams; we don't like our chats interrupted. "Hang on, I'll just sort this out," I say.

My heart leaps, literally, and I feel an intense emotion at the top of my throat. David is at the door. He has a key to my house, but he's never needed one to the shop.

I open the door and let him in. I don't kiss him till he's inside the shop; this is a small town and I never know which of my customers might be walking past — kissing a handsome man in my shop doorway is not what they expect of me.

He hugs me tight and I can smell his aftershave.

"What are you doing here? I'm so excited." I reach up and kiss his cheek. His skin is soft, closely shaven.

"I had to do some damage limitation. About the press."

I gesture quickly towards the open doorway where Mr. Williams can probably hear everything we say. "I've got a customer in the back."

I lead David by his hand into the workshop.

It's neat and organized in here, but with my varnishing bench, my woodwork bench, and the tall stand that holds my band saw, it's cramped with three people.

"Mr. Williams, this is my friend David. He's surprised me with a visit from Paris."

"How do you do?" Mr. Williams shakes David's hand and they exchange small talk and pleasantries. "I'll let you young people get on with it."

David is fifty-two; it's been a while since he's been called a young person, and it makes him smile.

■ ■ ■ ■

David and I are alone. I pull down the blind in the workshop so that no one walking down the road behind the shop can see in, and I kiss him for a long time.

"I can't believe you're here." I am blinking back tears. I didn't think I would see him for weeks.

"I have to try and shut this stuff down. It's everywhere, the bloody *hérosmystère.* If anything, it's getting bigger."

"Why here?" I ask. "Isn't it more important to shut it down in France?"

"I can get an injunction, very quickly and easily, in the UK. It'll damage my business if I'm suddenly a recognizable face; I can't be high profile in my personal life and invisible standing next to a client."

David's work can be very sensitive. He is at the top of the legal translation tree and stands, somber-suited and innocuous, behind some very important people during very delicate negotiations. He works for powerful people who need an expert they can trust with their lives.

"France is bloody terrible," David says as he wilts onto the chair beside my bench. "The press in France says what it likes when it likes; ours is far more controllable."

"Ours" is not lost on me. I walk over and stroke his hair, push his fringe out of his eyes. One day I will be responsible for his haircuts, booking him into the salon I go to, the one who — I think — cuts with more style than his barber in France.

I want so badly for him to be staying for a while. He doesn't have any luggage, but maybe it's in the car. He keeps a selection of "English" clothes at my house. He looks far more French when we're in Paris, dresses in a very different way.

David looks tired. Normally he doesn't look his age; he could pass for early forties. His hair is graying slightly at the edges but is mainly still brown and his skin is free of wrinkles. He spends a good deal of time in the gym and is toned and fit, his broad shoulders in proportion with his height.

"Were things OK in Spain?" I ask. This isn't the same question as "How was Spain?" We never discuss David's children or his wife; not because he wouldn't answer, but because we live in this play world, a make-believe bubble where he's just been away on business and now he is home. If we dissected his relationships, the moments he spends with his family, he would feel disloyal and dishonest.

David's wife knows that he's in love with someone else. She knows where he is when he's away. All three of us leave it at that.

David and I were the last people left at that party in Natalie and Jonny's garden. We had hung around talking. We had laughed and smiled and spun out our stories until there was no one left but us, and the hosts were sitting — tired — around their kitchen table drinking herbal tea.

"Golly, I am sorry," David said, shaking Jonny's hand and kissing Natalie on each cheek.

I reddened slightly as his skin touched hers, wished it was me.

"I had no idea it had gotten so late." David grinned at them. "How embarrassing; what dreadful guests we are. I shall see your friend here safely home and then toddle off to bed."

"Thanks for inviting me," I said out of politeness, when all I could really think about was how to avoid David going home once we'd gotten as far as my house.

It was a beautiful evening, scents of the neighboring gardens rose up on the air and few cars passed us in this end of town. We walked down the road and David reached out and took my hand. He twined his fingers into mine and we walked side by side, knowing already that this was how we belonged.

When we stopped to cross the road, it was the pause I'd been waiting for. David looked up and down the road for traffic, then, as he turned back, he reached down and kissed me.

All the hurt that had kept me company since college, all the hopeless relationships I'd made faltering false starts with, all the years I'd been mousy and shy and hidden inside myself; it all melted in an instant.

It took longer to walk back to my house than it should have. We stopped, giggling, to kiss under summer streetlights, our backs damp against dewy hedges, dusty on railings.

I felt completely different about my little house the second that David was in it. It felt like a home, like a palace. It felt warm and safe and settled.

We skipped drinks and conversation. We skipped discussion and promises. We undressed each other with trembling hands and a sense of wonder, both so aware that we would remember this moment for the rest of our lives.

I was almost tearful by the time we were naked and together in my bed. The frisson between us was everything I'd read of, imagined. I finally understood every piece of music I'd ever played.

In the last seconds before we made love, David lifted his lips from mine, his hair silhouetted in the light coming through my bedroom window.

"I'm married," he said softly, breathing into my face.

It was my decision to carry on.

In the morning, David spoke first. We were still wrapped in each other, covered by the white bedsheet he'd looped around us as we slept.

"I've never done this before."

There was a catch in his voice as if his heart would break. His arms were tight around me, my face against his chest; I felt him give a heaving sigh. "I don't know what to do next. I hardly want to leave."

The word "hardly" was a dagger. It meant that, whatever I'd told myself, whatever magic I'd hoped had been woven, he would leave. He would find his way back to his wife.

I must have flinched, shown my surprise — as ridiculous as it was. He pulled me tighter to him.

"It won't be easy but we'll sort this out." He sighed across the top of my head and my hair ruffled. "I can't stay here now, but soon. We will sort this out." He pushed his arms straight, moving me to where he could see my face. "We will be together."

We both cried when he left, not more than an hour later. We hadn't discussed any details, any practicalities. All I knew was that he lived in France with his wife and that I had to trust him. He had been struck as hard as me by this lightning bolt and I had to let him go and begin to unravel the complications it brought with it.

The sickness began three weeks after David left. He called every day, just as he said he would. It was frustrating that David couldn't give me a number to call him on our first morning together, but he posted me a mobile phone from France as soon as he got back there. It was 2002, I hadn't even begun to think about getting a mobile; I would have had no one to call on it. He bought himself a phone at the same time as mine; a hotline solely for use between him and me, a private courier of messages, a keeper of secrets.

At first I assumed I had a stomach bug. I

lay with my face on the cold bathroom tiles, close enough to the toilet bowl to lean over it and retch what seemed like a hundred times an hour. My head was thrashing and my throat burning with the acid of my continual vomiting.

I missed two of David's calls on the second day; I simply couldn't leave the bathroom for long enough to answer the phone.

After four days, even though I had graduated to sleeping in my own bed but with a bucket by my pillow, I realized that I would have to see a doctor. My face was gaunt with dehydration, my skin puckering and shiny with stress. The GP came to my house.

"Is there any chance you might be pregnant?" she asked.

"Not unless morning sickness can start in a couple of weeks and last all day and all night." I remember that I smiled as I said it.

She nodded, her eyebrows raised slightly. "You need to take a test."

My hands shook as I held the tester stick, waiting for the lines to connect in a chemical blue strip. In the three weeks since I'd met David, since we'd joined our covert world of phone calls and messages, one-line emails and snatches of conversations often interrupted, my life had taken a sea change.

When David finally called very late that night, I was still astounded, still teetering between elation and fear. I picked the phone up from beside my bed.

"I'm pregnant," I whispered into the dark.

Chapter Five

Last night, while David slept, I crept downstairs and sat with my cello in the sitting room. I rested its cool polished wood against my bare legs and thought hard about the things that matter to me, the things I really want.

Knowing David was upstairs and making sure that I focused on that, accepted it, I tuned my cello and picked a tune, pizzicato, across the strings.

I played — in a muted voice and without my bow — the first bars of Bach's Cello Suite no. 1. At college, Nikolai always said it was the very best arrangement of notes for finding out what you or your instrument could do.

"Even in Bach, you have no trust," he would say and lean his arm into mine, his hand covering my hand, pushing the bow hard across the strings. "Listen to what happens when your muscles believe, when they concentrate. You can do this with me but not alone?"

He never expected an answer from me, his questions were rhetorical and directed at my playing arm, my rigid wrist. The one-to-one sessions we had were never as painful as the group lessons, the ones where he would use the five of us in his quintet as ammunition to destroy one another. I knew it was all for our own good, but often I would be sick with fear before the lesson.

David has taught me to trust again, that he will always find time to call me whenever he can, that he thinks of me daily and spends every possible moment with me. It has mattered so much to be that valued by another human being, but I still cannot find a way over this wall that keeps part of me hidden from him.

I played — without my bow — in a whisper that I knew David wouldn't hear. I didn't play for long — three or four minutes at most — but when I got up this morning, I felt those notes hiding around the sitting room and I was quietly positive.

When I come down for breakfast, David is bent over his laptop, his shoulders solid with stress. I put my hands on them, palms against the knotted muscles. Over his shoulder I can see Twitter filling the screen.

"Bad?" I ask him, not wanting to say too many words, not wanting to make it worse.

"Fucking *hérosmystère;* it's viral. Have people nothing better to do than send these stupid messages around? It's in every French-speaking country."

"Oh." A penny drops for me.

"Oh, what?"

"When I looked it was trending in Canada and Vietnam. Somewhere else, as well. Belgium, that was the other one. I get it now. At least it's only in French." I know that doesn't help; it will be in French when David's children read it.

"There's one in English and one in Arabic." He points at the screen, at a jumble of shapes in a list of words. "There you are." He runs his finger under the text: #بطل غامض "Hashtag *al-batal al-ghamidh,*" he says.

Whenever I remember how many languages David speaks, how very un-ordinary he is, it makes me glow. It is a wonder how someone so intelligent can find the things I say funny. I've never stopped being amazed that he thinks I'm interesting.

I stroke my flat palms down his shoulders. The worry is coming off him in waves.

"Do you want me to stay here today, close the shop?" I have no intention of being anywhere else but here with him; it's an empty gesture.

"You have no chance of leaving this house today." He stands up and pulls me into his arms, kisses my hair. "I've got people working to shut this down. It won't be that bad, but I will have to go up to town and supervise them tomorrow." His sigh is longer than it should have been.

I try to look up at him but he holds me tight, his chin resting on the top of my head.

"Today belongs to us, darling girl. Just the two of us."

I don't know what I thought would happen the night I told David I was pregnant. I hadn't imagined anything past the first sentence. The relentless nausea, the prickling purple and white goose bumps crawling across my skin, the blurred vision, filled my world.

"How many weeks?" he asked after a silence like the gap between lightning and thunder. How many weeks: the terminology of experience.

"How many weeks do you think?"

"It can't be . . . I'm not. I don't think it can be mine."

"Well, there wasn't anyone else." I was surprised by the curl in my voice, the cold anger. Later it dawned on me that this was the growl of a lioness.

"Have you done a test? Seen a doctor?"

"I'm lying on my bathroom floor with an ice pack on my face. I've been here for a week. It did occur to me to see a doctor." This wasn't the conversation that people have in films, in books. This wasn't supposed to happen.

"I'll come now," he said. "It'll be OK. We'll sort it out. I'll be there by the morning."

David was with me by first light. We had spent one night together and hundreds of hours on the phone. It was an odd basis for a family, but it was ours.

"This is my fault," he said. "I should have asked about contraception. I should have been more careful."

"It didn't even occur to me. Like it couldn't biologically happen, all reason just switched off. I'm shocked at myself." I could feel the heat rising up my face that meant I would be sick again any moment. I was lying in my bed, David stroking my hair, kissing my face. "I need to go to the bathroom."

"Shh, it's OK, hang on." David rushed out, came back with the bucket I'd had by

79

the sofa. "You need to rest. You look really ill."

He rubbed my back as I heaved into the bucket, strands of clear spit dribbling from my mouth. He rinsed out my flannel in the bathroom and brought it back to wash my face.

"There, we'll sort this. Get it over with before I go back. You'll be OK." He traced the knobs of my spine with his fingers. I was alarmingly thin from the vomiting, and his fingers clicked down my vertebrae like a xylophone.

"I can't get rid of it. I'm not having an abortion." My conviction surprised me as much as it seemed to surprise him.

"What? You can't go through with this. I'm a stranger. You don't know me at all. I don't know you. I know we have this crazy . . . connection . . . but, we can't. We just can't." He buried his face in his hands. "What about your business? Your career?"

"I'll manage. People do."

"No, no they don't. People manage because they have a partner, a support network, family around them. You don't have any of those things."

I had decorated my bedroom in cool whites. I looked around the room from my bed and saw what he saw, a rootless person, an isolated orphan, an only child. There were no photos of nieces or nephews, no cards from well-wisher relatives. The room was elegant but empty. It made even more sense to fill it with our baby.

"I want this baby. I'm going to have it."

He stood up and walked across the room. He stood by the door and put his hands flat on the wall to either side of his head. He almost reached the ceiling. His head hung down in despair.

"You can't, Grace. You can't. We can't." His voice was low and quiet. "Everyone loses like this. Everyone. We will have a baby one day, I know it. But not this baby, not this time. I'm so sorry."

I leant my head forward off the bed and retched again.

David dashed across the room and got onto the bed behind me. He held me tightly to him. Even though it was only midmorning, I fell asleep in his arms. David's long body stretched out beyond mine, he tucked my head into his shoulder and my heels lay on the curve of his knees. He had been traveling since the early hours and we were both exhausted.

He was still sleeping when I woke. He looked peaceful and so very beautiful. I pictured those same dark lashes on our son or daughter, the same untroubled softness to his or her skin. Something in me didn't really believe that David would still feel the same, now that he had rested and relaxed a little. I was certain he had just been afraid.

I went quietly to the shower to make the most of a rare respite from the sickness.

The noise of the water must have woken David. He stepped into the shower with me and we made love so tenderly, so gently, that I knew everything would be all right. I couldn't tell whether there were tears on his cheeks or if it was just the spray from the shower.

We got back into bed, still damp. The afternoon sun was warming the room, the windows were wide open. I had a slight headache but wasn't sure whether it was from the upset and confusion of earlier in the morning or the sickness creeping its way back in, overtaking everything but the baby.

"I'm so, so sorry it has to be this way, Gracie," he murmured against my back. He pulled me tighter. "I'll be with you every step of the way. I'll come back for your appointment and I'll stay until you're better." He sighed. "And then I'll be here as much as I can, as often. I can't bear this; it's too awful for words."

I deliberately stayed silent. I didn't trust

this new fire inside me; I couldn't predict what it would make me do.

"It's my baggage that's the problem. It's my issues that are crippling me." He placed his face flat against my skin and it was obvious that he was crying. "I can't do it to the children I already have. Not now. They are six and eight. I can't risk their being raised by someone else. Or our baby. What if we separated? What if someone else took the role of my baby's father because I'm in another country and I can't be here?" He turned me around to face him, looked into my eyes. "I want to pick our child up from school, Grace. I want to go to sports day. I can't have furtive conversations on a mobile phone with my own child. And I can't abandon the children I have now."

Reality was cold and crawling through me. I tucked my chin into my chest to stem the rising tide of vomit that swelled in my throat.

David held me closer and continued to speak. These were words for the dark, words that revealed sores and secrets. They came out incongruous and alien on this bright August afternoon.

"I was a little boy who no one loved." He spoke slowly and evenly; it was clearly hard for him to talk about. "My parents separated when I was eight. My father remarried and began to spew out new children. By the time my mother died and I had to go and live with my father and stepmother — I was twelve at the time — he'd changed his whole method of parenting, taken on board all the responsibilities and roles he hadn't even thought about for me."

I wasn't ready for this. It was unexpected. David seemed so composed, so whole. It was hard to imagine him as a small and lonely boy.

David broke off from his story as a wave of nausea hit me. He wiped my face and went to wash out the bucket.

He came back into the bedroom and sat beside me on the bed. "They sent me to boarding school. While my three brothers stayed at home and enjoyed every indulgence imaginable. On the odd occasion I came home, I shared none of their privileges or — worse — their closeness. I didn't belong to anyone. During the school holidays, I mostly went to my mother's parents in France — it got me out of the way — but even there, I was an English boy in a household that spoke only French; I was still a cuckoo."

I pulled the sheet around me and closed my eyes tight. I didn't want this invasion of history smashing down the world I had built in my head.

"And I swore I would never do it to my children, Grace. I love them. Whatever happens between me and my . . . in my marriage, I can't start another family until my children are old enough to understand, until there's nothing left for me to miss of them."

I hadn't considered any of this in my bare and skeletal plans. I had only thought of my rosy-cheeked baby, of its downy hair and sweet face. I had only imagined David and me, side by side, watching it grow, helping it to flourish.

"You're an artist, Grace. You make beautiful instruments; you play the cello. There'll be something amazing of you left behind for future generations. I'm just a pen-pushing bean counter who happens to speak a few languages; I can't make anything, do anything. The only things I can leave for the world, if I get it right, are my children. And I can't mess that up. I can't."

The world outside my fantasy was ugly and real and intruding.

"I have to go, baby. I have to go and clear my desk, get things out of the way. I'll be back as soon as I can and we'll sort it all out. OK?"

It wasn't OK, but I said it was.

CHAPTER SIX

David is going to London to sort out the consequences of phone calls he made yesterday. The injunction against British papers reporting on the mystery hero is almost watertight. He is hoping that the disinterest in the British press will help quiet the story in continental Europe. At the moment, the world seems to be caught up in the romance of *hérosmystère,* the idea that David is some superhero figure, protecting Paris by night, mild-mannered businessman by day. The close-up clips of David being pulled off the track and the train shooting into the station are played over and over and still make me feel sick. We are trying not to think about it, trying not to let it darken these precious days together.

Nadia has been watching the shop for me. Her summer holidays are boring her and she has been edgy and easily irritated. I remember the same feeling, when six weeks was a lifetime of separation from one's routine, when the pleasure of sleeping late and doing nothing paled in days. Six weeks pass like lightning for me now.

I automatically check under the counter for Nadia's mess. I haven't even made myself a coffee. I know it will be there and I know I need to clear it away before a customer comes in and the bow cases need to come out.

Nadia's detritus is her usual style. There are two dirty teacups, one stuffed with a screwed-up crisp packet, the other still half-full of cold tea. They sit, with the nibbled-out corner of a sandwich, on a blue sketch-book.

I take the rubbish out, sighing as I do it, even though there's no one there to hear me. I carry the cups in one hand and use the sketchbook as a tray for Nadia's left-overs. Her habits are at odds with her appearance; she is always immaculate, her long black hair straightened every morning, her makeup flawless and consistent.

I put the book down on my workbench. I didn't know that Nadia draws, and I open it to see what she's been doing. I don't think she'll mind; as a violinist she has been open to the scrutiny of an audience since she was

small, and, anyway, Nadia is good at everything.

It isn't a sketchbook. It's a diary. At least,
a diary of sorts. It doesn't have dates and
times and ordered sentences of reporting.
My diary when I was seventeen was neat,
sensible; my handwriting reflecting my per-
sonality.

Nadia is angrier than I ever was. These
pages are covered in scrawls and illustra-
tions. Every profanity known to man is writ
large and colored in with furious scribbles
of blue Biro. It is the crazed, looping scrawl
of internal monologue and is clearly supposed to be private.

I should shut the book. It is not mine to
read. It almost feels as if someone else's
hands are flicking the page corners, watching weeks of Nadia's life fall flat against
each other. I stop on a block of text. And I
read it.

Fuck you, Harriet. Fuck your high-and-
fucking-mightiness. I wish you knew what
they say behind your back and I really
wish you knew about me. I'm your best
friend and I am so bored, bored of you
pretending you have a perfect life and I'm
bored of you not listening. You only care
about yourself and your stupid boyfriend.

Here's a newsflash, Harriet, a word from our sponsors — you're a dick and your boyfriend is worse. WANKERS.

The final word is in huge blue letters that take the form of bubbles and butt up against one another. I know that Harriet is Nadia's best friend, but I had no idea they'd fallen out. I do remember, though, the ricochets of teenaged relationships, the switchblade of friendships and taking sides.

I flick forward a few pages. I can barely believe I'm doing this and I cannot convince myself that I'm not looking for a mention of my own name.

I find David's first.

Today we mostly have to pretend that David isn't married. Yes we do. True story. If I want to get paid, anyway. Grace is in France. Thank God, she would do my head in if she were here. Blah blah fuckety blah, twit twit, blah. Do I think it's sweet that she still loves him after a lifetime? No, no, no, dear diary. I think they're cocks.

I'm torn between laughing at how like Nadia it sounds and being annoyed that she thinks we're less than cool. I tell myself, under my breath, that no one ever read good things about themselves in anyone else's diary. That doesn't stop me reading on.

He's nice, the married boyfriend. And he's not pushy or annoying. And, fuck, he is fit. But the giveaway is that he knows exactly how to talk to me without being an arsehole. And he's not a teacher. He doesn't work with kids, but he knows exactly how to talk to a teenager without being a massive dick. You know why, Grace? Because he lives with teenagers. True story. And you fucking know it. He lives with teenagers and he lives with their fucking mother, too. Who cares? Not me. But it does make me laugh that you think I don't know. I couldn't give two shiny shits whether he's married or not. Everyone's doing it. That's true, isn't it, dearest mummy and daddy? Everyone's divorcing or pretending. Which one of you has the boyfriend or the girlfriend? And how long will it be after one of you moves out that you'll try and pretend you just met them? And I'll shout in your fucking faces because I already knew, you massive arseholes, you haven't shared a bedroom for a fucking year. Just get on and divorce already.

Nadia's writing screams loudly in the empty shop. I am, literally, openmouthed, truly shocked by this revelation. The idea of Nadia's perfect parents divorcing is awful. The idea of her being so sad and so angry is utterly horrible. The irony and the guilt hit me at the same time and each equally hard. I wonder if perhaps she's wrong; teenagers can get the wrong end of the stick very easily. She's been remarkably perceptive about David, though.

I turn towards the end of the book; the entries are random and there are empty pages sandwiched by blocks of sharp text, squashed together and furious. On the second-to-last page, I find words I won't ever forget.

How does she expect her kid to learn music if she's too fucking uptight to play and the kid's dad can't? By fucking magic?

It's simple and cold. It's true.

It may not even refer to me; I know that Nadia's mum played a pretty decent level of piano when she was younger and that her father doesn't play anything. Does Nadia even know that I want a kid, would she care? It doesn't matter. Whether she is talking about me — and it isn't meant for me, anyway — or not, I know that sentence will haunt my dreams.

When I read on, I am absolved. *When they put up a statue to Pushy Asshole Parents, it'll be you, mother dearest. Without your fucking Botox. And without your makeup on. And Dad aswell.* She makes *aswell* one word.

I am absolved, but no less guilty.

I hear the door and look up, expecting it to be David. It's Nadia. I close the book and move it over to the rubbish bin, sweeping the sandwich crusts off the cover as she comes in.

"I didn't expect you today."

"You did," she says. "You told me to come in all week."

"I definitely didn't say come in today. I've got someone coming to look at a violin in an hour."

"Whatever." She shrugs and takes the book from my hand. "I knew I'd left this here, anyway."

"I didn't know you drew," I say as she puts the book in her bag.

"Yeah, sketches. Odd bits of shit here and there. You didn't open it, then?"

"No, of course not. It's your book."

And just like that I have lied to her.

I get home to a happy house. David is sitting at the kitchen table, spreadsheets and emails flying across the screen of his laptop. The radio is on in the background, quietly filling the house with the news from the outside world, reminding us that we're wrapped in this cocoon together.

"Good day?" he asks me, looking up from the computer and smiling. He has a gin and tonic with ice and a small slice of lemon in it. Beside his computer is a bowl of peanuts. He looks like he belongs here, wrapping up his working day.

"I did something a bit wrong. Something I shouldn't really have done."

"How so?" he asks, his hand over his mouth while he eats the nuts and speaks at the same time.

"Nadia left her diary under the counter."

"You didn't? Did you read it?" He is laughing.

"Don't laugh. I feel awful. I really shouldn't have. I only opened it because I thought it was a sketchbook." I reach out to take a peanut from the bowl and David puts his hand over the top of it. He pulls the bowl towards him. "Mine," he says, and grins at me.

"I didn't read much."

"Maybe she wanted you to? Maybe it was a cry for attention."

"Do you think?" I grasp at the straw he has offered.

"I always think, every time I meet that girl, that no one listens to her. Her bloody awful parents; they're so lucky to have her and they take bugger all notice of her except to boast about her exam results." There is something in David that seems to be able to isolate the exact thing that makes people tick, identify with them so quickly and effectively. I suppose that is what makes him successful in his business.

"You're much more perceptive than I am. I see her almost every bloody day and I just sit there feeling jealous of how gorgeous and how accomplished she is. She always comes across as so perfect to me. I wish I'd been like her."

David disagrees. He illustrates his point with one wagging finger. "Uh-uh, no. That girl is so angry, it seeps out every pore. She's mad as hell. Angry at everything."

"She said nice things about you."

"Of course she did, I'm amazingly nice."

"She said you're 'fit.'" I put speech marks around the word with my fingers.

"Because I am."

I make another fruitless assault on the peanuts. "Her parents are getting divorced, apparently."

"No surprises there. That woman is so incredibly uptight. I've only met her on a handful of occasions and it's just money, money, money. And her cheeks don't move when she speaks."

It's true. In the last couple of years, Nadia's mother has obviously resorted to Botox, perhaps to try and cement together her crumbling marriage. I'm not sure it's worked on any level.

Mine and David's relationship, although unconventional, has outlasted some married couples I know. Nadia's mother and father are just another pair added to the pile of fatalities we've seen grow so high over the years. Even Natalie and Jonny who first introduced us went their separate ways two or three years ago.

I'm not naive enough to think that the frisson of separation has no role in our passion for each other; it makes for a tender relationship when you are forced apart so often, but that's not, I'm convinced, the main driver of our longevity. Few couples started with the same pain as David and me, fortunately for them.

After I'd told David I was pregnant, he had been unable to leave France for almost a month. He called; at least once a day, every day. We mostly cried on the phone, oscillating between moments of sunlight where I thought we might find a tangled solution — a half-truth of a future — and the cold dark fact of the life he'd had before we met, the bottom line that drained us of options.

He shouldered the blame squarely, pointing out that he was the one with the existing family, with the marriage, not me.

But it takes two.

The sickness went on and on. I began to see it as a respite from thinking. It was almost a comfort.

The day I started to make the tiny cello, I knew I wouldn't have a termination. I cut out the pieces that would make my baby's first instrument and my confidence started to take shape alongside them. I had to accept that I would do this alone and that David, however intense his pain, however valid and logical his reasons, would have to live with my decision.

When I started to map the points of a minute spiral onto the piece of wood I'd chosen for the scroll, I knew that I would give David up if necessary. I could walk away from him if I was forced to choose between him and my baby.

The mathematical calculations needed to reduce something from the size required for an adult to one that would fit an infant were intricate and important. I had to shrink each anatomical part of the cello without altering the acoustics and the physics of the finished piece. Each side of the scaled-down instrument had to work as a sound box; the interaction of the wood and the movement of the strings had to be as exact as on a full-size cello.

There was no point in our baby starting with a less than perfect instrument; the whole idea was that he or she learnt the true beauty of sound at the same time as they discovered the rest of their senses. This wouldn't be music from a tinny speaker or a scratchy low-grade recording but full, rich notes that would speak to their little soul.

The long columns of numbers, the formula and algebra, brought solidity to me. I was relieved that there were still inalterable constants in the world. Working out the Fibonacci series of the scroll brought such calm and order that I was able to breathe smoothly for the first time in weeks.

Outside my workshop, I took to looking at women in the street, women with children, wondering how they managed, how they looked so normal. First I would look at their faces; were they just people like me, or were they in possession of some knowledge I was yet to understand? Would I join them on an equal footing on receipt of my own perfect infant?

Next I would look at their hands. Did they have wedding bands? Did they have a groove or a light strip of un-sunned skin where the ring used to be?

With a confidence that wobbled and wavered, I used to follow them down the street thinking, *If they can do it, so can I.*

David is in the kitchen cooking. He sent me upstairs to have a bath while he filled the house with piquant smells and the illusion of a completely normal life. I lay in the warm water, soaking off the smell of varnish, the dust of my workshop, and listening to pots clatter in the kitchen as if he is always here, and only here.

I go downstairs to see how far he's gotten with dinner. I am wrapped in a bath towel, a second smaller one around my head like a turban. I love this domesticity, this casualness.

The scene I could hear through the floorboards is over. David is packing his laptop into its case and I know straightaway that he is leaving.

"My son knows."

I am completely blindsided. I stand very

still in the kitchen, my hands hanging down. I don't know how to speak or what I could even say.

"He saw the video. On a Twitter link." David does the zip up around the case. It is a long, loud noise in the shocked room. "In France."

I imagine the scattering of hissed French words that must have gone on in here while I was in the bath. An image of them spread like tiny insects pops into my mind; fragments of conversation scuttling under the fridge, vowels rolling between the cooker and the cupboard, consonants scurrying under the kitchen table like spiders.

"How do you . . . Did he . . . ?"

"His mother called me a few minutes ago."

"What will happen now?"

He walks over to me. His face is ashen, his voice stilled. He sighs; an impassioned and terrible sigh. "Gracie, I don't know. It's like a fucking bomb's gone off." He takes a deep breath.

I imagine the explosion rippling through his family: the questions, the shouting, all of them wondering what on Earth was going on in the video. I wonder if his wife asked him if it was me. I assume, although I have never asked, that she knows nothing about me beyond that I exist.

I know a little about her. I know she is French and a lawyer. I know she has three children, a home in Strasbourg, and a family life I dream of. I know she is the red-headed woman I met briefly at Jonny and Natalie's party; the woman who went home because she was feeling unwell.

I know she and her husband have an agreement of silence, a contract of behavior that puts their children first. I do not know how she will react if this peculiar trust is broken. David doesn't either.

"What will you do?" I ask. After so many years, we both know the answer isn't that he stays, that we take the opportunity to announce ourselves, boldly and clearly, to the world. Experience has taught me that I have to be mindful of his children, that I too must want the best — and only the best — for them.

"I don't know how long I'll be gone, sweetheart. There'll be a shitstorm to sweep up. He saw the video, he recognized me immediately and — more than that — he's old enough to work out that I was *avec une amie* if he watches it too closely."

David draws me into his arms. "My darling girl." More tortured sighs. "It'll be all right in the end. And?"

"If it's not all right, it's not the end." I

know the words. I still believe them, even if I sometimes have to paint a smile on my face to get them out.

I compare every difficulty, every slope or hill, to our first two months together; ten weeks that were so awful that — if we got through that — we can get through anything. We can survive. It will just take patience, time, and trust.

CHAPTER SEVEN

My parents gave up everything for my dream of being a cellist. Their holidays were seaside weekends in caravans or cheap B&Bs, their social lives — if they'd ever had any — dwindled to chatting to other parents in the car parks outside rehearsals or exam rooms and, later with all the pride that anyone could feel, concert halls and studios. They had no treats or luxuries, all those were mine. Their needs were so frugally met that my dad paid more for my cello than he did the family car. And every joy they found, every triumph, was mine or connected to me. They kept long hours; my mum had a cleaning job early in the morning to make extra money for lessons, for strings and bow rehairs, and traveling to concerts. My dad would listen to me do my first practice of the day while he made my breakfast, his blue mechanic's all-in-one unbuttoned down the front. "So I'll feel the benefit when I go out," he'd say, and then do the jacket part up over his old white T-shirt.

My mum worked in a shop all day and was home in time to make my tea, and listen to the next two hours of my practice. They were ordinary people, a bit older than most parents, who ate ordinary food and did ordinary jobs. All their wishes were saved for me.

When I sent them the tickets for the recital, having already told them over and over what it meant to be one of the five musicians representing Nikolai Dernov, my mum would have gone up and down our street, knocking on every door and telling them what I was doing, what I'd achieved. Our neighbors would have had, for the most part, no idea what she was talking about, but her pride and enthusiasm would have told them everything they needed to know.

In her last letter to me before they were supposed to have come to my concert — to Nikolai's showcase — she described, in words dripping with guilt — certain she shouldn't have "wasted the money on herself" — the dress she had bought for the evening. "It's the palest blue, love," the letter had said, "and so long I have to wear heels under it. You've never seen me in anything like this before and nor has your dad!" She was dressing like a princess because she thought her dreams had come true.

It still breaks my heart that she never wore the dress.

Being pregnant softened me, just as it hardened up my resolve. I was thirty-two, so much had happened in the last twelve years and, for the first time, I allowed myself to regroup. I explained to David, over all the nights on the phone, how my dream of music college went so wrong, how I thought I would never heal from the humiliation, the shock and the disappointment at being asked to leave. I simply hadn't been good enough, and that had taken me completely by surprise. I told him how Nikolai Dernov had ripped through my confidence with his frustration at trying to teach me and how playing in front of anyone had destroyed me ever since.

Losing my parents while I was still in my twenties compounded my sense of failure and I had, increasingly, used staying in and playing the cello — alone — as a coping strategy, weaving a wall of safety around me through my music. It had become so much a habit that I'd stopped noticing that I did it.

Starting to make the little cello for my baby changed me. I allowed myself to celebrate, although I could still barely keep any food down and spent most of the day sipping at water and wishing the world would stop swimming in front of my eyes.

I didn't share the celebrations with David — they were just for me — and I didn't tell him — then — about the diminutive cello.

My pregnancy books told me that a fetus starts with its spine like a stringed instrument begins with its back and then grows a shape: ribs, shoulders, neck. I've never started a project with such enthusiasm. Or such love.

I shaped the outline of the tiny back, cut it to a classic Brescian silhouette; it was barely longer than my hand. I planed beautifully striped maple into ribs so thin they were supple in my fingers. In the front of the shop, the phone rang.

"Ms. Atherton?"

"Speaking."

"My name is Shelley. I'm your midwife."

Everything was real. We, the baby and I, had an ally.

"You've been referred to me by your GP. You're eight weeks?"

"Nine. Nearly nine." Eight weeks and five days. I was proud enough to count my achievement in hours.

"We wouldn't normally book you in so early, but your doctor was worried about hyperemesis."

"I'm sorry?" A flash of worry for my baby, the growl of the lioness inside me.

"Excessive nausea. She has you down as horribly sick."

I was relieved. "All day long, all night, too. It never leaves me."

"That's very wearing."

To hear someone be concerned about my health and yet positive about my pregnancy was fantastic. David worried constantly over my discomfort but assumed it would be over very soon.

"If you could come into the center in the next couple of days we can go through your details, get you checked in as a patient. And then . . ."

I felt the slight pause in her voice.

". . . we'll get you an early scan. Just in case. Hyperemesis is very common in multiple pregnancies."

"Twins?"

"It's a possibility."

Two days before the scan, at nine weeks and four days, the sickness stopped as suddenly as it had arrived. It felt as though the nausea had finally been defeated, squashed under the buoyancy of my excitement.

David and I had been a stuck record. Every conversation took us over the same ground, made the distance between us wider but the longing for each other more intense.

I was checked in by a different midwife from the one who had called me; Shelley was busy with a delivery. I imagined being in that same position, in this same building, in just seven months.

The scan room smelt of metal. I climbed onto the bed and a smiling radiographer smeared my still-flat belly with cold, clear gel. He rolled a steel bulb, a giant ballpoint pen, firmly over my stomach. The speckled screen became the womb shape I recognized from my books and leaflets, and there they were.

Both of them.

Two identical kidney beans.

Both as dead as cherrystones.

CHAPTER EIGHT

David's and my history has been pushed behind boxes like the little lost pieces of that cello I made so long ago. It is an uncomfortable past, but it is the only past we have; we can't change it, we can only build on it. Everything that has happened to us forms the investment that keeps us moving forward. We waded our way through such sadness that it has bonded us like little else could.

Now I help David make his arrangements to leave. We are only twenty minutes from the Eurostar terminal at my house and when we go to Paris we always take the train. This time, David has to go all the way to Strasbourg in a hurry, so a plane is the only option.

I pull up in the drop-off lane at the airport. This will be a tense and hurried goodbye. David will want to get it over with.

"Thanks for driving me, darling. Sorry

I'm in such a bad mood; I'm rubbish."

"It's fine; I totally understand. And I'll still be here whenever you get back."

We're outside the car now and I stand on my tiptoes to reach up and kiss him. He takes both my hands in his and kisses the backs of them.

"Come in with me; come into the airport. Let's have a few minutes more."

"No, I'll get a ticket. Or towed."

"You won't get towed." He scoops me into him, presses me against him, and kisses me long and hard. "I'll pay your ticket. Come on. Give me five more minutes."

I think about pushing him away, laughing, and telling him to be sensible, but instead I hook my arms around his neck and we continue to kiss. He lifts me slightly off the ground. "I wish I wasn't going. I wish I'd just arrived and we were going home."

He never says that. Normally it is outside of the rules to compare one life to another, to make empty promises or comment on things that can't be. His nerves are making him edgy.

"Come on," I say, and take his hand. "I'll come and wait while you check in, but if this car's gone when I come back, you'll have to get off the plane and sort it out."

"Deal," he says, and I lock the car with

the remote fob.

He just wants to be in close proximity to me when we get in. We aren't really there for long; a lifetime of planes and trains means that David has all this down pat and rarely wastes ten minutes. Around us, holidaymakers wait in lines and small children sit sulkily on suitcases. David isn't the only person in this queue with nothing more than a laptop bag as luggage, but he's the only one of the people dressed in suits who is involved in a passionate goodbye.

We don't usually make this sort of fuss. We're good at parting, just as we're good at getting together again. I suppose, under the circumstances, I'm suddenly the stability. Mine is the house that he can predict, the home where things are still the same.

Two American teenagers, all backpacks and baseball caps, are pointing at us.

"You're offending today's youth with your public displays of affection," I whisper into his ear.

"They're just jealous."

"Come on, go through security. You can do it." I make a gentle gesture of pushing him away.

He scoops me back up. "I'm going to miss you so much. I love you."

"And I love you, but I'm going to get a

ticket." I'm not a natural rule breaker; it makes me uncomfortable. "And those kids are staring. Maybe we should just go home?"

"I wish, darling girl," he says. "You can't imagine how much I wish."

The teenagers are making faces by the time we pull apart. I walk away from David without looking over my shoulder. Looking back at him is too hard; I never do it.

I swing past the supermarket on my way home. I live differently when David is away. I buy easy food, the food my family ate rather than David's salads and fresh fish. I play my cello.

It's late now, getting dark. I wander through the aisles looking at the people, wondering who else has just left their lover to go back to his or her family.

It is testament to my lifestyle that I spend longest in the wine aisle. The choice of fruit and vegetables was easy; I spend enough time in France to be constantly disappointed by the English supermarkets and I long for the pungent strawberries and the smell of ripe melon that wakes my senses in France.

I pick a few bottles off the shelf in a midprice range; not the cheapest plonk that will leave me with a hangover and stained lips, but not the sort that David would buy either. Ahead of me is a group of teenagers. They are clearly shopping for a party and their trolley is fairly typical. I can see crisps and bottles, the ubiquitous large dark plastic of cider and the clear glass of vodka. I hope there're a lot more of them outside.

"Grace." One of them, tucked in the center of the group and out of my eye line, is Nadia.

"Nad, hello. Fancy seeing you here." I point with a grin at my trolley. Four ready meals and five bottles of wine, a packet of cheese crackers and a bag of apples. "Party?"

"It's Harriet's birthday." Nadia points to the girl next to her. "This is Harriet."

"This is Harriet, my best friend, you mean," says the girl, and laughs. Her accent is cut glass, she clearly goes to the same school as Nadia.

"This is Harriet, who wishes she was my best friend," says Nadia.

I smile at both girls and remember Nadia's diary entry. I hope I don't blush.

"I don't want to sound all middle-aged and so on, but do you think you've got enough booze there?" I raise my eyebrows but make it clear that I'm friend not foe.

"It's not all ours. We're going camping. A bunch of us." There are three other girls with them and two boys lurk farther down the aisle.

"And it's not for Nadia at all." Harriet makes a face. "She's far too goody-goody to drink it."

Nadia shakes her head. "I gave up drinking; a bit ago. And Harriet can't bear it."

"Can't bear how boring you are now." Harriet's smile is viperous.

"Have you got hot dogs, then?" I ask, trying to change the subject. "You need hot dogs. And bacon."

"I'm a vegetarian," says Harriet, who shoots me a look that makes me glad she's not Nadia's best friend at the moment. Harriet has long blond hair and a superior air. There were lots of girls like her at my school too; part of me despised them, but part of me yearned for them, to be one of them. I feel for Nadia.

"Am I still working Saturday?" she asks.

"Ah, I'm not sure. David's gone back. Early."

To her credit, she doesn't flinch. I wonder if she'll tell Harriet where he's gone as they leave.

"Doesn't matter, I'm coming in, anyway. I have something I want to talk to you about," she says.

"OK, Nadia. That's cool," I say before I remember that she will want to talk about my playing in private. Then I hate myself so much for saying "cool" in front of the glamorous Harriet that I can't think which is worse.

In a space between my flying thoughts, I realize that Harriet will have judged me long ago. She will have looked me up and down; taken in my flat pumps, my jeans, the T-shirt that is slightly faded. She will wonder why I haven't got makeup on or why I keep my hair so short. Perhaps she'll decide I'm a bit too old for little silver hoops in my ears and the slight short spikes that I still tease my hair into. She'll trip her judgmental eye down my arm and, at the same time, check for nail varnish and a wedding ring.

Perhaps she'll be more impressed when Nadia tells her I'm a mistress.

When I get home I choose an apple, cut it into fours, and put it on a plate with a few crackers. I open a bottle of wine and carry it all into the sitting room.

My whole body itches to play my cello, but I want to find the right piece. I bite into the apple and leaf through my music. I have shelves and shelves of sheet music. All of my past is recorded in them, notes in the gaps between the staves or little drawings where I need to remind myself to lift my bow or move my fingers into an odd position to catch the gap between one note and the next.

Sometimes I find little scribbled notes such as *buy cheese* or *meet Mike Monday.* The writing shows how old I was when I wrote the message; I've been collecting sheet music since I was young. I don't even remember who Mike is.

I take my cello from its stand and unscrew the spike. I don't have to measure it, although I know how long it took to get right when I was a child. I tighten the bolt and pluck through the four strings to see how far astray they've gone in the last two days. They're not bad. I adjust the fine tuners on the tailpiece and don't have to use the pegs; it's not that far out.

I get twitchy without playing. It is something I've done most days of my life since I was eight years old. It's more than a habit. David always notices the twitchiness and it's another reason that we both wish I could just play with him here. I haven't told him that I picked a tune when he was in bed; I think I meant to.

I tighten my bow, rub it with rosin, and

begin to play. I am, and have, all that I need.

My special interest in music, and the things I love the most, are traditional tunes in variations written by composers. "La Follia" is one of the commonest examples: there is a popular — and wonderful — version by Corelli, the one David took me to that night in Paris. There is a crazy and striking one by Vivaldi. Liszt, Beethoven, and Handel have all written versions of the theme. I love that these musical themes and all they stand for can trickle down through centuries, that they never dull. There is scarcely a composer who hasn't borrowed a tune from folk music; from Bartók and the Romanian folk dances to Vaughan Williams and "Greensleeves." I've been collecting and playing them for decades. If I'd finished my music degree, my dissertation would have just trotted onto the paper by itself with list after list of examples and all my experiences playing them and all the reasons they are so wonderful.

I find the music for the Vivaldi version, but I haven't got the energy to play it. The end calls for some serious physical jerks and I'm not up to that today.

I sip my wine and try to call a piece to mind. I know it as soon as I see the folded dog-eared corner of the music. "Libertango"; an Argentinean tango seething with passion and darkness and brought to life by Astor Piazzolla. This piece isn't tender or mournful or sotto voce; this piece isn't even decent.

I play it first as it appears on the sheet music. Then, after a huge gulp of wine and wiping beads of sweat from my forehead, I play it to a piano backing that I have on CD. I play faster and faster and it swoops through my head like a drug.

I put on another CD; I'm halfway through my wine bottle: Grace Jones singing "I've Seen That Face Before," that's the "Libertango" too, and I play it loudly over the top of the recording.

I'm breathless and laughing by the time I finish and I text David.

take me to argentina. it's a need not a want.

He texts back almost immediately.

the french press have found me.

CHAPTER NINE

I don't do anything else with my evening but drink wine and search the internet. I finish the bottle before I find what I've been looking for. I misspell things in French and cannot get my computer to put accents in the right places. The search would be easier in English, but of course the UK sites are silent on the story.

It's hard to admit, even to myself, but what I've been waiting to see is a picture of David's wife. I wonder if I'd do it if I wasn't drunk. I feel a sudden stop inside, a jolt of reality, when I find the photograph.

David's wife has aged really well. She has barely changed from the night I saw her at Jonny and Natalie's party. My memory of her was accurate; tall and thin, well turned out and elegant and, thankfully, not like me in any way. I have always been confident that David wasn't just looking for a younger version of his wife, but it's nice to confirm it. She and I are, in every way, different.

In the photograph I find online, they are side by side. Nothing in their body language suggests any sort of intimacy, past or present. They stand, almost shoulder to shoulder, with their hands by their sides but not touching. She is every bit as strikingly attractive as he is. Her mouth is set in a straight line of determination or distaste.

David's wife looks angry, but then I would be too if my family's privacy had been invaded by the media, if the world were asking awkward questions of my husband. The caption below the picture names her as PROMINENT HUMAN RIGHTS ADVOCATE DOMINIQUE-MARIE MARTIN. She was introduced to me at Natalie's party as Marie. I have always assumed she had taken her husband's surname, but she obviously hadn't. David only refers to her as "my wife" or as his children's mother. Only now I realize that I didn't know her name before this moment.

I open a second bottle of wine and resume my search.

I have searched the internet for David's wife before. I used *Marie Hewitt,* her husband's surname and her second name. I didn't find anything of note, and of course that satisfied me.

By searching *Dominique-Marie Martin,* I unfold court cases and international transgressions that she has resolved. Her eye for injustice is respected worldwide.

I click through the online image files of her. She doesn't put a foot wrong in the pictures; her clothes, her shoes, her hair, all flawless. There are no photographs of her children — and I'm grateful for that — and no more pictures of her and David together.

David employs a PR specialist to keep him out of photographs and media comments; it is imperative that translators at his level stay in the background. There are a few corporate shots of him — beautifully groomed and with an incredible presence — but nowhere near as many as there are of his wife.

I wonder how he would feel about me searching, digging into the side of his life that is hidden, crossing a boundary we laid down by tacit agreement. It feels grubby to know about the woman he is married to.

When I was little, Pandora's Box was one of my favorite stories; and now, I wish I'd listened.

I'm drunk and maudlin, but at least there is no one to watch me. David's wife has always had the best of him — no one's fault — but from the cheap seats, that's how it feels.

The day we lost our babies, David left France to get to me in such a hurry that he forgot to take the wedding band from his finger. In the aftermath of our sadness, as we waited to be sent home, the midwives referred to him as my husband and credited the loss to both of us rather than just to me.

It was David's loss too. David had been immovable in wanting to end the pregnancy, only because he knew from experience that he would love the babies just as much as I did by the time they were born. Were to have been born.

Our lives had moved miles while we had been inside the hospital; we went in as two separate people fighting over a possibility and came out, less than twenty-four hours later, as a couple stripped of choice.

We left the hospital in daylight, cinema eyes blinking in our disbelief. When we got home, truly depleted, David had to ask if I take sugar in my coffee.

During the night, I woke to find that what had become in three short visits "David's side" was cold and empty. I walked quietly into the sitting room. He was sitting on the sofa, hunched over a glass of whiskey on the coffee table in front of him. The room was dark and his face was lit by the jumpy light of the television, the volume stilled to the silence that had engulfed the house.

He looked up as I came in. "I am so fucking sorry. This is all my fault. I did this."

I sat down next to him, pulling my dressing gown tightly around me. My shoulders were rounded with the weight of disappointment.

"It's one of those things," I said. I didn't mean it, not then.

"It isn't. I did this to you."

I knew his "you" was plural.

"Jesus fucking Christ." He drank the whiskey in one swig. "I'd give anything to turn the clock back. Absolutely fucking anything." He was more than a little drunk.

Beside him, I shrugged; a silhouette of acquiescence.

"It was the stress. I put so much stress on you. This is all so fucking wrong."

I leaned into him and he put his arms around me. I told him about the tiny cello and he wept. I let him hear all my wishes, all my promises to myself that I had bottled up inside in case they made him hate me.

The only person he ended up hating was himself.

"I feel so guilty. I've smashed up so many fucking lives. We can never get them back."

"It wasn't that," I whispered. "It wasn't

me worrying that killed them, because I didn't really believe you. I wasn't going to go through with it."

"Gracie, it was my fault. I should have supported you. I should have found a way. I will find a way. After this, this fucking hard lesson, I . . . I'm not going to be such a prick again. I've been so selfish." David reached forward and poured more whiskey. "Who the fuck do I think I am?"

He raised the glass towards my lips and I nodded. I hate whiskey. I swallowed hard, a huge mouthful on purpose, and felt the discomfort as it tore down my throat. I took another.

"I have to tell you something. It's so fucking fucked up. I'm so responsible for all of this. Such an arsehole." He put his hand over mine and squeezed my fingers.

"Wait." I got up and got another glass. I half filled it with whiskey and drank. The pain at the back of my nose made me feel human, as if there was some capacity for reaction left inside me. My eyes smarted, my nostrils burned, and I drank again.

"I wanted to tell you this when we met. On our first night. But it was the most magical night of my life — I couldn't break it. I couldn't break us."

He started to cry properly and he held my

face against his cheek. His tears stuck our skin together.

"I didn't know you last winter. I made decisions then that didn't include you. I'll never do that again."

His large hands covered his face, he was trembling.

"Grace, my wife is six months pregnant."

I was flattened. There was simply no more I could do or comprehend. His words eviscerated me.

"I've explained to her that I've met some-one else. She understands that our mar-riage, as it was, is over. But I can't let the child down, Grace. Please, I'm so sorry. Please say you can forgive me."

I started to push him away, but he held me tightly.

"I thought I wouldn't have to tell you until everything was over. I couldn't think any-thing through; I was so scared of losing you. I still am."

David continued his thinking out loud. Their baby, the vital healthy baby, had been a last-ditch attempt to rescue a relationship that had died despite it. He couldn't find a moment where he could tell me.

I still wasn't ready to be told.

There were many promises carried on the sad breeze of that night, decisions made in the shadow of our heartbreak that we still stand by.

David was able to stay for ten days; one of our longest unplanned stretches of time together. We built our relationship from those ashes, taught it to stand on shaky feet, to walk with its injured legs.

In the weeks and months that followed, David and I began to believe that we would have time — a future — in which to grow our own family, to make everything work. It seemed important not to rush, to let our lives unfurl and stretch together. Part of us felt there should be a proper period of mourning for the babies we had lost, part that we should have a stable base before we thought about planning a family. Having a child alone was not what I wanted, and missing a child growing day by day would have tortured David.

But some romantic notion of mine, something buried deep beneath everyday logic, believed that our children would make themselves known when the time was right. David shared my confidence to the point that we decided not to use contraception, not to deliberately avoid another pregnancy.

Secondary infertility — the unexplained inability to conceive following a previous pregnancy — is a cruel mistress. I have undergone every test known to man in the last few years and there is no obvious reason why I can't conceive.

We know that there is nothing wrong with David; his third child was born in France just twelve weeks after we lost our twins.

CHAPTER TEN

I wake early and hungover. I regret my evening's activities on every level. When I wander into the sitting room and collect my glass and the half-empty second wine bottle, my cello stares accusingly from the corner.

I didn't text David back last night; that's the last thing he needs. I have set the next few days aside to work on the final polishing of my Cremona cello, smoothing away the last tiny blemishes and touching in any streaks with a brush almost too fine to see. It will be meticulous work that requires my full attention.

The competition isn't until October, eight full weeks away, but the cello will need to be packaged and couriered two weeks before the display of instruments and the judging even begins. To be shipped, the varnish must be rock hard. Even the gentlest of movement will cause it to rub against the soft inside of the case — however well it fits

— and the slightest mist or smear would cost me the competition.

Once, the shop and my cello were all I had, but meeting David put that in perspective, showed it for the empty life it had been. When he and I move in together permanently, I will have to leave my shop behind: we will have to live in France as it's where his children are, at least for now. Their first language is French, although he tells me they speak excellent English. David and I decided that he will talk in French with our children so they don't feel left out when their half siblings are chattering away to one another. Having a waiting list for instruments would mean that my customers will come to me, wherever I am in the world. I know that the chances are slim — even though David reminds me constantly that they're the same as anyone else's — but it's got to be worth a try. Most of all, when I think about Cremona and the competition, I love that David has enough faith in me to think I can win it. It's infectious, that kind of belief, and he has me excited with him. I've gone too long in my life taking no risks, not daring to jump in case I fall. David will catch me.

Much as the cello needs me, I can't face it until later, if at all, today. I call Nadia and ask her to come in. The camping trip has been cut short by in-fighting and squabbling girls; she's quite happy to earn some money and hide away from them.

I officially take the day off. Before I go back to bed for an hour, I check the internet to see where the story has got to. David seems to have gotten it under control. Hopefully it will become tomorrow's chip papers and all blow over before any lasting damage is done.

Later, I go for a long wind-blown walk on the downs. I climb breathlessly to the top of a steep hill and realize I have taken very little exercise in recent weeks.

The view from the top is stunning, fields of ripe yellow rapeseed scattered with the earliest poppies run from just below me right into the distance. This year has been rainy and the verdant trees have made the most of it. The colors are those of a child's quilt, sewn together by bushy hedgerows and five-bar gates of storybooks. I try to take a picture of it on my phone to send to David. There is no signal up here and, anyway, the camera is too small to see the detail my eye can take in; it doesn't do the view justice. I will have to tell him about it when he comes back.

As I reach the car my phone signal comes back and his text arrives.

things mighty fucked up, sweetie. doing best to firefight. exhausted.

I presume it will be easier for David to get away if I go to Paris. I make a mental note to speak to Nadia about it when I see her. There is still another fortnight left of the summer holiday and I'm sure she could do with the money.

can you get to paris, meet me there? I press send but the signal is still erratic and the message refuses to go.

I call into the shop on the way home.

It's a yellow summer dusk and the street-lights are just going on in the market square outside the shop. The window looks beautiful. It is softly lit from behind — Nadia has closed up and turned off the main lights for me — and really adds to the charm of this little town center. I have put together a display of a music stand, a double bass, a cello, a viola, and a violin.

I change the music on the stand to keep it topical or seasonal or sometimes funny; an "in-joke" for those who can read it. This is such a perfect summer, such a very English mix of sweet-smelling rain and warm sun, that I have Vaughan Williams's "The Lark Ascending" on display at the moment.

I change them often: Christmas carols and concertos, adding a little incongruous tinsel to the more classic look of the window display; hymns and votive tunes for Easter; the occasional piece from popular culture. For the football World Cup, I bought an anthology of national anthems and changed it every day to the team that had won the night before. That made the local paper; it's all good publicity for the shop.

I unlock the front door and tap the code into the alarm to turn it off. I go to collect Nadia's empty drinks cans and cold half-full teacup from the counter. The blue book is there again.

Perhaps Nadia thinks this is the only place she can leave it without it being read. I feel awful about that and walk away, into the workshop. I will go back in a minute and remove the sweet wrappers and apple core that are on top of the book.

The cello looks perfect. I am insanely pleased with it. I turn on the spotlight over my workbench and lay the cello on its side. I fiddle with the lamp until I can light the front of the instrument without a curve of glare reflecting from the perfect polish of the belly.

When I'm satisfied that it is, literally, in its best light, I take a picture for David.

I attach a message to the photo and press send. our winning entry. can't wait to see you. can't wait for our holiday in italy with this beast. miss you.

Afterwards I send another almost immediately. i can get to paris any day next week. just text.

All the time, the pale-blue notebook is boring into my head. I am compelled to read more but disgusted with myself at the same time. Excuses creep in: I am reading it to try and understand her; to find out what turns this girl I talk to every day into the molten fury she is inside; I only want to help. Even the excuses cannot overwhelm the fact that I know it's wrong and that I know I will read on.

I can't get going with my sanding and setting up of the cello while there is rubbish in the shop front; I will have to tidy it. I sweep the apple core and wrappers from the top of the book and into my hand. I walk away again, back into the workshop to the bin that Nadia can never be bothered to use.

I sit at my workbench and absorb myself in cutting the bridge. I've left my chinagraph pencil in the shop and I need it to fit the bridge. I wonder why I can't just have the courage of my convictions and be honest about what I'm going to do.

When I walk past the book a third time, it's too much; a biblical temptation. I sit behind the counter in the chair Nadia will have sat in to write it. I think about David's comment that perhaps she wants me to read it, and I open the book near the back.

Me and coke are over. Ceebs w/ the fucking chaos. Harriet can keep it and ~~everyone~~everything that goes with it. Fact.

For one naive moment I hope she means Coca-Cola. I realize with a horror that flings my hand over my mouth that she means cocaine. I tuck the book under the counter, still open where I can see it but invisible to anyone who might look through the window.

I'm done. Harriet and her wanker boyfriend piss me off too much. Yes, Charlie, I mean you. I'm not playing anymore, dicks. Charlie and Harriet, march off together, get married, see if I fucking care, have coke for confetti that catches in your hair. I'm out.

It's doing my head in. It was bad enough at school but now, now everyone's parents are away and we're in party central. I drink too much, because the coke won't let me stop, and then I feel shit the next day and then we all get pills off Charlie because he always has them. And then I go home and my house is full of total arseholes, yes, dear parents, you. And then I take the last one of Charlie's pills and then I have to go and get another one — that means I have to be on my own with Charlie. With #Harriet'sBoyfriendCharlie.

The depth of her rage is frightening. I don't know which is the real Nadia — the one who shows the world an impenetrable confidence, the girl I can trust with my shop and the thousands of pounds' worth of stock, or this tortured, seething teenager. It breaks my heart that it might be this one.

I hate Charlie. I hate his white hair and his see-through skin. I hate his face. His eyes make him look like a white rat, pink eyes, piggy eyes, piss eyes.

I wonder for a moment if Charlie is an adult, an older man, if there's even more behind this anger. I can't imagine how he would get drugs otherwise, not around here. Then I remember the white-haired boy sulking on the outside of Nadia's group in the supermarket. He was skinny and his trousers were tight enough around his calves to make him look frail. I noticed him first for that and then for the long white fringe sticking out from under his cap, covering half his face. He didn't stop and chat, he moved off when the girls got into conversation, but he must have been Charlie.

Mums fucking love Charlie. He's posh and he's loaded and he shakes their hands and he says what they want to hear. And he's not one of those boys who drive around the town center in suped-up shit-wheels doing ~~handbreak~~handbrake turns.

Mummies don't want them in the house — them *is overblown, shaded in the bubble letters she uses for emphasis, like the child she still is at heart* — oh fucketyduckety no, not the townies, not the boys off the estate. They might have sex with our lovely clean girls. They might not be posh boys like Charlie. And do you know, dear mummy, who those COMMON boys get their drugs off? Do you? Ha-fucking-ha, they get them off Charlie. Charlie. From Charlie. I fucking hate Charlie. And I hate Harriet.

I am reading slack jawed. The beep from

my phone makes me wake from the horror and close my mouth.

> maybe can do paris. not sure. have client borrowing apartment, so nowhere to stay at moment. hotel? you ok?

I wonder if I should text him about Nadia's diary. He has enough on his plate, but I have no idea what to do and David knows about teenagers. No, if I call him it should be about us, about what we do next, how long he will be away, not about my Saturday girl and her cocaine habit.

Perhaps David will just tell me that's what kids do nowadays. They may have done it in my day — I wouldn't know. I would have been hiding behind my cello, staying in and being the perfect child, sliding scales up and down the fingerboard, dreaming of concerts and taffeta dresses.

I try to be logical. Nadia has, after all, said — written — that she won't be doing it anymore. I have no way of knowing how old the entry is — I can see it's sometime this holiday but nothing beyond that. It could be weeks ago. She may have completely stopped.

If I tell her I've read it, I will lose her trust and — I realize with a selfish stop — my

Saturday girl. I imagine for a moment that I don't have Nadia in my life, that I'm not party to her moods and her defensiveness, her sudden sunshine and sharing. I would lose a good friend, too.

I flick through a few more pages. This isn't the last page, but it is near the end of the dog-eared part that has been written in. I see the word *wasted* elongated and decorated across a few pages but no more long passages, no more scrawled rants. There are long swaths without anything in and then a sudden drawing of a Christmas tree, profanities hanging from it like baubles. There are pages more of writing after that.

I need to reply to David.

i'll just come over — any day. we can get a hotel. it's fine. all good here. going to play cremona cello in next two days. I almost write *wish it could be with you* on the end of the message but hold back. That is not going to happen on so many levels.

I ask Nadia to work in the shop while I set up the cello. The bridge feet are cut and flat, the pegs fit perfectly, and the tailpiece is ready. Today I will put the strings on, test the sound, and make the last adjustments to the sound post.

I have bought an expensive case to carry

this cello in. The outside is navy blue and very solid, very smart. The inside is scarlet, the cut-out piece in the middle the perfect size for the instrument. This will be the case it travels to Italy in.

I had wanted to take it, maybe meet David in Italy, but I've taken a lot of time off work lately and my jobs are mounting up. I haven't even started Mr. Williams's violin. The cello will have to go with a courier like everyone else's; David and I will meet it there.

"Will it be finished today, Grace?" asks Nadia, pointing at the Cremona cello.

"It will, which is exciting." I pass her a duster. "But you are needed front of house."

I point out that I'm not paying her to keep me company, but it falls on deaf ears and she lures me into letting her stay in the workshop by making me coffee. I wonder whether I should try and get her to discuss the things I know. But today will be complicated enough.

She doesn't look how I expect a drug user to look. I know nothing about cocaine, apart from that it isn't fair trade and isn't very good for you. Her skin is bright and clear, her makeup immaculate. The line of black kohl on her upper eyelids has been applied with a perfectly steady hand and peters out into two ticks at the outer corners of her eyes as neatly as the purfling bee stings on my cello.

"Are you all right?" she asks, and I assume I'm staring.

"Yes. Perfectly. I'm just excited. Excited about the cello."

"Me too," she says, and I feel the sweat on my palms.

Then, out of nowhere, "Grace, can I tell you a secret? Something no one else knows. Mainly because I don't know who to tell, not because I don't want to."

I hold my breath. I try to gather my thoughts and make sure that I react sensitively and supportively. The whole cocaine idea is so at odds with this sweet girl in front of me that I feel I know nothing about her, too.

"I'm writing a symphony." Her face is calm, solemn; her deep eyes earnest.

It takes a few moments for the penny to drop. My first reaction is just shock that it isn't her cocaine use that she wants to confess.

"You're kidding?"

She shrugs, shakes her head. "No. I'm not kidding. I've already started it. Well, some of it; melodies, themes." She waves her hands around dismissively, a disorganized conductor of an abstract piece.

"That's amazing." I marvel at her self-belief, her scope. I could never have had the bravery to attempt something as huge as that at her age, at any age. Nadia is prepared to scale this challenge; she knows she has the tools she needs and she has the ability — the confidence in her music — to use them.

"Wow, I'm so impressed." I shake my head; partly in disbelief, partly in brutal envy.

"You don't think it's silly?"

"Oh my God, no. Who would? I think it's phenomenal." What she fears is the outside, the criticism of others. She is scared of letting their limitations embrace and confound her, but, in Nadia, this will pass.

I am entirely the opposite. It dawns on me like a cacophony of trumpet blasts; like something so obvious I should have seen it from the start. I hold failure to me like a talisman; I firmly believe it's the only thing I am guaranteed to achieve. Sadly, understanding our differences isn't the same thing as being able to fix them.

I stare at Nadia like she's a stranger. "I think it's wonderful."

"You don't think I'm biting off more than I can chew? That I might not finish it?"

"God, Nad, by the time you're eighteen, you'll have written a symphony. People will still be able to hear it, to play it, long after you're dead."

"That's cheery."

"But you know what I mean."

She smiles slightly. "Thanks, anyway. For not saying it's stupid."

"There's a story about Mozart," I say. "I'm sure it's not true, but it's great."

Nadia nods her head for me to tell it to her.

"Someone asked Mozart how they should start writing a symphony. Mozart said that they should start with something simpler, a concerto perhaps. He said that a symphony required experience and understanding and commitment and was obviously far too much for this composer."

Nadia looks at me, pulling a face. She's worried the outcome of the story will be a criticism of her.

"So the composer said to Mozart, 'But you started writing symphonies when you were eight.' And Mozart said, 'Yes, but I never asked anyone how.'"

Nadia laughs. The story has made her feel good.

I remember Nikolai telling me that story at college. We were in a practice room. He was pacing the floor, listing my limitations. I was bent over my cello, my arms limp down its front, my bow defeated in my hand.

Nikolai tried to get me to feel the music more deeply. He sat behind me, his arms wrapped along the length of mine, his breath hot in my ear. We read the music together, beat out the rhythms, hummed the melody line. It wasn't ever enough.

Nadia will not need to go through that. She understands the depth of her talent and she is listening to it, letting it carry her along, allowing it to lead.

Nadia wanders into the front of the shop with her duster, satisfied by my reaction. I busy myself with the Klotz school violin I need to have ready for tomorrow. Peace settles over the shop for the first time in a while.

Nadia is humming; I can't quite get the tune, but I'm sure I know it.

"What's that?" I walk into the shop to hear it more clearly.

"I'll show you." Nadia reaches up and takes down one of the violins. It's her favorite of the ones I've made myself — a copy of a little Bohemian I once bought at auction.

She turns the fine tuners on the tailpiece to get the strings spot-on. Her face takes on a different set; a certainty and a determination.

"Listen," Nadia says, and starts to play.

The tune is magical. I do know tiny licks of the main theme; it has borrowed from folk tunes and tangos, it has stolen arpeggios from history and diminished chords from old stories. It is the start of Nadia's symphony.

The music is extraordinary. It soars and swoops and dives. It has light and joy and then sudden and fierce bursts of shade and fear. It is the perfect balance of a tune you're sure you know and then a sudden realization that, no, this is new; this is comfortable and appealing and easy to learn or play, but it is new.

I understand quickly that the piece is autobiographical and wholly about Nadia, or at least about her life. There is the sharp jangle of a sitar spiking through and then a sudden pizzicato of picked notes as percussion. There is the repeated use of a bass refrain that I can tell is taken from pop music.

Above all, it has a strong melody, a line that I know I will wake up humming in the night. That is the mark of a truly great piece of music. I have no doubt, suddenly, that Nadia can sustain this right across all four movements of a symphony.

Plenty of people attempted symphonies when I was at college. Nikolai discussed it with me but I brushed it off, certain I'd have time to come back to it later. Some of the works were good and published, some were great and unpublished. Others were execrable and the result of a growing ego in tight combination with little class or style.

Nadia's symphony will be so exceptional, people will have difficulty believing it was written by a student. I am sure of it.

"It's beautiful." I am in awe. I can't fathom how someone so young can understand so much; understand and then have the instinct — it can't be the experience — to translate that into music, to apply a structure. "It's absolutely wonderful."

"That bit, that I just played, that was the first movement, and I've nailed the next two — I think. I don't know about the fourth yet. It's evading capture." She grins and I can see how happy it's made her.

I nod and smile. "I'm so impressed, Nad."

She speaks with her back to me as she puts the little Bohemian back on the rack above her head. "I've perfected three parts so far; two violins and a cello."

I put one hand out to steady myself, my fingers flat against the leather of the counter.

"You, me, and . . ."

I can't imagine who else. I can't see how this could get worse. My mind is flying, the top of my back wet with the sweat that is prickling down my neck.

". . . Mr. Williams."

I sit down behind the counter.

"Tomorrow night at your house. You cook dinner. First outing for your cello. First performance of my first movement."

I feel sick. "You can't do this. How dare you?"

She shrugs. Her face is flat with hostility.

"What about my privacy? You can't just decide something and steam ahead." As I say it, I see the blue book. Its corners wave at me like tentacles, its pale cover threatens to reveal everything.

"Well, I have," she says, and picks up her bag to leave. "And Mr. Williams is fucking thrilled."

CHAPTER ELEVEN

By the next day, my house smells like a home. I decided to embrace Nadia's supper idea and I've made a cake for dessert, one I can decorate with strawberries and cream and make summery. The baking has filled the whole place with warmth and comfort. I should do it more often. Measuring and mixing and stirring has cleared my mind of the things that frighten me, the horrors of the evening to come.

I decided to live a lie, for all of today; after all, I have managed it with David for almost nine years. Today, I am the kind of person who has dinner parties, albeit for the oddest of guests. I am fearless and I am able.

I realized last night that I hadn't really cleaned the house since David left, and spent the first hours this morning hoovering skirting boards and wiping down basins.

Everything is fresh and clean. I am occupying my mind with cleaning, baking, anything except music. Nadia and I have made a pact and she is due any moment to begin the process that will lead, she guarantees me, to my being able to play this evening.

She is sunny and cheerful when she arrives, and I wonder if getting her own way always makes her feel so positive.

"So this is how it works," she tells me. "I promise faithfully to stay downstairs, sitting-room door shut, getting ready for tonight. OK?"

I nod; now I am the child.

"And you sit in your bedroom with the door shut there, too. And you play these four notes upstairs." She hums four clear notes, little bells that pop into the air.

They are the four open strings of a cello, and the rhythm in which she hums them is the exact rhythm I pluck them through after tuning. *Bom, bom, bom, bom,* like a marble rolling down four even steps.

"And then play this." Four more, an octave higher, and I hear myself checking the tuning of a viola. "And then . . ." She hums G–D–A, and E, the strings I pluck when I tune a violin. "That's twelve notes. That's a tune."

"You're funny," I say.

"I'm not funny," says Nad. "I'm clever.

It's bollocks to say you can't play my tune in front of anyone — I've heard you a million times."

It's true. I have tuned cellos, violas, and violins in front of Nadia so many times. I can't deny it, despite how much I want to.

"And then play it with your bow, a few times through, and then play something else. And I promise, promise, promise, I won't open the door. Either door." Upstairs, with my heart a metronome in my ears, I consider Nadia's proposal.

"Enough!" Nikolai Dernov screamed at me in one of our last rehearsals. "I tell you over and over that you can do this. You can make that slide without sounding like a baby, like a stupid child. You can trust your hands." He leaned his face into my mine. "Do it again."

The others tried not to look at me. Catherine and Shota stared at the music stands, the other two concentrated on the straight lines of their bow hair. Everyone blocked out the embarrassment.

I tried the shift again, loud in the tense air. There were no windows in Nikolai's studio, no way of looking out and remembering that the other world was still there, that this intense atmosphere wasn't all there was. A strip of glass ran around the top of the walls to let light in. It didn't open, as far as I ever knew, and it was too far up to see out of. Every day the studio felt more like a cell.

Nikolai's nose wrinkled up, his eyes narrowed. He made small spitting noises as I attempted to spider my fingers from fourth to fifth position. "You are so clumsy. You don't even try. I sent a boy away from here." He squeezed the top of my arm so hard it hurt. "I sent him away so that you could have his place and look what I get. You were not worth it."

My stomach knotted into a ball so tight I thought I would have a heart attack. I kept my mouth shut, my feet pressed into the floor. Anything less and I would have screamed and run.

"You appall me." Flecks of his saliva hit my chin. The institutional mustard yellow of the studio walls blurred behind his looming face as I tried to focus my eyes away from his.

"Stop."

It was Shota. I glanced sideways at him, I could not look up. *No,* I pleaded silently, *please don't make it worse.*

"Leave her alone."

He had edged to the front of his chair as

if he was about to stand. He held his viola by the neck and his bow was balanced across the lip of his music stand. He pointed with his free hand at Nikolai. "Leave her alone."

"Get out." Nikolai's voice was like ice. "Get out of my room."

I hoped he was talking to me but he wasn't, he was staring at Shota.

Shota stood up, faced him eye to eye. Nikolai was not a tall man and Shota's shoulders were far broader.

"All of you get out. Except her." Nikolai pointed at me. "You will stay until you can do it. Even if we sleep here."

"I won't leave her here on her own. You can't keep doing this." Shota moved closer to Nikolai. I had never been so afraid.

I found my shaking voice. "Please go. All of you. I'm sorry."

Nikolai stepped back from Shota. "Well?" he asked him.

"I don't want to leave you here." He stretched his free hand out towards me.

"Please. I'll come and find you as soon as I come out." I began to feel that I could cope with anything as long as Shota and the others weren't watching. I made a show of straightening the music on my stand, pretended to be circling my shoulders, relaxing my muscles, when really I was concentrating so hard on not crying that my teeth hurt.

"I'll wait an hour," Shota said, his eyes steely, "then I'm coming back."

I did not notice the hour pass: my skin was tight across my shoulders, my elbow aching from the pressure Nikolai exerted through my bow. There was a red ring around my wrist where he'd held it, steering back and forward across the strings relentlessly. The doorknob of the studio rattled. I remember that they automatically locked from the inside to give the players confidence they would not be interrupted.

"Grace!" Shota was shouting through the soundproofing of the door; his voice was muffled.

"What are you going to do?" asked Nikolai. He stood up and walked towards the door. "What will you choose?" He shrugged his shoulders theatrically and there were sweat patches under his arms, darkening his gray shirt.

"I'm not done, Shota," I called through the closed door. I looked at the tramline welts on the fingers of my left hand; they would sting like mad later when the nerves started to recover. "I want to stay."

Nikolai raised his eyebrows, his wire-rimmed glasses moved up and down on his nose, and he nodded once.

"I'll see you in the morning," I said through the door, my whole body feeling so faint, so insubstantial, that I might have been able to vaporize and disappear.

Shota thumped the door from the other side.

Nikolai yanked it open. His outrage left a terrifying silence between us.

The corridor was dimly lit compared to the practice room, and suddenly Shota looked small in his shadow.

"How dare you?" he boomed into the passageway. "Who do you think you are?"

There was a shuffling pause where Shota gathered his thoughts. "I was worried about Grace." I could barely hear him.

"If I were you, Mr. Kinoshita, I would be worried about my own position in this conservatoire. My own future." Nikolai had his baton in his hand; he pointed it at Shota like a wand. "And I would mind my own business."

"I needed to see that Grace was OK." I couldn't see Shota now from where I was sitting, but I could imagine his face, the mix of fear and determination. My heart pounded.

"I am." I found the words from the tangled lump caught in my throat; they sailed like

mist into the corridor. "I'm nearly there."
My fingers pulsed with pain at the thought
of playing any longer, of trying even harder.

"Satisfied?" Nikolai's voice was spiteful;
he relished the victory.

I heard footsteps outside in the corridor
and Nikolai's silhouette visibly shrank in
the frame of the doorway. Shota was gone.

"Is there anything else you'd like to stop
for? Any more friends dropping by?" Nikolai's face was white with anger.

It was pointless to tell him that it wasn't
my fault, that I hadn't asked Shota to come
back. I could only put my bow on the
strings, hover my left hand over the fingerboard in submission.

It worked; Nikolai's fury lost its focus and
he settled back on his stool behind me, his
fingers wrapped around mine. Our fused
hand sliced one more time down the strings
and I thought I would die.

"There!"

Nikolai hadn't needed to tell me. I heard
the note, the sweet strung-out smoothness
that fluttered through the world from my
strings. The perfect transition that pulsed
like the blood in my veins, our veins. A thing
of wonder.

"Do it again."

He lifted his fingers off mine. He was still

close enough that I could feel the heat radiate from his face, but he was no longer touching me. I moved my fingers down the strings. Over and over. I had never heard a sound so pure.

Nikolai breathed out a long, exhausted sigh. "That is the music I knew you could make," he said. He got up, bent his creaking knees and stretched out his back. He picked up his jacket from the chair. "Go to bed now," he said, and left.

I couldn't go to bed. It took an hour of holding my fingertips under a cold tap to stop the bleeding, another hour to stop from crying. But I'd done it, I'd found the note that had made him happy.

I remember all of this now because I could do it, even when I truly believed I couldn't. I think of what Shota did for me, of how I went to find him in the morning and, with the great formality of inexperience, he asked me if I would be his girlfriend and how, clumsily, I'd accepted.

Now my bedroom door is shut to protect me, not humiliate me. I can walk out of it anytime I choose and no one will come in unless I ask them. I leave the hurtful memories in the past and edge the bow onto the strings. I remember what I can do. I trust

Nadia to keep the doors closed and I play.

I put fresh flowers on the kitchen table —
big white daisies from the hipster florist near
my shop — and set the whole thing up as a
formal dinner party. The tablecloth is white
and I only have to hide one red wine stain
with a glass.

I do have a separate dining room, but I
have rearranged the furniture in there. I
have folded down the leaves of the table and
heaved it to one side of the room. Three of
the dining room chairs form a small semicir-
cle, three music stands unfolded and set up
in front of them. My music is on my stand;
Nadia and Mr. Williams will bring theirs
with them.

One chair is set apart from the other two
and, between them and tied to the lamp
shades, is a large white bedsheet. This is
Nadia's deep psychological plan and makes
me wonder what they're teaching at A-level
nowadays.

This is the first time I've seen the Cremona cello out in the real world. I get my
phone and sit on the floor next to it. Nadia
would call the photograph that I am compelled to take a cello selfie. It's a great
photo, a good one of me and a beauty of
the instrument. I fire it off to David and

wonder what his Sunday holds.

I have decided not to say anything to Nadia about the diary entry, at least not tonight. I'm the last person to make a judgment on her condition, I'd imagine. At the moment, though, I may be the only person who cares.

In the evening, Nadia is the first to arrive. She's looking beautiful. Her hair is loose around her shoulders and down her back and she's wearing a black skirt, puffed out and very short, a black jumper and bright red tights. She has her violin case on her back and, to my surprise, a bottle of wine in her hand.

"I thought you'd given up drinking." It is suddenly important in the light of everything I've read.

"Your trolley was full of white," she says. And then explains, "In the supermarket. So I bought you a bottle of white."

"Thanks." She is a box of surprises, a zigzag of child and woman.

"What's for dinner? It smells really good. You don't usually cook, do you?"

"Not when it's just me. Pointless. By the time I've cooked it I can never be bothered to eat it."

"I'd be the same, I expect." There is

something in her tone that makes it clear she has no intention of ending up like me.

We walk through to the dining room to get her violin out. Even having her stand in the same room as my cello with her violin case is making me feel dizzy. I breathe deeply.

I sold her this fiddle. It's a beauty. Her parents' budget was fairly high; they ended up spending £30,000. I'd love her to play one I'd made, but I have to admit that this instrument really does suit her playing style. It has a quiet sound; it's not a pushy violin. It's for playing in trios and quartets more than for orchestra work. Nadia wanted something that would serve her well for her music college audition and this little Italian violin is certainly that. She already knows that she will get offers from Manchester, Oslo, London, and Paris. The choice of where to study will be hers.

"Drink?" I ask her.

"Can I have a glass of water? Or Coke or something?"

I look at her twice and then remember that she doesn't know what I'm thinking.

"Is that OK? Grace?"

"Sorry, yes, of course. Fizzy water?"

"Fine. Are we playing before we eat?"

I nod. "Definitely." I pour myself a large

glass of wine. I'm going to need it.

Nadia accepts the glass of water and sips at it. She narrows her eyes slightly. I can see she's about to ask me something she thinks is a little near the knuckle.

"So," she says, "Mr. Williams. Gay?"

"Nadia." I tut as if it's something I've never wondered about. "How would I know? It's none of my business."

"But?"

"Well, I assume so. Although I'm not sure. He might just be a camp old sort, you know, and straight. Does it matter?"

She shrugs. "Of course not. I was just interested. Bet you are as well."

"I know his partner died eighteen years ago and he's not met anyone since. But beyond that, I don't know much about him at all."

"Mission, then. I'll find out." She nods at me just as the doorbell rings.

Mr. Williams has dressed up for a concert. He is wearing a beautifully tailored black suit, a white shirt, and a gold cravat. His black lace-up shoes are shined until silver arcs of light are reflected in them from my ceiling lamps.

I feel horribly underdressed. I did stop to think about my outfit but settled on blue linen trousers and a pale yellow tunic top. A

158

silver necklace with large drops of Polish amber lifts the look a little, but it's still casual compared with Mr. Williams.

He has put his violin case down on the floor and takes two bottles of wine out of a cloth bag he had over his shoulder.

"One of each, dear, couldn't decide."

They are nice wines; he has chosen with care. David would approve.

"Thank you, that's so kind. Would you like a gin and tonic or wine or . . . ?"

"Gin, and it would be lovely, thanks. I play better after a sharpener, I find."

"I'm sorry I couldn't get Alan's fiddle ready in time for today." I am genuinely sorry. It would have been very sweet for him to have played the new version of Alan's violin at the same time as I tried the Cremona cello, but I couldn't get both done. "It's really coming on, though. It's going to work brilliantly. I'm going to cut a new bass bar and I've started thinning down the neck. It'll sound great."

"I have every faith in you, dear," says Mr. Williams, and accepts a large gin in a tumbler. "Smashing. Bottoms up."

We all take a drink. I feel guilty about mine and put it down on the table; I need all my senses sharp to judge the sound of this instrument. I've got to get it right.

The Cremona instruments are judged on their appearance first; they're not looking for anything out of the ordinary — they're looking for perfection. They want to see an even color and a clear depth to the finish. They want to see the flame of the wood magnified by the opacity of the varnish, not obscured or altered by it. What the judges want is, oddly, not what any customer would want. Customers want their instruments to be individual; they want to see character and distinctiveness. If I don't win and wanted to sell my Cremona cello to a player after the competition, I would have to make it look older, give its high shine a little sanding down, flatten a corner here and there.

If I win, the competition organizers will buy the cello from me. They would pay their set price, higher than most makers would ever ask for an instrument, and that would become the value of my cello and all subsequent ones. All the winning instruments, over all the years the competition has run, are displayed in a museum in Cremona. I am determined to keep believing I can join them. I don't know who'd be prouder, David or me. I look around the kitchen and realize Mr. Williams and Nadia would be part of that equation too. I am not as alone as I once was.

We take our drinks through to the dining room and start the tune-up. Mr. Williams and I both tune to the A string of Nadia's violin, partly because she has perfect pitch and partly because she will play the lead violin part. The whole string section tunes to the A string of the first violin, even the basses. I tell myself that this is just tuning, something I do in the shop, something I do all the time in front of customers. The sweat is clinging onto the edges of my hair and my hands are shaking, but I'm holding on.

I assume Mr. Williams thinks the giant bedsheet, strung between us like a ghost, is part of playing a new instrument. He hasn't even commented on it. Perhaps he doesn't find it odd.

At last we're all ready. I can tell just from the tuning I've done and the process of getting the bridge in place, the sound post right, that this cello is going to be unusually good.

"Do you want to just play something solo first, Grace? Something to christen it?" Mr. Williams asks.

He can't see me behind the sheet. He cannot see the panic on my face, the fear in my eyes. I am keeping my ragged breathing deliberately quiet. I will do this.

"Let's just get going."

Instruments made of wood wake up as vibrations start going through them. They never sound as good on the first bowing as they will after a few hours' playing in. The mark of a great instrument, as opposed to a good one, is that it will continue to get better over time. Years of playing will open up depths of sound the wood is keeping in its rings, its knots, its pattern.

I'm shaking; I can feel my lungs tighten, the muscles between my ribs constrict with fear. So much work has gone into this; it is the bearer of my hopes and dreams.

I think of my future children, their music practice, my need to coach and coax them.

I think of Nadia and her loneliness among all the noise and chatter, about how much she needs me to prove to her that she matters.

I think of Mr. Williams and his losses, how we need to grab things while we can, hold them dear.

I think about David, his low, calm voice, his kind eyes, how much he loves me.

Together they push Nikolai out of the picture; they diffuse his frustrations, the memory of his pursed, angry mouth and how he shouted at me.

Nadia has only written out the shortest

part of her symphony, but even in this fledgling state it is extraordinary. I stare at the music, swimming in front of me, and realize that it opens with just the cello.

I am alone. I am responsible for my own sound — my own life — this is the moment I decide whether I am heard or not.

The first note I play is a low C, melancholic and full.

It's beautiful. It is the lowest string on the instrument and, without my fingers on it, produces the deepest sound — the lowest note my cello can make. It vibrates around the room and when it's finished, there is nothing but silence.

It is as if the note has left a hole in the air that carried it.

I look up. The sheet is gone, crumpled onto the floor. Nadia's mouth is open wide in wonder at the clarity of the sound. Mr. Williams's grin is so big that his eyes have almost disappeared into the concertina folds of his wrinkled skin.

Rather than fill the tingling air with fear, I start to play.

There are only two bars of solo before the violins join in. This piece is everything Nadia had played to me, with layers and layers more. It is complex and simple, pointed and angular and — simultaneously

163

— soft and gentle. Its themes are clear and accessible, its phrases perfectly timed.

There is a beautiful dialogue towards the end of this short section, a fragment that showcases — perfectly — the relationship between the instruments. The cello calls and the violin answers and then they turn — elegantly — and continue their discussion the other way around. They compete and tussle, and then they are smooth and harmonious, dependent on each other. It is us, Nadia and me, unmistakably and clearly. She has written about us.

I have never been so touched.

I don't know whether to jump up and throw my arms around Nadia or to fling myself at her feet.

She throws a tissue into my lap. "You need to blow your nose."

I realize I am crying. The tears threaten to fall onto the shoulder of my competition cello. I manage a smile and blow my nose loudly.

"What next, Grace?" asks Mr. Williams. We are high as kites; we need to carry on.

"Piazzolla's 'Libertango.' I'm in a very 'Libertango' mood."

The "Libertango" is the perfect piece and I have missed playing it with other people so much. The CDs that I play along to are a pathetic substitute and I am joyful to have real humans take their place.

My bow slides gracefully across the strings, my left hand shoots up and down the fingerboard, squeezing the high notes from the top register, pulling long, cool, low notes like toffee from the bottom two strings.

I am in Argentina, it is a smoky café, the smells and the dark are what I expect from such a country. I imagine the close and humid air inside the room, the yellowed ceiling; the drinkers lined up along the bar, ancient men perched on stools, one toe touching the floor and the other hooked behind the horizontal brass bar that keeps the legs of the old wooden stool in place. The orchestra of my imagination is a small man hunched over a wheezing accordion and a violin player, tall and swarthy; a man who looks dangerous. Maybe somewhere behind the scene is a woman with bells or castanets, and loud square heels on black shoes. She will dance as we play.

Outside my fantasy bar, through the louvered doors with peeling paint, there is a forest of green. There are vast cliffs sweeping down to crashing rivers, wide rolling plains of short yellow grass, waterfalls that drown out all other sound. Across the whole country the heat remains the dominant force, smothering the people, the plants, the animals, in an escalating pressure.

Nadia joins the tune. Her violin is high and reedy compared to the voluptuous sound of the cello, but she makes it work for both of us.

I picture the red swirling skirts of the dancing woman, her tumbling black hair slick with oil or water, long tattered ribbons tied around her wrists and floating against the fabric of her skirt.

Mr. Williams picks up the simpler line, playing a steadying beat to liberate the two of us, Nadia and me, to play our hearts out. I lean farther forward over the cello, feeling the heat in the strings; Nadia stands and the elbow of her bowing arms flies in and out with the speed of a machine.

We are an engine, the three of us, and we play with exactness, precision. We play like we are making a pact with the devil. We run through the music three times, stretching out the tune because we can't bear to hear it end. Somehow, on the last note of the third turn around, we just stop. The silence is deafening. It feels like smoke.

"Bravo! Bravo!" shouts Mr. Williams.

Nadia is grinning like a demon. We are untidy, sweaty. We are all excited and aflame.

"The sound, Grace." Mr. Williams points towards the cello with his bow. He holds his violin by its neck, the rounded bottom of it on his knee. "I can't believe the sound of that instrument."

"It's fantastic, Grace. Amazing." Nadia really means it. Her makeup is slightly smudgy on one eyelid where the speed of the music left her sweating.

"I didn't think it would do that." I shake my head, pat the front of the cello like it is a horse.

"Imagine what it's going to sound like when it opens up." Mr. Williams is invigorated; there is a shine to his smile that makes him look years younger. "My late partner adored the 'Libertango,' any tango, actually."

Nadia doesn't miss her chance. "What was your partner's name, Mr. Williams?"

"Leslie," he says, or perhaps he says "Lesley." I smile inwardly at Nadia's enthusiastic frustration — it is painted across her face. She is the same Nadia, the same girl. Perhaps her diary entries were complete fantasy. They were certainly all her own business.

In this ordinary white dining room with its ubiquitous pine table and chairs, the mundane beige carpet, the few photographs and paintings, magic has happened. The cello has enchanted us to believe we can fulfill our promises, work through our dreams, banish our fears.

I really have faith in this cello.

I know it can win.

Chapter Twelve

The night is a runaway success.

We play on for over an hour, running through personal favorites and crowd pleasers, even though our audience is imaginary.

We eat far too late and the salad starter I'd prepared has pools of oil and vinegar in the damp leaves where the dressing has separated in protest. We drink and laugh and play some more; the music joining and bonding our odd little trio.

The cello continues to open. I will give it at least three hours' exercise a day between now and when it gets packed into its case and shipped to Italy. I resolve to go to the gym more and improve my muscle tone to do the cello justice.

It is late when they leave. I am tired and extraordinarily happy. I want to thank David for the encouragement, to be able to share this success with him, but he's an hour ahead in France and it will be one thirty in the morning.

I think about texting so that he will have the message in the morning, but it doesn't feel like enough — and I have too many superlatives to say about my cello. I have too many promises to make him about the things I will play for him.

Already I am trying to list adjectives to describe the cello's sound. Normally, the words I'd use are abstract nouns — *profundity* or *broadness* or *subtlety.* The music this instrument makes warrants real, heavy words. It keeps making me think of food: of chocolate, of treacle, of dark burnt toast and melting yellow butter.

I decide to ring David's phone. He won't pick up — the phone is permanently on silent unless he's here — and it won't disturb him. I haven't heard his voice in days and he will be needing to hear mine, too.

I press the green button — his is the only number I call from this phone, a redial will only reach him. The bill goes straight to his account, something he insists on as he could be anywhere in the world and our long nighttime chats cost a fortune.

I know where I will start my monologue. I will talk first about the cello and its sound. Then I will explain what happened, that I wasn't playing alone, that there has been a miracle. He will be able to hear the smile and the enthusiasm in my voice — he'll be able to hear that I've also had a few drinks — and he'll know that I'm managing well in his absence. It will be one less worry for him in the morning.

David's answerphone is set to come on after four rings. I count them off as I hear them. After the third, to my surprise, he answers.

"Hey." He is whispering, his voice is thick with tiredness.

"I thought you'd be asleep."

"Hang on." I hear him get up from wherever he is and I hear the quiet closing of a door behind him. "That's better," he says, his voice only fractionally louder. "Are you OK? Everything all right?"

"More than all right; I played the cello. It's perfect, it's so beautiful."

"Oh, my darling girl, I knew it would be great. What did you play?"

I love that David knows the things that matter to me, that he asks the right questions and listens — really listens — to the answer.

He hums the melody of "Libertango." "Is that the one?"

"Yes. Love it."

"Good choice." He is still whispering.

"And then there's more." I need a run-up to tell him. "Can you talk? Where are you?"

"I'm in Paris. Things are difficult, really fucking difficult. I can't talk for long."

I hear a door open and shut in the background. Something moves and makes a scraping noise — a chair, a coffee table?

"Sorry," he says, and I imagine him sitting back down, brushing his hair away from his eyes as he always does when he's tired. He sighs as if he's about to let go of a huge and heavy sentence of his horrors, but he doesn't.

"Shall I come over?" Now is not the time to tell him about my triumph. It will be better in person.

"I don't know when. Or where." He sounds like someone else, someone smaller. "I've got a client here. I'm on the daybed."

"I could book a hotel. Tell me the day."

"I can't do an overnight. It's complicated, but I'll tell you when I see you. I'm sorry, darling." He sounds so desolate.

"Is everything OK? Really? Are you and your . . . ?"

I was about to ask him if he and his wife were making some kind of reconciliation but he interrupts.

"God, no, nothing like that. Jesus, that

ship sailed a very long time ago." He pauses and understands my silent worries. "Nothing's changed between us, sweetheart. There's just been a lot of mopping up to do."

I throw myself onto the sofa. I have a small glass of wine still sitting on the side and I drink it while he speaks.

"Look, I could do tomorrow. Late lunch. Maybe into the evening. Can you get here? Could you bear to, just for one afternoon?"

I think quickly through the train timetable. "I can do that. I might look like shit after five hours' sleep or something. Can you cope with that?"

"You'll still be more beautiful than every other woman on the street."

I smile. Even now, David manages to make everything about me. "OK, see you tomorrow."

"I'll book Le XVIII" — he actually says *dix-huit* — "for two at two o'clock?"

"You're on," I say, and smile.

"Love you, sweetheart, see you there."

Le XVIII is our favorite restaurant in Paris, and full of memories and conversations. When we first met, we skulked around in less populated arrondissements while we found our feet. Bumping into someone he knew in those early days would have made us both feel so treacherous, so awkward. David meets a lot of clients, past and present, wandering around the streets near his apartment. Most of the American, Russian, and Middle Eastern businessmen he deals with stay near the Trocadéro in the tranche of five-star hotels running down towards the Arc de Triomphe.

On one of our first dates in Paris, when I was new to the city and even David was still exploring those outer reaches, was out to the Pont de Clichy. It's an ugly area. The bridge itself — once you've navigated your way from the Metro and beneath a flyover, past cut-price supermarkets and grubby launderettes — is utilitarian. It isn't, as one might imagine, a piece of tongue-in-cheek Brutalist architecture — it's functional, grim, and ugly. The walkways of the bridge look more like something from an American movie about rail tracks than a pedestrian pavement: the water below is muddy, gray, and eddying.

But across the river are leafier boroughs, far more inviting, and in one of those streets, bordering the river, is Le XVIII. If the waiters there have any judgment about us — and I'm sure they're well aware at least one of us is married to someone else — they are far too professional and old-school-Paris to say so.

Le XVIII is a lovely restaurant. I'm pleased to be going there. It has everything that impresses me about the formality of Paris. The waiters are aloof and handsome — there are rarely any women front-of-house — and the food is never disappointing. The decor and the smells and the slightly arrogant ambience come together to produce something so — totally — Parisian. No one could think they were in any other city in the world.

I'll book a hotel as well, low-key but near the restaurant. David has already said that he can't do an overnighter, but he may well be able to stay late into the evening.

I switch on the computer. I may be able to save a few pounds by booking my Eurostar ticket now instead of buying it at the desk in the morning. I can certainly look at the hotels since I'm far too excited to sleep.

I did promise Mr. Williams that I'd work on Alan's violin over the next few days and I desperately need to keep playing the Cremona cello, but those things will have to wait. I could hear the tension and the stress in David's voice tonight; I need to know he's all right.

I will email Nadia and ask her to open the

shop. She didn't mention any plans for to-morrow.

In the shop inbox is an email from Dominique-Marie Martin. I know the name.

It takes three full seconds to realize that it is from David's wife.

One, two, three.

I open it.

Dear Ms. Atherton, it begins, as harmless as any other.

Please forgive the intrusion of my writing to you — it is not something that I ever saw myself doing.

I have known about your affair with my husband, obviously, since the night you met. Meeting a pretty girl at a party and then not coming home that night is a constant giveaway with David.

While I am not minded to explain the nature of my marriage, I am sure it comes as no surprise to you to realize, or perhaps to have confirmed, that my husband and I enjoyed a very satisfactory, indeed mutu-ally beneficial, arrangement. The only part of this that you need to know is that it ex-ists to protect our children. Specifically, we had a firm agreement that David would have no further children.

My husband is now, to my and his own utter humiliation, having his vasectomy reversed. He believes himself to have found, and please rest assured that this is a direct quote, "true and everlasting love." The object of his lust is a twenty-five-year-old "model" named Marie-Thérèse.

My husband's recent "heroics" on the Paris underground prompted him into action when his girlfriend — an active Facebook user like most twenty-five-year-olds — watched the video of the two of you at Porte de Pantin Metro. As a consequence of this, he has left the family home and moved in with this girl in his Paris apartment.

I have no desire to enter into any dialogue on these matters. I have sent the same email to his PA — who has served him selflessly for twenty years — and a family friend in Germany. I have not bothered with any interim or unimportant girlfriends, and I did not want to humiliate any of you by putting you all on one email.

How you choose to continue your relationship with David is entirely your affair and absolutely none of my business. I do, however, need to point out that, should you and he also decide to have a child, I will do everything necessary to protect my own children's inheritance, rights, and stability. That is my only concern.

At the bottom it is signed, simply, Dominique-Marie Martin.

I am nineteen. I am in the long corridor of the halls at music college. I am going up to the third floor where my best friend's room is because I desperately need a shoulder to cry on and I can't find my boyfriend.

My eyes are so blurred with tears that I cannot make out the color of the paint on the walls or the numbers on the doors.

My cello is in a case on my back; my poor, silenced, mistreated cello. I have come from Nikolai's study where I had a tutorial. Nikolai has been warning me that if I do not practice, my position at the college would be in jeopardy. He has told me for weeks now that I am a disgrace to the beautiful instrument my parents saved so hard to buy for me, I am a liability in his quintet, and — worse — I have jeopardized Shota's very career.

I have practiced. Practiced until my fingers bled. I get up in the night every hour, on the hour, to put more methylated spirits on the ends of my fingers to make them tougher. I book music rooms when it is dark, when everyone else is in the bar or at a club. I practice while they socialize.

Even when I am alone with my boyfriend I talk too much about music, ask him how he would play pieces, hum refrains under my breath. I am doing everything I can not to leave. I am trying harder than anyone can try.

Today Nikolai declared that it is not enough. I am leaving. He is going to the principal tomorrow to explain that he cannot teach me because I don't have the talent. There is nothing more — or less — to it than that.

He has been pushing me more and more. I can no longer eat before Nikolai's sessions, my throat tightening and my stomach shutting down. I have been required to stay behind after every rehearsal, and Shota and I argue about it more and more.

"Your relationship with that boy will cost him his career," Nikolai told me tonight. "Pitching himself against me is a mistake. You only have one heart and it needs to belong to your cello, not to some stupid boy who thinks he can have you."

My face burns with shame; the idea of Nikolai knowing about Shota and me at all leaves me more humiliated than ever.

Nikolai squats behind me, he pushes his

palm flat against the small of my back. "Here," he says, and presses against my spine. "This is the center of you; this is where you will generate the sound. This is near to your soul."

I sit up as straight as I can. I'm dizzy from hunger and from Nikolai's shouting.

He holds my bowing arm out straight with his right arm, and draws his fingers back until they circle my wrist. "Now," he says, "draw the bow back and feel the song in your soul. Let go."

But I just close in more tightly as the inside of his arm meets the back of mine, as his body makes another attempt to push me up straight, to give my arms and spine the combined power they need to make the sound he wants.

My posture solved for the moment, he moves to my left hand position, pressing my agonized fingers flatter — but not harder — onto the strings. The slide when we make the shift down the wound alloy strings feels like they will separate my flesh like cheese wire.

I cry out in pain, certain there will be blood streaming down the fingerboard. Nikolai covers my small hand with his, each of his fingers mapping mine like a glove, his cheek fleshy against mine, and I can smell his breath in the air in front of my mouth. "Once more," he whispers, and his voice is uncharacteristically gentle against my neck.

"I can't." I pull away from him. I cannot get any closer to this man who pushes me and tries to teach me; this man I want to please more than almost any other, but whom I fail every day. "I just can't."

Nikolai shouts at me the whole time I am packing my cello away. As I slide in the spike and tighten the bolt, he tells me who I could have been. As I clip the case shut he lists the reasons that I will never be a player of any note at all. As I struggle my arms through the straps to get out of the room, he lays out — in pointed, painful detail — every fracture and crack that will tear across my parents' hearts. The concert we have worked for months on is next week and I will not be playing in it. My parents will not be in the audience.

My time in the college is over.

I search out my boyfriend. I stumble up the stairs and into the corridor. His door is on the right. I knock on the door, wishing myself inside. There is no answer.

I know he isn't there — it is too small to hide. Only a month ago, I left my virginity in Shota's room, in that tiny bed. It was part of my effort to feel normal, to be like all the other students. It was my attempt at finding the passion that Nikolai says I will never have.

It didn't work.

Shota has left his family in Japan to come here — he is alone. College means as much to him as it does to me. He is my kind of boy.

I pull myself down the corridor, crying so hard I feel sick. Catherine's door is near the end, farthest away from the stairs. I get closer and her door opens. It is Shota who backs out of Catherine's small room. It is Shota who pulls on his coat and blows a kiss back through the open door. It is Shota who isn't carrying his viola, who wasn't in Catherine's room to practice music.

I turn and run. I call my mother and I leave.

I never ask Shota how long he has been seeing Catherine. I never question Catherine about what is really happening. I never speak to anyone from college again. It is years before I can even think about it without crying and decades until I will play the cello in front of anyone else.

I read and reread the email. I am not hysterical or naive. I am not, any longer, stupid. I breathe deeply and calmly and remember that this has been written by an angry wife, a betrayed spouse.

I concentrate on the things I was doing before it arrived. I know I can't ring David — his phone will be on silent and he will be asleep now.

I book a hotel in Asnières-sur-Seine through an internet site. It is midrange — for Paris — and functional and a short walk from the restaurant. I book my ticket for the Eurostar and work out where I will leave my car and, therefore, what time I will need to leave home.

The most awful thing that David's wife has done is to pretend that he has had a vasectomy. It means, presumably, that she knows I am desperate for a baby. It also shows that she doesn't know about our two precious miscarriages. They, the lost babies, are what we have that excludes his wife, and that is what I hold on to. I hear myself mutter, "I know something you don't know," to no one in my empty house. I go to bed.

I set my alarm for half past five but am awake, wide-awake, at four.

I am determined not to make the mistakes I made at college. I'm not going to jump to conclusions, conclusions that have painful, spiny echoes for years.

I have no reason to trust David's wife and every reason to trust him. The logical conclusion, and the one I want to reach, is that she has seen the footage of the two of us together and needs to lash out. My email address is easily found — it is on my shop website. There aren't many female violin makers in this end of the country, and even fewer who have their own shops. She would need little information about me to find me and I presume that little information was given up by David in response to the media sitting outside their house day and night.

At half past four, the birds start singing outside and the sun creaks slowly into life as if a hinge is lifting on the horizon. With it my spirits begin to rise. The daylight brings a rationality, some common sense. Perhaps David has told her that I am a twenty-five-year-old model called Marie-Thérèse; maybe he is deflecting blame from me. I am even more convinced when I google and find nothing but a maze of Picasso and perfume under that name. Maybe he wants to direct his wife's vitriol at a cut-out image from a magazine, save himself from listening to her cursing me. I hope fervently that he has really moved out of his family home, even though it will hurt his children and even though it is not, strictly, in the rules.

For a moment I imagine the rest of his things here in this half-empty bedroom. We will have to share our time between here and Paris for a while but what utter bliss that will be.

I dress carefully. I want to look a little Parisian; as if I could fit in there, belong there, if need be. I want to look like I haven't put too much effort into what I choose; David isn't keen on high heels and too much makeup.

I choose a dress that is very short but balances out with sleeves, which are long and slim, tapering tightly in at the wrists. It doesn't need any jewelry; it is beautifully designed just as it is. It is enough. I don't wear tights — my legs are brown from the summer — and I dig out the loafers I bought in Paris this spring.

I check myself in the hall mirror; I look good and it makes me feel confident.

I pick up my bag and check for passport, shop keys, money, and phone. With every mundane thought, everything is calming down, getting more normal. I will see David in just a few hours.

The last thing I pick up before I leave is the cello. I am taking it to the shop so that Nadia can play it if she wants to. She's no cellist, but she is a capable string player who knows how to get a tune out of it and, more important, knows how to treat it well. Any practice at all will help the sound to open up.

By the time I get to the shop there are one or two lights on in shopwindows along the street. The butcher's shop up the road keeps long hours, and the owner waves hello at me as he carries meat from the wagon parked outside. He doesn't seem to think it odd that I'm standing outside my shop at six o'clock in the morning, dressed to kill and carrying a cello.

I daren't leave the cello in the shop. It would only take one unsupervised child, one busybody father, to do something catastrophic to its perfect shine, its flawless varnish. I leave it out of the case so that it is obvious to Nadia but arrange it, safely, in the corner of the workshop where no accident could befall it.

CHAPTER THIRTEEN

I get to Paris far too early. I knew I would. I booked so late that I had to buy the most expensive ticket; the only upside is that it is completely flexible. I can stay over this evening or go back later on today. I squeeze my fingernails into the palms of my hands as I hope that I'll stay, and David with me.

I try to doze on the train but I'm too tense. Instead I leaf through the paperwork for the competition. I have two weeks before the cello must be sent off. A month after that, David and I have twelve blissful nights booked in a beautiful hotel in Cremona. In the daytimes I will network and chat to makers and dealers from all over the world; David, of course, will do his part with translating for me and generally entertaining potential clients. In the evenings we will listen to world-class recitals from some incredibly big names. In the nighttime we will sleep curled up to each other and try to put all this anxiety behind us.

The Gare du Nord is its usual squash of sounds and smells. Tourists bump by me on their way to the taxi rank on the right; trying to move out of the stream of people into the left side of the station is like trying to swim against the tide.

I give up fighting and let myself be popped out onto the sidewalk like a cork on the sea. The sunshine is fresh after the cloying air of the train and I breathe in deeply. There is a taste in the air of this city that I'm sure I could identify against any others.

I walk down the road. This isn't the most salubrious of areas; in my experience, the parts of cities near stations never are. I walk past a few massage parlors and a row of restaurants that are boarded up. A couple of men are handing out phone cards outside a *tabac* but they ignore me because I'm white. They assume I have no one to phone in far-off countries.

The bus system in Paris completely defeats me; even David only uses the few routes he is familiar with. I check on the app I have for the Parisian public transport system, but there doesn't seem to be a clear route to where I want to go. The app tells me it will take not much more than an hour to walk and I have at least that to kill. My overnight clothes and a miniature version of my makeup kit are all in a small leather backpack over my shoulder. It isn't heavy or awkward to carry and my shoes are flat, comfortable and sensible. The walk will wake me up and I can make it beautiful by going through Pigalle, up over the hill of Sacré-Coeur and down into the winding streets of Montmartre. The second half of the walk will be far less pleasant, but I'm prepared to try. I think I look sufficiently like a native to risk the bleaker areas out towards Pont de Clichy.

I'm glad of the exercise; it is probably the hilliest route one could find in Paris and I find my shortness of breath invigorating. I push myself hard up the steps of Montmartre, turning at the top to take in the view.

I wander into the Montmartre Cemetery; one I haven't been in before, and I ground myself by looking at the sculptures and the history and the declarations of love or respect.

I check the time; I can't put it off any longer. I walk at a decent pace for the next half hour or so. I can tell by the area, the buildings, the people and their purpose, when I'm very close to the restaurant. I go into a pharmacy and pretend to be looking at sunglasses while I check my hair and lipstick in the mirror on the display stand. I look tired. My cheeks are sun-kissed and bright from the walk, but my eyes are dull and puffy.

The heavy restaurant door has a long brass handle running down one side of it. I don't get a chance to push it open before the attentive maître d' scuttles forward and opens it for me. I look past him into the gloom of the restaurant. It really is spectacular, all dark green houseplants on mahogany aspidistra stands, and rails of polished copper along every horizontal surface — except the tables, which are draped with starched white napery.

David is at a table in the far corner. He is tasting wine and talking enthusiastically to the waiter. He holds the wineglass up to the light and swirls the red liquid around in it.

David looks up and sees me. His face lights in recognition and he stands, his arms out and open. There is no guile, no pretense and no worry on that face, no tension in the skin around those beautiful eyes.

David is an innocent man.

I am so relieved I almost cry in the restaurant doorway. I walk towards him and he holds me close; everything is just as it should be.

"That must have been a rotten journey, Gracie. I'm so sorry to mess you about."

"Do you mean I look like shit?" I ask him and smile. I have dropped my voice in case the waiters speak English.

"You look incredible. As always." He kisses me and pulls out my chair so I can sit down. "And actually, I have to say — you look incredibly Parisian."

"It's because I bought this outfit here. The shoes and the dress."

"The dress is a knockout. You look sensational." He leans towards me. "And the cello's a triumph?"

I grin. "It really is."

David rocks back in his chair and shrugs; he is wearing his Paris clothes, he looks every inch the Frenchman. "I knew you'd do it. And you'll win the competition. I know it, darling girl."

He turns his attention to the menu, orders champagne for us both. It arrives swiftly, wrapped in a white cloth. David shakes his head when the waiter offers a taste. He gestures that he should just fill both our glasses.

"To your success," he says and stares into my eyes. "I'm so incredibly proud of you."

"Your wife sent me an email. Dominique-Marie." It comes out of my mouth without permission. This is not a moment to spoil.

The champagne is crisp and cold, biscuit yellow and perfect.

The man opposite me is glowing with love, holding my hand across the tablecloth and sending pulses of electricity through my skin.

The waiters are dipping and bobbing like birds, arranging cutlery and smoothing napkins.

"She said she would," he says. His gaze doesn't move from mine. His mouth doesn't twitch. There are no Hollywood beads of sweat on the Cupid's bow of his top lip.

"Is it true?"

"I don't know, baby. I don't know what she said."

"Have you left her? Them?"

He clinks his champagne glass against mine again and drinks. "I have."

I don't know what to say. I don't know why he didn't tell me.

A waiter comes past with two menus. He runs through the plat du jour and he and David laugh a little over something. David waves him away.

"She said some awful things." I can't name them. The words are stuck in my throat like cotton wool. My tongue is made of glass and will splinter if I say the words.

The shards will choke me, lacerate my throat.

"She's angry, Grace. And really hurt." He sucks his lips together. "This wasn't what we'd agreed would happen. It wouldn't have, you know; if fate hadn't pushed things around." He gives his trademark sigh and pushes his fringe up from his face. "Shall we forget about it for today? Try and enjoy ourselves? I'll tell you about all the fucking crap in my life, you tell me about the cello and about what we're going to do in Cremona?"

There are vipers crawling through the skin on my face. Tiny malevolent snakes wriggle through capillaries under my eyes. I can feel the pain of their scratching scales as they worm their way across me.

"Grace?"

An intense pain runs around the outline of my chin, it settles at the hinges of my jaw. It fights and bulges behind my eyes. I open my mouth to relieve the pressure and words fall out.

"She said you had a vasectomy."

He closes his eyes. I can see his face moving, his thoughts regrouping. I watch his tongue at the very edge of his mouth; I see it rub and wet his teeth. It pulses minutely, involuntarily. I can see the taste buds pop-ping from the end, from the blunt point. His lips are the exact shade of pink a man's lips should be, his tongue a shade or two darker. His teeth are straight and white and they shine where the light catches them.

"Grace, let's take this somewhere else." He is counting out euro notes onto the table, leaving twice the value of the drinks we've had, to signal to the waiters that it is us, not them. We are wrong.

David is elegant and in control as he helps me out of my chair and takes my arm. He stands back at the door to let me go first and steers me through onto the pavement.

"Where's your hotel, Grace? What did you book?"

My hands are trembling when I take my notebook out of my bag. I don't trust myself to open it and unfold the printout of my booking. My possessions will scatter onto this Paris street, every precious piece of paper, every ticket, each memento that is tucked into the leaves of this book will blow away.

David reads the address out loud.

"It's OK, sweetheart." He takes my hand. "I can explain. Please, don't cry."

I am not as frozen as I thought. One tear has melted out of me and is slowly threading down my face.

David wipes it away with his thumb. "Come on, Gracie. Let's get off the street, talk properly."

I have shared the worst moments of my life with this man. There must be an explanation. There must be words and reasons.

David is the only one who feels the drop I felt, the sheer careening chaos of falling, flailing, into the void we have never climbed out of. He is the only person besides me who knew our babies, who was aware of them, who was physically close to them.

He is the only person I have been able to use as a foothold, a handhold, a fraction of safety to keep me from hitting the ground. Please don't let him be the one to cut the rope.

"Grace, Grace." He is talking quietly, stroking my arms. We are outside the hotel. "Just for a moment, I need you to concentrate. We'll check in, find our room, and then sort this out. OK?"

I move up the stairs without speaking. I follow David into the hotel room like I've followed him into a hundred hotel rooms before. If I speak, if I open my mouth, I will shatter.

The room is remarkably good for midrange Paris. In any other circumstances I would be impressed. Instead I will just remember the Louis Quinze sofa, the thick red drapes with gold rope ties, as the room where I lost my life.

The themes of art, of classical music, fly through my mind. Man against man. Man against nature. Man against himself. For each theme I see a piece of my life fly away; I am flayed by the loss of my career, my children, my future.

David sits me on the bed, moves closely in beside me.

"It's not what you think. I swear to you."

I spread my fingers on my knees, straighten them out as far as they will go, feeling each knuckle press rigidly into the finger next to it. I stare at my fingernails. I try to breathe normally.

"It was before I met you, three weeks before I met you." He springs off the bed, falls to his knees in front of me and takes my hands. As he kneels he looks up at me. "Don't think I'm not really fucking ashamed of thinking they weren't mine. Of even telling you that they weren't mine on that first day. I replay that conversation over and over." His head drops down; I see the swirl of his crown, the few gray hairs that spiral out from it.

"I'll never forgive myself; it was an utterly

brutal thing to say. But at the time I believed it."

He lays his head on my lap. "I had a checkup that week, a routine follow-up. They warned me, no — they didn't fucking warn me — they reminded me. They'd already told me once that I mustn't have sex without contraception for weeks, not till the last . . . well, you know. Till they'd all died, gone."

My fingers are still. They are white and I am cold. My legs have goose bumps. The short dress seems ridiculous now; childish and frivolous.

"And then you were broken. So completely fucking destroyed. What could I do?" He looks at my face.

My mouth wobbles, my chin is shaking. There are no words.

"I asked them at the hospital; I made sure there are ways to still have a baby. To get around it. They can stick a needle into my balls, pull out swimmers." His face twists into a peculiar smile. "They do it under a general." He wants that last piece to be a joke.

Words roll out of my mouth. They are diminished; we both have to strain to hear them. "Have you any idea what I've been through. The invasion? The tests and the scrapes and the fucking pain?"

"I've been with you at most of them, Grace. Of course I know." He stands up, strides around. "Don't you think that fucking hurt me? Can you imagine how it felt to watch you stirruped up and poked and prodded? Knowing all the time that I could stop it, but that if I did, I would cause you the most pain possible?"

He slumps into a chair on the other side of the room. His head is in his hands.

I stand up and open the door to the en suite bathroom. I am sick before I even have a chance to shut the door behind me. Vomit splatters into the lavatory bowl as if all the poisonous years are erupting out of me.

I don't want to lose my poisonous years. I don't want to lose our past — however fictitious. Without it I have nothing.

When I come back into the room David is openly crying. It occurs to me, for the very first time, how easily he cries. How sexy he looks when he does it. No rivulets of snot, blotched skin or racking, gut-spilling sobs. David cries softly; fresh, straight tears lengthen his perfect eyelashes and then light two trails of sadness down his blemish-free cheeks like a well-set varnish.

"I was going to get it done, one way or another, as soon as my kids were old enough. As soon as the time was right for us to start a family." His eyes are pleading with me.

I wonder if my heart has stopped beating. I can hear nothing from my own body.

"I was going to get it reversed or — if it came to it — we'd have IVF and use the harvested sperm. It was always going to work in the end. In the meanwhile, it just meant that no one would get hurt."

I sit back on the bed and he comes over. He rolls me gently onto my side, lies beside me and scoops me into his arms. I can smell his beautiful scent and his neck is soft against my skin.

"I'm so fucking sorry, baby. I loved you too much to tell you."

He kisses my face, tiny butterflies of kisses landing and leaving, leaving and landing.

"I can't believe I've hurt you this much. That I let it go on so long. I'm so sorry."

"Eight years." I have shut my eyes against the pain, the weight of it all, and my words echo out into the purple darkness of my closed eyelids. "Eight years."

"I'm so fucking sorry."

"She said you have a girlfriend."

CHAPTER FOURTEEN

I know I will hate myself for sleeping with David, but I am too tired, too punch-drunk, not to. I need someone to hold me, to press their skin against mine and reassure me that I'm still alive. Despite the fact that he is the reason I am so totally destroyed, he is the only person I can think of to protect me.

As soon as I say the word "girlfriend" I know it is all true. I accept the fact slowly, in drips that mottle all our previous conversations like mold. My conscience dashes backwards and forwards; looking for a clue here, a suspicion there, finding a cold, hard infidelity at the end of my search.

The scales slip from my eyes one by one. Not the scales that blind me to him; the way I feel about David will take more than one day and one conversation to dismantle, but I can suddenly see the situation and its bleakness as surely as if they were standing in the room.

I need to put off speech for as long as possible. I need to stem the relentless shower of words that threatens to submerge me, that already cuts off my air.

I yield to David's tentative kisses. I allow his mouth to move from my neck, to my face, to my mouth. And then I am kissing him back with a hunger, staving off the fierce pain of having already lost him, of having never really had him.

We do not speak except in gasps. He tells me he loves me. I answer. It would not be true to say I don't love him.

This is my last of him, I think as we make love, and I cannot imagine how life will work without him in it.

I wake in half darkness, in the hotel bed. The curtains are still open and the sulfur light of streetlamps outlines everything in the room. David is sitting up; his feet are on the floor and he is doing up his shirt.

I have woken up heavy with knowing and full of shame.

Before I speak to him, I tell myself that I had little choice, that the alternative to sleeping in this hotel with David was sobbing my way — alone — back to England. That is what I tell myself, but the truth is that I just wanted a few more hours, minutes, of him.

"David."

"Sorry, darling, I didn't mean to wake you. I have to go." He turns and touches my arm. It is a gesture I know well, one from my every encounter with him. David touches me as if nothing has changed.

He takes my hand and kisses it. He holds it for a second afterwards, breathes in my skin.

"I'll see you soon. Really soon. I'll come to England as soon as I can. I'm sorry I've cocked all this up."

I feel dizzy, as if I have imagined every part of the day and night.

"I thought . . ."

He smiles at me, kisses me softly on the cheek. "God, you're beautiful. What did you think?"

"Your wife said you have a girlfriend."

He hasn't confirmed or denied it, and I hold that fact to me like a talisman. It slips through my fingers like smoke.

"Look, nothing's changed between you and me. We're the same as we ever were."

"Do you have a girlfriend?" My head aches. I need the loo but I can't get up. If I move he will leave, I know it.

"Gracie, I have a wife. That didn't affect us, did it? Not ever." He turns up his collar to put his tie on underneath it. "Nothing's changed. I love you. And . . ." He puts his hand on my shoulder. "I don't want to lose you. I never have."

"You are sleeping with someone else, aren't you?"

"It's not that. It's not a sexual thing. Look, fuck, this is hard to explain — I need more time. I have met someone, yes, but it's different. It's different from my marriage and it's different from us."

Cold air blows in through the open window, but it isn't that that makes me shiver.

"I thought I could live without you, darling girl, I was really going to try. I thought I was. I promised Marie-Thérèse that I would give you up. But I can't."

I sit up in bed. I put both my hands over my mouth and try to hold in the disbelief.

"When I saw you in the restaurant, looking so fucking beautiful, I realized I could never give you up. You're totally fucking unique."

If I stay silent, this strange man in David's skin will stop talking. If I use my silence to bargain with him, perhaps he will return my beautiful boyfriend to me.

"It's just like when we first met. No more, no less. I've been enchanted by her. Just as I was by you. Still am by you."

He leans towards me, tries to kiss my back.

I wrench away from him and then immediately regret the distance I have made; the inches between us that will split like an iceberg, flaking chunks of cold falling into my life.

"Don't be angry. I'm being honest with you. It's all I can be. It's all I can do."

"Are you asking me to stay with you? While you make a baby with this girl?"

He stands, pulls on his trousers and tugs at his belt. "I don't know what will happen. My arm's been forced, you know? I didn't ask for any of this."

"What about my baby?" My voice is a ghost in the room.

He puts his fingers to his temples, closes his eyes. "We were fucking great together, you and me. Fucking great. I didn't mean to meet Marie-Thérèse. I certainly didn't mean to fall in love with her. You have to understand that none of this was planned." And then he adds, as if I am a child of limited understanding, "Please take that on board. This. Was. Not. Planned."

A noise comes from within me, half hiccup, half sob. It is a belch of humiliation, a pain that refuses to turn into anger no matter how much I want it to.

All I can feel is loss. I am desperate for

him to tell me none of this is true, delirious with the need for it to be a hallucination. Or even just a mistake.

"Grace, I've lied to my youngest child his whole life to be with you: he's almost nine years old. I don't have to lie anymore. I've left; my family is destroyed, devastated. My kids won't even speak to me."

He sits down again. I edge away from him in the bed and he puts his hand on my knee. Beneath the thin white sheet I am naked and his palm traces the bones of my leg.

"Every single thing I ever said to you was true. Every fucking word."

"But you were sleeping with other people?" The depths of me beg him, without words, to say no.

"You never asked me that, Gracie. You never asked for it to just be you. You knew I was married when you signed up for this. You knew it was never just you."

He exhales a sigh of frustration. "Don't ask me to give her up, darling, I can't. I only wish I fucking could."

Inside my body, a bold — vivid — me screams that I would never ask that, that he's welcome to her. They're welcome to each other. The hidden me screams at him and slaps his face; pulls his hair and rips his clothes.

The outside me just starts to shake with impotence.

"You're cold, baby. You're shivering." He gets up and shuts the window, an everyday act of concern, of kindness. And then he starts again with his litany of how much he loves me and how much he loves his girl-friend — only eight years older than Nadia — and what he's given up.

The shaking won't stop. My hands tremble and I cannot trust my legs when I try to stand. My tremulous voice croaks that I need to go to the bathroom and David has to help me, half carry me, through the door.

He pulls the door closed behind me in a peculiar gesture of modesty, given that we have just spent hours having sex in the room he is standing in.

I whisper that I have finished and he helps me back to the bed.

"You need to get some sleep, baby. You're not doing yourself any good like this. Not either of us."

My lips are too dry for sound to come out; it will catch on the sandpaper of my skin. I stare at him with round eyes and he responds by tucking the sheet around me, covering my body with the duvet.

"I've got to go, darling girl. I'm so sorry, I really have to. I'll call you."

My mind goes with him, back to the Trocadéro, into the art deco elevator and behind its ornate iron doors. My imagination travels into the cool, white hallway of his apartment, feels the breeze of the river coming through the long window, traces his striding legs as he crosses the elegant sitting room.

The last thing I picture, before I fall asleep still shaking, is his arrival in the arms of a beautiful young girl. My mind puts me through the pain of watching them kiss, and I turn away before they make love.

The journey home is the kind that people make when someone dies. I cannot concentrate; I cannot separate my reality from my imagination.

Just as I manage to process that he is not coming back — that he has gone — a plan we had made together for the weeks ahead pops into my mind and I am back at square one. I am still the person I was when I set off walking from Gare du Nord to meet my boyfriend. My default setting is hardwired for David to be in my life, to consume my thoughts.

As soon as I relax, I remember with a jolt everything that has happened in the last two days. It is a fresh and violent shock each time.

I try, in the gray seat of the train, to picture moments from our past, to pull on a clue and get it in my grasp. There are no clues. There was no preamble to this discovery. David and I never discussed who he was when we were apart.

I wonder how long he has been in love with Marie-Thérèse. I try not to think about how long they have been sleeping together.

The part of me that lived in the glamorous Parisian apartment is over. The would-be cosmopolitan high achiever with the handsome boyfriend, the brilliant career, is dead. Worse still, I don't know when that person died.

Was the girlfriend staying in the apartment when I wasn't there? Have we been tumbling into laundered sheets on alternate nights, watching separate concerts and booking different restaurants but living the same life?

She knows about me. David said that he had promised to give me up.

Give me up.

Give me up to what? To whom? It feels like he has given me up to an abyss, a churning crater that I can't understand.

The train thunders through its same

route. The sketched fields of northern France, the poppies, the orange farmhouses and small white vans, give way to the black of the tunnel. I wish for the rock to shrink, to grip the train and squeeze us until we are all just black. All given up.

In the bright light of the other side, the cliff rises up to my right and the weald of Kent declares its green slopes. The closer I get to home, the worse I feel. There is nothing left. This is worse than college, worse than the miscarriage; both of those events — although I couldn't see it at the time — left fragments of hope, translucent ghosts of future to grasp at. This is the end of my world; the undoing of the past of it and the obliteration of what might have been. This is the end of "one day."

I cannot go back into my house. I cannot sleep in a bed that has "David's side."

I drive to the shop instead of home. I clench my teeth and grip the steering wheel; it takes every piece of me to concentrate on the road. My mind wrestles the whole way back, trying to find a reason not to drive into the walls, off the corners. I tell myself that I need to find a place where I can only hurt myself, where there is no risk of taking anyone innocent with me.

I unlock the door, slam it tight behind me.

I shoot the bolts across the bottom to make sure I have cut myself off from the outside world and any rescue. This is where I want it all to end, where I have chosen to be.

I walk through to the workshop.

In the corner is my Cremona cello. It shines under the striplight. Its perfect varnish is an allegory for all the veils I have chosen not to look behind, all the smoke and mirrors of my life.

I pull back my leg, bent at the knee.

I point my French loafer to the ground before I swing my foot forward and through the front of the cello.

What we know as a cello is actually called a *violincello,* hence the grammatical shortening to *'cello.* It is part of the violin family, whereas a double bass is technically part of the viol family.

The separate pieces of a cello are held together using hide glue. Hide glue is made by boiling down connective tissue of animals. The glue is water soluble and can be undone at any time. Science has not come up with a more appropriate adhesive for violin making.

Two of the commonest — and most serious — injuries to any string instrument are sound post or bass bar cracks. When force is applied to the outside of the instrument, the tender belly cracks across the stronger interior pieces. Lines running down from the bottom of an f-hole to the base of the instrument are usually bass bar cracks on the right or sound post cracks on the left. The belly, being softer wood than the maple back and ribs, has always been more prone to damage than other parts of the instrument.

The cello is one of the few instruments with the vocal range of a human.

CHAPTER FIFTEEN

The first voice I hear belongs to Mr. Williams. Behind that there are other voices, but I can't make them out.

I don't bother to listen. I can hear Mr. Williams cooing and worrying. His voice is a blanket and I use the safety of it as an excuse to close my eyes again.

Nadia's voice is like breaking glass. "Holy shit, Grace. Way to go."

Behind her, Mr. Williams continues his noises of peacemaking and platitude. The words are indistinct, but the sounds are enough on their own.

"You couldn't fucking make it up." She is taking little or no notice of him.

I feel the gush of air as Nadia drops herself down somewhere near my face. I open my senses if not my eyes and try to understand where I am.

I am in a bed that is not mine. I can tell

this from the softness of the pillows ballooning onto my cheeks at either side and from the warmth of a heavy duvet smothering my whole body, cocooning it. I can guess, without too much effort, that this is Mr. Williams's house.

I have a horrible feeling, a memory as faint and elusive as smoke. I know why I'm here. A guilt, a horror and a crashing sadness fill my mind.

I am less clear on why Nadia is here and I wish she'd go away.

"I'm assuming it's got everything to do with David." Nadia is relentless. "I've read the article."

I open my eyes. It is definitely an older person's house. The walls are beige and covered in a variety of landscape paintings. The light is gentle and filtered through unlined curtains with a pale pattern of stripes.

"What article?"

"I assumed you'd read it. I thought that's why you . . . you know. Why you smashed everything up."

"Nadia. These questions can wait." Mr. Williams shoos her out of the way and I catch sight of her face without turning my head when she stands up. She has come out without her makeup on and she looks young, soft.

"Grace, dear, can I get you a glass of water? I have some here on the nightstand." He sits on the edge of the bed.

I move my eyes slowly to the left. There is a carafe with a clean glass tumbler upended over its mouth. I nod.

Mr. Williams lifts the glass to my lips and I let him because every inch of me hurts. It is a dull pain, muscular and deep. "What article?"

"Shh, really, Grace. All things in good time. Let's get you back in the land of the living first."

I struggle upwards, raising my shoulders off the pillow. My head feels as if it is made of lead and I can barely support its weight. The inside of my mouth feels swollen, the skin on my face tight.

"Jesus, Grace. You look awful." Nadia's voice is very loud.

"That's enough, Nadia," Mr. Williams intervenes. "Go and make yourself useful. See if the oven's up to temperature yet for the bread."

Nadia leaves, presumably to do as she is told. I am so glad she's gone.

"Is it David? Is he in the papers?" My voice sounds like someone weak and old. Someone defeated.

"You really must have a drink and get sorted out first, Grace." Mr. Williams helps me shuffle up onto the pillows. I am wearing a white T-shirt, too big for me. I have never seen it before. "It is David, yes. It's about him. But waiting ten minutes isn't going to change it."

"Is he OK?"

Mr. Williams nods. "He's fine, which is a lot more than I can say for you."

The burning in my eyes feels like I am crying, but nothing lands on my cheeks. I remember — in a photographic flash — a tableau of me, weeping on the shop floor. Literally on the shop floor; my front flat against the carpet, my hopeless arms and legs spread out. Occasionally I whacked the rough carpet with the flat of my hands, scuffed against it with the tops of my feet as I screamed. I don't want to think about it.

"I was drunk." This new version of me is as thin as paper.

"I know."

"I went down to the shop cellar when I got back from Paris. There's a sofa down there, a little sitting room with a low ceiling." I don't know why I am pointing out these details.

"I know." Mr. Williams nods his head slowly. He still has the water glass in his hands and he offers it towards mine.

I wrap my fingers around the glass. Its coldness is comforting; I am surprised to find I can still feel ordinary sensations. "I don't know what I drank. I wanted to die, I think."

The ends of my fingers are covered in tiny scabs, carpet burns from clawing at the floor, scratching at it pointlessly with my desperate empty hands.

Mr. Williams doesn't speak, but he nods his head. I catch his eye but have to look away; the sadness in his face is crucifying. His hand trembles slightly as he takes the glass back from me.

"It was a terrible thing that you did. So awful."

I squeeze my eyes tightly shut as if that will close my ears, my memory.

"I can't believe you could harm the violins, all those beautiful instruments."

Horrible pictures streak in front of my closed eyes. Inside my head I see my foot going through the cello, I hear the grating wood bending against itself, splintering into matchsticks. I think I can imagine myself doing more. I hope — halfheartedly — that I didn't take the neck of a viola and swing its body and shoulders into the violins hanging from the racking. I wish with all my being that I am just pretending I kicked over all the cellos and swept the workbench of instruments.

I feel sick as I smell the memory of the dust, the fresh open wounds in the wood, the spilt varnish, and the leaking glue. I pray that these things are all hallucinations; I put my hands to my face and sob. I know they are not.

I retch and lurch forwards as the clearest image comes to my mind. My French loafer, my thin ankles, my bony knee, stamping down furiously on the fragile body of a half-size Italian violin; an instrument that had survived two world wars, outlived countless owners.

I truly hate myself, and the retch turns into a full-blown vomit.

The vomit spills onto the clean bed linen. Mr. Williams jumps into action with towels and buckets, but the damage is done.

I lie, helpless, in a pool of damp red, clouds of dirty, stinking pink surround me and I can feel dribble hanging from my chin.

Mr. Williams starts to talk. I think he does it to change the subject, to pretend that I am not covered in my own sick and incapable of doing anything about it. The stench of putrid wine and acid feels right, feels like it fits.

My life is over.

"I'd come by the shop to see if you were back." He is rubbing the sheet with the corner of a towel. It makes no difference to the color.

"I looked through the window and assumed you'd been burgled. Burgled? Vandalized? I don't know. Something." He drops his head down so that he isn't looking at me. "There was chaos, smashed instruments everywhere. The glass front of the counter was shattered, smashed to smithereens with everything else."

Nadia's disembodied voice comes up the stairs. She's shouting something about bread and ovens. Mr. Williams walks over to the door and calls down some instructions. I don't care what they are, I just want her to stay downstairs, to stay away from me.

I start to cry, although I don't know whom I'm crying for or why. It is a totally pointless exercise and it will bring nothing back.

"So I called the police," Mr. Williams continues. He wipes my pillow with the towel but leaves the spit drying on my face. My jaw is slack and open like a doll.

"The police broke in and that's when we found you." He stands and folds up the towel. "The ambulance came, but they were fairly certain you had just drunk yourself unconscious. We brought you back here last night after they'd had a good look at you in the hospital."

" 'We'?" I wonder, just for a moment, if "we" means David.

"Nadia. One of her friends saw the police cars and called her. She and I took turns watching you during the night."

Flakes of wood and shards of varnish drop into my memory as he speaks. The screams of strings snapping and the wailing of the fractured wood won't leave me. I am fighting for breath.

"I called a locksmith; they've made good the shop front . . ."

He was obviously going to add that everything is safe, before his voice trailed off as he realized there is nothing left to save. I have destroyed it.

"Mr. Williams?"

This is the worst of my pain. This is the worst moment of my life.

"Alan's violin? It was on the workbench."

He shakes his head. It is one death too many; there are no words.

Nadia speaks in whispers through the dark. Her voice is soft but intended to wake me up. She calls my name gently and sits down on the edge of my bed.

"Are you awake?"

"Yes."

She lies back on the pillow, on top of the covers, and shuffles herself down the bed so she is lying next to me, perched on the very edge.

"I was really scared."

I haven't heard this voice for years. The angry fledgling-adult Nadia is gone; this is the voice from inside her, beneath the barricade. "I thought you were going to die."

"I'm really sorry."

She sniffs and I can hear that she is stifling tears. I tug the corner of the thick duvet. I feel the weight of her in its resistance.

"Come under here if you want."

She wriggles, pulls the duvet over her.

I can feel the pillow dip with the weight of her head, but the room is dark and I can barely see her. I choose not to peer closer — this is not a moment that requires scrutiny.

She curls herself up, a prawn shape with her knees towards me. Her face is close to my ear.

"Are you OK now?"

I remember being young. I recall — with startling and sudden clarity — the time when everything was either black or white, when I hadn't yet learnt about the middle ground and how wide it is.

"I'll be OK."

She moves her head onto my shoulder, her hair near my face, and I wonder if this is what it's like to have a child.

"But really? Really OK?"

I reach one hand out and hold hers. I squeeze her fingers.

"You won't kill yourself, will you?"

I have to pause before I answer. I have to be sure. "No, I promise. I won't kill myself."

She lets go of my hand and hugs me; I hug her tightly back.

I realize that this is exactly what it is like to have a child; I am thinking about her instead of me. She needs me even more than I need my self-indulgence. It is a novel experience for me.

The room is warm and comfortable. I don't know the time, but it is very dark and I presume it is somewhere in the small hours of the morning. I don't want to ask Nadia, I don't want her to look at her phone. I don't want the outside world to come into this moment.

In the silences between our conversation, I try not to think of what lies outside this room. I try to forget the devastation that I've deliberately caused. When I think of Alan's violin I feel an actual physical pain in my stomach. It tightens and worsens when I focus on the fact that every bit of this is my fault.

"Are you sure you're OK?" Nadia asks me in the dark, and my thoughts collide with the promise I made to her not to kill myself.

"I will be. I will be." I wish I believed it.

"I need you, Grace," she says, and my broken heart flickers.

When I'm certain Nadia is asleep, I climb carefully out of bed. The bed is pushed up against the wall on the side I am sleeping on and I have to get myself to the foot and drop out that way to avoid waking her. The carpet is soft and thick under my bare feet.

My legs feel weak and my knees take a few moments to lock into an upright position; I keep one hand on the end of the bed. I feel as if I've had the flu and been bedridden for days and yet been looked after, nursed.

I run through a calculation, trying to work out what day of the week it is, how long I've been back from France. I have no idea. I could be a day out either way and I wonder where my phone is. The date will be on the home screen; it will be a first step to coming back to life.

I wonder if there will be a message from

David on the same screen, the first six or seven words visible without opening the message, maybe tantalizing, maybe straightforward. The thought that there might be nothing belongs in the same black hole as the destruction of my shop, and all the beautiful instruments.

I quietly open the bedroom door. Mr. Williams has obviously prepared for my waking up in the night and there is a lamp on atop a side table on the landing. The lamp has a round china base, like a vase, and a shade with short tassels around the bottom; there is nothing like it in my house, but there was in my mother's and my grandmother's. I like the memories it brings.

The door of the bathroom is open, clearly so that I don't go into the wrong room. I walk down the hall, into the bathroom, and shut the door behind me. I pull the cord of the light and the room is flooded with a brightness that makes me blink.

The bathroom is tasteful and very clean. Stark-white fittings are softened by touches of mahogany; the loo seat, the light pull, the laundry box. It is very masculine and surprisingly smart.

Next to the bath is a full-length mirror and I know I am going to stand in front of it and criticize myself. I don't want to; even

I know that what I see will be shocking and pathetic. But I owe it to the instruments, to Mr. Williams, especially to Alan, to start facing some unpleasant truths.

I make sure the door is locked, then pull the white T-shirt up over my head and drop it on the floor. The pants I am wearing are my own and I realize that someone must have taken them out of the bag I took to Paris. I turn and face myself in the mirror.

My arms still look healthy. My muscles are taut and round, sinews run down the outside of my upper arms and in at the elbows. I work hard on my upper-body strength for my playing and for my making. I follow strict exercises in the gym to make my arms as flexible, strong, and responsive as they can be. Their robustness has protected them — a little — from the trauma that the rest of my body has undergone.

The only way I am going to start to rebuild my life is on a ladder of honesty. This is where I start; this naked vision of me. I accept — for the first time — that I limit what I eat because of David. That isn't fair; I control my food because of me. The net effect is that he coos and compliments my sleek body, my tiny breasts and my flat stomach, but the decision to do it, to be that thin, is mine. The responsibility is mine.

My body is a mass of shadows. The bottom of my rib cage sticks out in a xylophone of lines around my chest. My hip bones stand proud of my abdomen, and their marked contours make my belly look even flatter, almost concave. There are tiny bruises on my hips, the last marks that will ever be left on my body by David. The bites and kisses are not the result of punishment; they are a consequence of passion, and of my having so little body fat.

There are pools of darkness in the recesses of my collarbones and the rude health of my muscular shoulders is out of proportion.

I have not been kind to this body. And I have not left it the resources to deal with two or three days of starvation or however long it's been. Suddenly I am overwhelmingly hungry.

There is a bathrobe hanging on the back of the door. I wrap it around me. It is white and soft and swamps me. I rub my face against its collar. The belt goes around me twice and I wonder whose dressing gown this once was.

This is a lovely house. It is Victorian and great care has been taken to restore everything just so. The banister is polished and smooth, the carpet on the stairs elegantly fitted, and the oak of the stairs immaculately swept on each side of the runner.

It is easy to find the kitchen; a light has been left on in here, too. I assume it is an invitation to help myself to a cup of tea. Near the kettle is a tray laden with bits and pieces. There are cheeses in greaseproof paper under a glass cloche and a basket of biscuits and crackers with cellophane stretched over it. There are even two jars of pickles, one light and one dark, with teaspoons balanced on their lids.

I make a cup of tea and carry it to the table on the tray. There are two side plates and two napkins on the tray; presumably in case Nadia was hungry too. There is a note and a sweet little sketch of a basket. The note says, *Homemade bread in basket on side, bread knife on board. Please eat.*

The bread looks gorgeous. I carve a bigger slice than I mean to and paste it with butter from a tiny porcelain dish on my tray. My teeth leave marks in the butter, it is so thick. It is absolutely delicious.

It beggars belief that someone can be so kind after everything I have done. Mr. Williams trusted me and I have totally betrayed him. My first job tomorrow will be to find the little homemade violin and repair it. I pray that I haven't done anything to it that can't be fixed.

I have mended some terribly badly injured things in the past. I have undone other people's repairs — sometimes hundreds of years old — that have added to already existing problems. I can fix Alan's violin but, depending on what I have done, it may take years. I try, screwing my face up tight and putting myself back in the shop inside my head, to remember what happened, but I really can't.

I unwrap the cheeses from their paper. The first is French — Époisses, one of my favorite cheeses — and I cut into it and taste it before I have a chance to associate it with Paris or with David. The other two cheeses complement the Époisses and each other. There is a solid yellow cheddar and a rippled Stilton. This little meal has been put together, chosen, with such incredible kindness. The kindness doesn't make me cry. The kindness makes me strong.

"You found your supper?" Mr. Williams closes the kitchen door behind him. "How do you feel?"

"Awful." I smile at him, my mouth still full of cheese. I swallow. "And guilty and shallow and pathetic. And grateful."

He makes a face, wobbles his head from side to side in an *if you say so* gesture. We both smile. "It'll come out in the wash," he says, "apparently."

"David used to say, 'It'll be all right in the end and if —' "

Mr. Williams interrupts me, "It's not all right, then it's not the end." He nods his head. "It's an old one. But a good one."

"I will fix Alan's violin."

"I know." He has made himself a pot of tea and he pours a cup. He adds a tiny dash of milk; *un nuage* the French call it — "a cloud." "There is a lot to do. You have months of work just to get the shop up and running. What will you do for money, for an income?"

I shake my head. I can't believe he is still thinking about me, still worrying on my behalf. "I'm OK for money. And I could always take out a small mortgage if I run out, I suppose. I don't have one on either property." This was part of my maternity-leave plan; not my *rebuild my life from the ashes of madness* solution.

"You may need to wait and see it before you decide."

I remember that he knows what's happened in there, while I am only guessing at most of it. I feel a little less optimistic. "I have to keep it from my clients; I'll be finished if anyone finds out. I mean more so than I am now."

Mr. Williams takes a small slice of the blue cheese. "I wondered if perhaps your insurance would cover it all."

"I really doubt it. And, do you know, I'd really rather not ask." I pull the folds of the dressing gown farther around me. "Was this your partner's robe?"

He nods. "It was. He made it himself. He was a costumier, dab hand with a sewing machine."

"He must have been a big chap." I gesture at the length of the gown and the doubled belt.

"I suspect that's why he made his own, only way to get one to fit. He was six-foot-six."

I wonder if Mr. Williams felt safe in Leslie's arms the way I had in David's.

"I understand what you're going through, I really do. I know how frustrating it all is, the cloak-and-dagger, the subterfuge. You need to know you can trust your partner. You need to know it's worth it."

I look down at my cup and blow the steam away. I don't want to look at Mr. Williams when he's this close to my soul, when he is trying to understand my life.

"I was with a married man for forty years," he says.

CHAPTER SIXTEEN

Mr. Williams and I sit for a long while in the kitchen. We are different now; we have lost a barrier.

"Leslie's wife knew he was gay when she married him," Mr. Williams tells me.

I am still trying to compose myself following his revelation; it is important, I think, that I — of all people — don't appear shocked. Surprised is more accurate and, when I examine that, my surprise is simply because I thought he was a better person than me.

I pick crumbs of cheese from the breadboard to focus my gaze and wonder at my arrogance. Of course Mr. Williams is a better person than me; his relationship was under completely different circumstances.

"It was unusual — in those days — to be that honest. It suited Jean to marry a homosexual; she had no interest in" — he lowers his voice and I am reminded that he is of a different generation than me — "that side of things. And for Leslie, well, one couldn't just push off with a chap back then."

Mr. Williams's turn of phrase makes me smile a little. I feel privileged to be wearing Leslie's dressing gown in his absence; I feel like I am part of their lives.

"We were together for a long time, more than most people, but they are painful rules to live by. How you have to learn to stand in the queue, how you must know your place."

He puts one hand over mine. The skin on the back of his hand is drawn and tight; the wrinkles look like translucent bark. His knuckles show through it as four white dots.

"And at his funeral, it had to be all about Jean. I was just another guest, just another close friend. Jean and I kissed cheeks politely; she loved him too in her way. Alan and his wife stood on either side of me, holding my hands tight. And I kept from shouting out."

He squeezes my hand and I smile at him.

"I'm so sorry. I'll fix Alan's violin. Whatever it takes, I'll do it."

"It's wood, my dear girl. It's lovely and it was clever of Alan to make it and, yes, it was precious for a while. But it's wood, it's not flesh and blood."

I cannot believe so much compassion can come from one lonely old man. I want to tear out my heart and give it to him. I want to make everything better; turn back time and bring Leslie and him forward, to now, to let them be together. But then what would happen to Jean?

It dawns on me like daybreak that there are no winners in love affairs, however well-meaning.

"I'll mend it. I've done a terrible thing and I'll mend it."

He shakes his head. "It's not important. If you want to make it up to me, you'll mend the Cremona cello. The one with the great big hole through it, the poor thing." He looks right at me. "You'll mend it, and you'll take it to Cremona in time to win. Then I'll forgive you; when you show me what you're made of."

It's a lovely thought, so sweet, but pointless. "It can't win now, Mr. Williams. They wouldn't accept it. They would know it's been fixed no matter what I did. That ship has sailed, I'm afraid."

"There must be something we can do. We'll sleep on it."

I look out the kitchen window and see that the dawn is just starting to crack over the garden. A line of orange edges the hedge and whispers pink into the sky.

"I'm sorry; I've kept you up all night."

"Twice." He smiles. "But that doesn't happen often nowadays." He pats my hand.

"Mr. Williams?"

He has turned to put the cheeses and milk in the fridge. He is an old man and it is time he went to bed, but I need to ask him one more thing.

"Nadia said there was an article? About David?"

He looks back over his shoulder at me. He is puzzled. "It's in your magazine. The one you brought back from France." He points to a magazine lying open on the kitchen counter.

I am slipping down the rabbit hole. There is a pounding in my chest. I recognize the magazine instantly. I remember the article, the photographs, the white-toothed smile and immaculate hair of David's wife, the soft-focus picture of his strong, healthy children in the distance; not recognizable but outlined in their vigor. The children are walking towards the camera under an avenue of linden trees. The picture captures the spring in their step, the vitality of their day, the buzz of their conversation. The sky is blue above their heads and there are no clouds.

On the opposite page to that freshness and health is a picture of the escalator in the Porte de Pantin station. The picture is in color on glossy paper; most of the photograph is of those dull, camouflage colors one finds in Tube stations — gunmetal gray, granite, galvanized rims of posters, grinding dusty teeth of the escalator itself.

At the bottom of the escalator is me. My skirt is the green of the linden trees in the other picture, vivid and fresh. Towards the top of the escalator, frozen in his giant steps and one knee raised in the race to the top, is David.

I remember.

I remember buying the magazine at Gare du Nord.

I remember realizing — almost straightaway — that I would not read it because this was not my normal journey. I had completed the steps I always take on my way home: a coffee from the stall at the bottom of the stairs, a women's magazine to improve my French by reading — in baby steps — recipes and fashion pieces.

I remember putting the magazine in my bag, rolling it up, all the images on the cover facing inwards.

I remember opening it in my shop. I laid the magazine on the counter. I had a glass of red wine in the other hand. I flicked through the pages mechanically, taking nothing in.

I remember that I stopped when I saw the picture of Dominique-Marie Martin, utterly recognizable, a face etched by distress onto my memory.

I remember trying to read the headline *La gentillesse commence avec soi-même, selon avocat spécialiste des droits de l'homme* on the page opposite my photograph and realizing that I didn't speak enough French to read an article about me. An article that the whole of the French-speaking world could understand.

I remember feeling absolutely trapped and, at the same time, utterly naked. And then, with a punch, I remember everything else I did.

Be sure your sins will find you out.

"Grace, Grace, dear. Please." Mr. Williams springs to his feet. "You've cried enough tears over all this. I thought you'd read this? In the shop."

"I can't read it," I say, and my words catch on my sobs. "I feel so stupid. I can't believe she'd humiliate me like this." I clap my hands over my mouth. Dominique-Marie is surely entitled to humiliate me in any way she sees fit. I have been humiliating her for eight years.

"I thought it was remarkably generous." Mr. Williams sounds genuinely surprised.

My instinct is to pounce, to yell at him for taking her side. I catch my breath and hold back for a moment.

"What do you mean?"

"Even the title. She has a point."

"Mr. Williams." I am spelling things out. My patience is thin. "I can't read French."

"Sorry, dear, sorry. You did say. The piece, the title says 'Leading human rights lawyer calls for kindness to begin a little nearer home.' It's about being *sympa,* having an understanding, being nice. It's about women standing up for other women, being kind to one another."

"It's not about me? About what I've done?"

"She doesn't even use your name. The photograph is from a news agency; it says it on the bottom. She just uses it to explain why she suddenly felt the need to pull the plug on her husband's long-standing affairs."

That "affairs" is plural is not lost on me.

"I'm exhausted or I'd read the whole thing

to you. Can we leave it till the morning?" He points at the lilac sky and the new day outside.

"I'm sorry. I really am."

"It's all fine. It will all be fine." He kisses me on the top of my head and walks out of the kitchen. His shoulders are rounded; I can see how very tired he is.

I peer at the magazine for just a few minutes more. I am going to have to exercise discipline, wait until tomorrow. There is no one to read it to me and I am simply not good enough to do it for myself.

I push the sleeves of the giant bathrobe up my arms and sweep the last of the crumbs on the table into my cupped hand. I shake them into the bin and fold the napkin I used.

I need to go back to bed.

Nadia stirs when I get back in beside her. She moves across so that I can get into the side that is not against the wall.

"You OK?" she asks me.

"It's been a long night."

"Tell me about it," she says, and pulls the duvet up to her eyes. Her long sigh explains that she is going back to sleep.

I am happy with that; I cannot process any more information just now.

■ ■ ■ ■

I wake at the same time as Nadia. I stretch my arm out and turn the alarm clock towards me; I still haven't found my phone. It is half past ten. I cannot remember when I last slept this late. The day is warm and the sunshine leaks into the room, all innocence and encouragement.

"Shit, it's half ten." I have no idea if this is a school day or not. I cannot — for the life of me — work out what day it is. "Have you got school?"

"I haven't got school."

"Are you sure?"

"Positive. Very sure indeed."

There is something wrong in her voice. She sounds like a child building up a wall of bravado, like someone trying to believe themselves.

"Nadia?"

"I'm taking a year out."

I don't know what to say. Thoughts clamor to the front of my mind, words jostle in my mouth. None of them are right. The pause while I juggle my ideas ends up too long and becomes an awkward silence.

"Why?" I ask.

"Shit got cray," says Nadia in a deliberate

238

parody of her generation. "Too much shit got cray." She puts her face in the pillow and starts humming loudly. I don't recognize the song.

I wonder if I should use my insider information. Is it drugs? Is that why Nadia won't go to school?

"All that work, Nad. The marks you got in your mock A-levels."

"And I'll get the same for the real thing. But not till next year." Her voice is muffled but assertive.

"What about your parents? What will they say?"

She raises her head and a broad smile beams from her face. "Not what will they say; what did they say? They already know."

"Oh." I cannot imagine Nadia's immaculate mother and distracted father taking this well.

"They went fucking mental. My mum actually screamed. I mean, screamed. At the top of her voice." She rolls over onto her back and looks directly at me. "And then listed all the people who will comment on it and who will make her ashamed."

"Perhaps —"

"No, wait. It gets better." She stretches out her arms and points, jabbing at the ceiling, invisible enemies and audience in the empty air. "Then she turned it into her fault. She made the whole thing about her. Where she'd gone wrong. Where my fucking father had failed — we had a good half hour on that one. Then my dad joined in, blah, blah, blah. And I fucking walked out *and . . .*" She makes the "and" loud and long, then leaves a dramatic pause. Nadia, as I have long known, is a consummate performer. "And they didn't fucking notice. For ten minutes."

"Sweetie, I'm sure they did." Her fervor is making me uncomfortable. I'm not sure what I'm supposed to say or how I'm supposed to support her. I'm sure if I had more experience with teenagers it would fall into place and I would be effortlessly able. I think of Dominique-Marie and the clouded, dewy ghosts of her perfect children in the photograph.

"They didn't. I'm telling you. I went through to the sitting room and sat on our fucking ugly sofas and listened to every word." She slips off track with the agility of a bird. "Our sofas are white leather and my mum had them imported from Italy. When she talks about them, you'd think she'd found the cure for cancer stuck down the side of the cushion. It's fucking amazing."

I give her a small smile, try to be on her

side. "And are they worth it?"

"They are fucking hideous. And they squeak." She smiles back. "And they make your arse sweat." She sounds like herself again.

"What did your dad say?" I close my eyes and sink into the warm pillow. I like this closeness. I like hearing her talk. Apart from David, I haven't been this intimate with anyone for years. There is a scant gap of three or four inches between us, and Nadia's animated delivery regularly crosses that territory with a waving arm or a gesticulating leg. It's a good feeling.

"Money. He listed every fucking penny he's ever spent on me." She props herself up on her elbows as if she needs momentum for this one, some forward drive. "I didn't ask to go to fucking private school. Really, if we're honest, I didn't even ask to play the cocking violin." She drops back down onto her pillow, point made. "And — the best bit — it was like taking a year out of school, sorry — my bad — taking a year out of his budget, was worse than fucking dying. Like if I stop now, that's it. If I take a breath and maybe work for a year, I won't be able to play the violin ever again. I won't even — if you're my dad — remember how to read.

"I actually fucking hate them. And

they . . . They despise me."

I want to tell her that they don't, that they're just misguided. But I know she will feel patronized; I know I would have just days ago if someone had given me advice about David. It's that fear of advice that has made me so isolated; not the actual situation at all.

"Anyway, if that's her taste in sofas, I do not want to see her boyfriend."

"Your mum's boyfriend? Are you sure?"

"Sure I don't want to see him? Or sure she's got one? Both; thanks, Grace."

I rub my face with my hands, my bony elbow crosses onto Nadia's side and she pushes it away.

"He will be perma-tanned, Day-Glo orange, and have really massive teeth. And I bet he wants to be my special friend."

"You're a weirdo," I say. "Aren't you more upset about their divorce? Don't you mind?"

"No. I don't mind at all. I just wish they'd get on with it. I hate them pretending all the bloody time."

A money spider crawls onto my arm. I move my fingers in front of it so that it can climb onto my hand. It isn't at all daunted by my enormity. I twirl it three times around my head like I did as a child. I pass the spider, on the tip of my fingers, to Nadia.

"Twirl it around your head like I did."

"Why?" she asks.

"It's good luck. It brings good things." I wish it did.

She moves the spider around in three long circles over her head. "There. I need some fucking luck."

"Because of your parents?"

"No. They are fine. They'll get on and do their own thing. They can't make me go back to school this year; if I pimp myself out as a wedding musician, I can even afford to move out if I'm driven to it. Nah, it's all the other shit."

"Harriet? Is that her name? The girl I met in the supermarket?"

"In the wine aisle." Nadia laughs. "A bit. Not so much. She's a twat."

Nadia rubs her eyes with her hands, scrunching her whole face up. She wiggles the end of her nose with her fingers.

"Boys?" I ask.

She waits. I can feel her debating whether to tell me or not and I know — because of that — that she will. I can wait too. I am warm and comfortable. The idea of leaving Mr. Williams's cocoon of a house terrifies me, although I know I must do it at some point today.

I take advantage of Nadia's pause in

conversation to look around the room for my phone. My bag is on the carpet, leaning against the side of the bed. It was here all the time.

I pull the phone out. My passport and purse are still in the bag. The shop keys are there too, and a shiver runs through me.

My phone has long since lost all power. I drop it back in the bag; I am not going to interrupt Nadia's moment to ask her for a charger.

"Yeah, there is a boy. Was a boy. I'm not seeing him now."

"But you were?"

She shrugs, turns over and puts her face back into the pillow. "It wasn't a relationship. I was just, you know, seeing him a bit. Now and then."

"Is he nice?"

"No. Not even a little bit." She visibly tenses, stretches her long body out. I feel the duvet move over her pointed toes. "He was a massive shit, actually."

"But you loved him?"

"No." She lifts her head and squints at me in disdain. "No, I didn't love him. I was a bit dazzled by him for a while. That's all."

She is so in control, so sure. I am certain that if she has decided not to go back to school, there must be a valid reason for it. I am not her parent, though; I am not responsible for overriding her wishes with my experience. I am in the enviable position of being able to trust her.

"He was a fucking predator, really, spider and a fly. He knew exactly what he was doing and I didn't. Bosh. I've learnt my lesson, though. He's not why I'm not going back to school yet. He's not that fucking important. Nor's Harriet."

The penny drops. Charlie. Charlie who Nadia hated so passionately.

"This boy. Was he Harriet's boyfriend?"

"Is. Is Harriet's boyfriend. Has been since Year Ten."

"Shit. I'm sorry. Poor you."

"Fuck it. It was ages ago. It was snowing."

She burrows her face farther into the pillow. I cannot see her expression, but I can read all I need from her angry shoulders, her tight back.

"This is none of my business but . . . did you sleep with him?"

She lifts her head from the pillow and fixes me with her stare. Her lip is wobbling and I can see it whiten as she tightens it and gets it under control.

She nods, a long solemn nod. It is the same one she gave me when she played her first antique instrument. She must have

been five or six years old; she played "Ol'
Man River." The sound was like deep water.

When she'd finished, I said, "Do you like
it, this old violin?"

She gave that same long, slow nod and
stared with her wide black eyes.

"And Harriet and Charlie got back together? Are together?"

She sits up, her whole body rigid. A
silence pools between us like blood.

"How do you know his name is Charlie?"

Chapter Seventeen

Nadia has gone. It was awful.

There was no way to explain, no way to excuse what I'd done. Perhaps I knew this was coming from the first moment I picked up that book and began to read.

I didn't read it to protect her. I didn't read it for her own good. I have just hurt her more than she thought possible. The last port she thought she had in a squall of teen-aged horror has betrayed her.

It is all about betrayal.

Before she left, while I was still fumbling with words and pulling on my clothes to follow her down the landing, she turned and yelled at me with such hate. Her words pelted me like hail, spiking into my skin and damaging my soul, but it was her eyes that hurt the most.

Her lip was curled into a snarl over a mouth still open with disbelief. Her eyes narrowed and focused and peered at me in a way that convinces me she will never forgive me, never forget what I've done.

Her parting shot left ripples of anger, palpable waves of thick air, in the hallway. She stood, framed by the front door, the outside world ready to take her, the door ready to slam behind her and emphasize that she was gone.

"You're a fucking train wreck of a forty-year-old who reads people's diaries and shags other women's husbands. But I thought I could trust you. What a fucking twat I am."

It wasn't the words, it was the way she delivered them; the pitch, the tone, the rhythm.

When she slammed the door, the house rattled. When we stopped shaking, the house and I, there was a huge hole where she had been, a rip in the fabric of my life.

Nadia has gone, is gone, and Mr. Williams and I are having a cup of tea. It is as far forward as I want to think.

"So the book was there, under the counter, and you dipped in and out a few times?"

"Twice."

Mr. Williams shrugs his shoulders, shakes his head slightly. "It's wrong, it'll always be wrong, but — honestly? People have done worse things."

"It's a bad time for her. Her parents are divorcing — very messily."

"I'm not sure there's another way," he says.

"And she's had a thing with her best friend's boyfriend. Although she says it was over by the spring. And I've read her secrets. Oh, poor little Nad."

Mr. Williams stirs the tea in the pot, replaces the lid, and taps the spoon twice against his saucer. "Can you text her? Try and explain."

"Ah, my phone's dead. I'd forgotten. Do you have a charger?"

Mr. Williams stands and rootles about in one of the kitchen drawers. "Will this work?" he asks and hands me a charger that looks nothing like mine.

I shake my head. "Maybe that's a good thing. Maybe she needs a while to calm down. Maybe I need longer to think about what to say to her."

"Many forms of sorry followed by *what's done is done*?" Mr. Williams smiles gently. "She'll get over it. So will you. Worse things have, honestly, happened at sea."

"Does there come a point where you wouldn't forgive my behavior, Mr. Williams? I must look a bit of a slimeball to you. Nadia's not wrong with her summing up."

"It's been a long life, dear. And if I've learnt nothing else, I've learnt never to be surprised and — whatever ever else may happen — never to cast the first stone."

There's nothing I can add, apart from my immense gratitude and relief that he is who he is. Mr. Williams waves away any praise I try to give him.

"What's next, Grace?"

I panic slightly, wondering if any of this could get worse, if I have anything left to lose.

"I meant in terms of improvement," says Mr. Williams, "reparation, if you will."

"I need to go home. Get changed. And then, I suppose, start trying to put things back together. The shop, Nadia."

"But not David?"

"Not David," I say, and I am certain. "Would you tell me what Dominique-Marie's article says, though? Could you translate it?"

He nods. "I've read it through a few times. I think I have it pretty much sorted. My French is rusty."

"Well, mine, as you know, is a liability," I say to him, and smile. "So anything will be an improvement."

We settle ourselves at the table, the teapot between us and our cups steaming in the breeze that blows through the open back door. Autumn is coming, the sun has taken on a harvest glow and the plants around the doorway are tangled and drying.

Mr. Williams clears his throat and I smile.

I don't know what to expect from this woman and her contacts in the media. I do know that if it were me, this article would be about revenge, with a possible side of saving face. I wouldn't shy away from apportioning blame.

"She starts off with the title. As I told you last night." He corrects himself. "This morning, this morning. 'Leading human rights lawyer asks for kindness a little closer to home.' Do you want me to translate exactly? Every line? Or the gist of it and the important bits?"

I know what he wants me to say; I can see it in his tired eyes. "Just the important bits is fine. Thank you."

He nods. "Good, much of the middle section is statistics; number of divorces in France, number of people to take lovers, that sort of thing. Irrelevant to us, I think."

I like that he says "us" as if this is "our" problem.

"It starts off about David. It says: *Dominique-Marie Martin's British-born husband was feted by all of France for being the* mystery hero in July's incident at the Porte de Pantin station. David Hewitt, a businessman, put his own well-being to one side and dashed onto the tracks to save the life of Muminah Yusef and her unborn child.'* Then there's a section about Mrs. Yusef — how she is now, that sort of thing."

He moves his finger along the paragraphs, his lips working soundlessly as he rolls the words around, tries them for fit.

" *'Unfortunately, Mr. Hewitt's concern for the safety of a stranger didn't extend to his own family. CCTV footage of the incident clearly revealed that Mr. Hewitt was accompanied on his trip to Paris by his British lover. This situation put into action a chain of events.'* Sorry," Mr. Williams says, "that's clumsy but it's the general meaning."

"Your French is amazing." I am deeply impressed.

"My first degree is in French. I read *French Politics* at Cambridge as an undergraduate. A jolly long time ago, mind you." He smiles. "And I love France. Leslie and I went whenever we could." His voice drops slightly. "You know; when we were able to get away together."

"I do know." I pat his arm.

" *'When Dominique-Marie first met her husband, she guessed he would always have difficulty settling down. He had left his first marriage behind him in England —'"*

I have to stop him. "What?"

"That's what it says. He was married before he met Ms. Martin."

I have my hands over my mouth. It is such a secret. I feel a little sick. "What else does it say? How old was he when he got married?" I am frantically doing mental arithmetic, trying to work out how old David might have been when he got married the first time, how long he might have been married for.

"It doesn't say any more, just that. Perhaps it's not even true?"

I shake my head. "Why would she lie? She has no reason to lie and, anyway, people would know if she did. Her children would know."

Mr. Williams grips my forearm in a supportive gesture. "I was playing devil's advocate, dear. I'm sorry. I didn't think for a moment that she'd lie."

David is fifty-two. His oldest child is sixteen. His eldest child that I know of. If I assume that David, the David I thought I knew so well, met Dominique-Marie a couple of years before they had their first baby, even then he would have already been thirty-four. Even if they met when he was thirty, he had years to be married before that.

I am speechless. In all our plans, in all our talking, it never occurred to me that I might become David's third wife. I had allowed him one error, one leap of faith that had landed badly. I was to have been the answer, the Right One.

"She doesn't mention that again. *'Martin was blinded to any lessons she might have learned from her husband's past and it didn't even begin to resonate when she realized he was having an affair. Martin was working hard and struggling with her second pregnancy when she first became aware that her husband's indiscretions might be a little more . . .'* ah, what's the word? I had this last night. This is what old age does to you, Grace. *'A little more consequential than she had first thought. With a disregard for cliché, Hewitt had a long-term arrangement with his PA and more than one casual liaison at business conferences and on trips abroad.'* "

Mr. Williams puts the magazine down. "Are you sure you want me to go on?"

I nod. I am still struggling to find my words.

" ' *"What I hope to achieve here,"* says Dominique-Marie at her beautiful home in Strasbourg, *"is an understanding among* women." Martin explains that her husband was a damaged child; a man whose background is a litany of sadness — none of which he is responsible for. Martin totally accepts the psychology behind her husband's need to "collect" women. "What I find so awful" — explains Martin — "is that women are prepared to settle for this second-best, to be part — literally — of a harem. We have undergone a global struggle to liberate ourselves, to become equal to men in the workplace and at home. We have not done this without solidarity."

" 'Now Dominique-Marie Martin wants to start a campaign where women defend women. "If we cannot trust our men to stay close to home and hold their families at their heart, we must bond together and support our sisters," she says.' "

"Oh, dear God." I have to interrupt him. "Now I'm guilty of crimes against my gender as well as against all that is good and holy." I have my head in my hands and my heart in my throat. "Couldn't I have had an affair with someone whose wife wishes me and all the other hookers some sort of life-threatening illness? I don't want her sympathy."

"I'm afraid you have it, dear. It's awful, isn't it?"

"It's awful because she has such a point."
We are both silent.
"The rest?" Mr. Williams asks.
"Précis."

He can't resist. "I thought you didn't speak much French."

I roll my eyes at him, but I'm very grateful for the levity. Even hearing my relationship with another woman's husband pulled apart for a magazine article is preferable to what I should really be thinking about, is kinder to me than the devastation and the upset in my shop.

"So, blah, blah, statistics. This and that and then . . . Are you sure?"

I nod.

" *'The situation in Martin's home was only going to escalate. I ask Dominique-Marie how she managed to continue with her marriage, knowing that her husband had numerous partners both here and abroad. "My husband and I had entered into an arrangement — nothing unusual — we would stay together for the children, but our sexual affairs, for the last five years, have been our own business," she tells me. Martin and Hewitt decided on a policy of honesty on which they could build a friendship. Martin believed this would protect her children from the trauma of divorce and that both parties could continue relationships* outside of the home.' This is making me uncomfortable too, Grace, don't worry," says Mr. Williams.

I nod at him to continue.

" 'Hewitt decided to start a new family with one of his lovers. Not, Martin explains, one of his longer relationships but a relatively new dalliance with a very much younger woman. At this point in the interview, Martin comes alive. Her elegant —' Oh, bugger that, Grace. I'm sure you don't want to hear some French bloke tattle on about how attractive David's bloody wife is."

I sigh. Deep breaths are keeping my tears at bay; deep breaths and a sudden horror at the cold facts of my life, of my lover. My skin is clammy. My tea has gone cold.

"She gets animated, about now, in this interview and her point is . . ." He concentrates on the text again. "Her point is 'that we shouldn't be raising our daughters to believe that this is all they're worth. That she — and her husband — would be horrified if this were the kind of relationship their sixteen-year-old daughter decided to enter into.' Basically, Grace, the rest of it is about how women need to be kinder to one another and how society needs to raise expectations of women, on the whole. Mostly that this is just part of the patriarchal system and its faults, that sort of thing. Enough?"

"Enough." It really is enough. I have never felt smaller. "It's true, though." I drop my voice to break a confidence. "Even Nadia. The whole situation with Charlie is in the very same circumstances."

"I realized that from what you said. Poor girl." He stands up and pushes his chair neatly under the table. "A tale as old as time, I'm afraid. Maybe this woman is right; maybe we can change it. I think it's just human nature, though." His smile is gentle. "And she'll have a job changing that."

I take my cue from Mr. Williams and get up. It is time to leave him and the safety he has woven around me. I will be forever in his debt.

"What will you do?" he asks me as I head upstairs to pack.

"I'm going to go home first. Get changed and so on. The shop can wait."

"That's very wise." Mr. Williams's approval means a lot to me now. "I'll run you down to pick up your car. It's around the corner from the shop, rather than right out the front. You won't have to go in."

I nod my thanks. "Then what? What will you do later?"

"I shall come back here and enjoy my solitude in a way that only those who live alone and have had houseguests can appreciate."

Mr. Williams drops me off by my car. It is still David's car. Its sleek lines, the engine size, the statement the brand makes; it is wholly David's car.

When I get into the car my phone charger is in the cigarette lighter socket. I resist the urge to plug it in. There is enough to deal with in the world I can see.

I avoid looking at the shop front. Mr. Williams has assured me that it's safe from any further harm. He had the presence of mind to roll down the blinds, front and back, while the police and ambulance were still there. I have to go and sort it out as soon as I have steeled myself, but at least my customers can't peer through the window and see the debris.

When he dropped me off, Mr. Williams insisted that he come to the shop with me as soon as I decide to go. I want to see it for the first time by myself, but I have agreed to text him when I get there and when I have had a chance to assess where to start. There is a lot to clear up in every corner of my life.

My house is calm. It is as I left it before I went to Paris. No one has been in here and nothing has been disturbed. David is evident in the photographs around the room. The choice of sofa was his, the music stand next to my cello was a gift from him last birthday, the oversize spider plant in the giant earthenware pot came back with him from a random trip to a garden center. He is everywhere.

Upstairs, his clothes are neatly stacked in the drawers. His toothbrush stands in the pot on the bathroom basin. There are two tubes of toothpaste, both half-used, that describe our particular preferences. My teeth are sensitive and I constantly feel they need whitening; David's are perfect.

My bed is neatly made. David's side is a shrine to him. His book is open at the page he was reading. It sits askew on top of a guidebook. The spine of the guidebook faces me; it is northern Italy. It is for Cremona.

Beside the books and David's beside lamp are innocent clues to him. There are two pens, both black and with the sharp, fine nibs that artists use; there are nail scissors and an empty eyeglass case with a navy-blue cover. His reading glasses must be somewhere else in the house. I know his habits; they will be on the side of the bath.

This is a trail of crumbs left by a person I thought I knew; there are other Davids in other cities and other countries. I have no idea how many. I am certain, though, that none of the other Davids can have been as real as mine.

My bath towel hangs on the back of my bedroom door and I take it through to the bathroom. My clothes are fusty and need washing; I drop them in the basket in the corner.

David's reading glasses are perched where I knew they would be and I walk past them and step into the shower. There are more reminders of this David, English David, in the shower cubicle. He has shower gel and shampoo. He has body lotion and a separate face wash. These are the traces of a vain man. Before today, I just thought he was thorough and taking care of himself.

I close my eyes against the stream of water and imagine him next to me. I cannot turn off the way I feel about him; no matter how many facts there are, how many suspicions that may become real, he and I were special. He and I were something different.

I dress in jeans and a T-shirt. It will be cold in the shop and I pull on an old sweatshirt that won't matter too much if it gets dirty. The weather is turning and I find socks to keep my feet warm after a summer of sandals and bare feet. I think forward to

Christmas. I am always alone at Christmas; David — quite rightly — has to be with his children. I wonder if this year, perhaps, Mr. Williams will join me. I dismiss the idea almost immediately — it takes a special sort of circumstances and a particular kind of person to end up as isolated as me. Mr. Williams is too kind and too generous with himself to ever end up this lonely: he will have invitations to other places.

In the corner of my sitting room I find myself. I remember what happiness I have had and how fortunate I am to have this world to escape into. I have ignored my old cello for almost a week, and a fine film of dust takes the shine off its shoulders.

I wonder what would have happened if my cello had been in the shop. If it had been my instrument on the stand in the corner. This cello has been my pride and joy for so long it is part of me. Our communications are never tangled, never misinterpreted. I ask, and it rewards me. It needs so little in return. I have only ever owned two full-size cellos, only ever needed those two. One, my parents bought me, the second — this one — was a gift from David.

I pull up my chair and test the A string. It is a little out; I relish the feeling in my fingers as I tighten the fine tuner and the buzz between my cello and me begins.

I know what music is on the stand. I know that I left the "Libertango" open, my pencil marks of things I need to remember decorating the staves. Here an extra-long bow, there a slide to fifth position to keep my fingers from feeling like they're webbed and will split apart.

I tighten my bow, curl my chin towards my chest and drag the horsehair hard against the strings. The sound that comes out is loud and gratifying. It is alive with possibilities. It is vibrating with opportunity. In moments I am miles away, years away.

I don't know how long I play for but it heals me. I know the cure is temporary and that there is much work to be done, but for now it brings me some peace.

I lift my fingers and examine the ridges that run through them from where they have pressed so hard on the strings. I have spent years hardening the tips of my fingers, coaxing layer upon layer of skin to protect me. Even a few days away from the strings softens them. The lines are pink in the middle and white along each side of the valley. They are my tattoo, my imprint. I remember how much I love this feeling. Pinprick scabs flake off from my fingerprints as playing, literally, removes the scars of the last few days.

I have work to do. I have to repair the damage. I have to try to right my life.

I used my cello to find control — to find peace — when I first left college. I would sit, upstairs and alone, and play scales. I played until I knew that there was no margin in the notes I made, not even the slightest variation or error. I played until I knew the scales were faultless, that they would have been good enough for Nikolai.

The idea crept in, for a while and with the optimism of youth, that I might go back to college if I showed Nikolai how dedicated I had become. I thought that perhaps if I practiced hard enough they might give me another chance. Most people who had stayed on — ones whom Nikolai hadn't kicked out — had struggled to keep up with me in rehearsals and in seminars. The problem was with my attitude rather than my musicianship.

My parents were worried by the amount of time I spent alone, by the repetitive nature of my practicing, by my utter loss of faith in the world. They were right to worry; I had slipped, with enormous ease, into a life of ritual and obsession. I began to genuinely believe that if I only played every scale perfectly, every day, my world would get back in balance.

Towards the end of that time I had stopped pausing for meals, I was sleeping less and less, but I was definitely nearing perfection.

The day I cracked it, playing all the scales of western music without pause and without fault, I felt free. I had set myself a Herculean task and had pulled it off; just over five hundred scales without a single mistake.

I went downstairs to tell my mum that I was feeling better, that she could stop worrying. She was on the phone.

My mum had twiddled the cord of the phone around her fingers. She was smoking a cigarette with the other hand and the ashtray was balanced precariously on her crossed legs. I could tell by her clucks and sighs and by the way she leant forward into the phone to speak that she was talking to her sister, my auntie Pauline.

Our stairs had upright banisters all the way down. I could sit on the step, on the swirled brown carpet, and listen to my mum without her seeing me. She was sitting on a dining chair that she had pulled through to the hallway. She clearly meant to be on the phone for a while.

I was enjoying being liberated from the

obsession I'd set myself. I took my time. Instead of rushing my mum off the phone to talk to me, I waited, listening to her one-sided conversation with Pauline.

"It's awful, Paul. Terrible to watch. She just gets thinner and thinner, sadder and sadder."

I knew she was talking about me, but, to be honest, I had known that before I sat down. My mother and my aunt conversed in terms of their children, as if they had had no background before us, my cousins and me. As if they hadn't really existed before we came along.

Pauline had three children, all older than me and far more experienced at getting into trouble; she could talk about them for hours. My mum commented and compared and stuttered for a space to speak. She leant back on her chair, her head against the cool wall, framed against the floral wallpaper in a tableau I still remember.

"I think there's probably a boy in this as well," she said, her voice lowered. "I can't see that it would be this bad without."

A short silence, during which I marveled at her perception. I wondered what she would make of Shota; how she would see my Japanese boyfriend, all alone so far from his parents. All alone apart from my friend

266

Catherine.

"Exactly," my mum answered Pauline. "She would be wanting to phone her friends or at least get in touch with someone. Instead, just this constant practicing, all day, all night. Poor little thing."

My mum listened intently. I knew Pauline would be giving my mother the benefit of her experience.

"It's her whole world. I've never felt like this about anything. Except about her, of course."

It was making me nervous, this strange one-sided conversation. Under my breath I started reciting my scales, my fingers flicking as if there were strings beneath them as I thought through the run of notes. I was imagining my major and minor arpeggios when I caught my mother's sob.

"We gave it all up for her. We could have done it like you, had lots of kids and eased the pressure on everyone. But you don't know that at the time, do you? You don't know how much that sort of decision will come back and haunt you." She shifted awkwardly on her chair and wiped her nose with a piece of kitchen roll she took from her pocket.

"We thought, we believed, that if we just had one child, an only one, we could give

267

her everything. Absolutely everything. But it isn't enough. I can't take away her pain. If I'm honest, I don't really understand her world."

I heard the dull clunk of the front door opening and closing at the other end of the corridor. My mum would have to go and make my dad's tea now he was home.

"I'll have to go, Paul," my mother said into the receiver. "Frank's home from work."

My aunt obviously ignored it. She spoke for some time.

"But that's how it was, when we were kids . . ." My mum was animated. "Remember when we got ready to go to school of a morning? *First up, best dressed,* they used to say. Not enough decent clothes for everyone." She wiped her nose again.

"And I wasn't going to put her through that. If we'd had another child, there'd have been no fancy cello lessons at all — we wouldn't have had the money. And I just wanted what was best for her. Only her. I don't know now if that was the right way to do it."

My parents' decision to only have one child was none of my business or my responsibility, but I didn't know that then. It wasn't until I was an adult that I understood that people do what they want to do, regardless of whether they later blame someone else. My parents were long dead by then and I couldn't ever talk to them about it. They would have been so sad if they'd known how I felt that day or that I'd heard the conversation at all. It hadn't been meant for me. At that age, at nineteen, I just felt a stinging guilt.

I went back to my room and my scales. I added consecutive octaves to my major, melodic minor, and harmonics; just to keep me in my bedroom a little longer.

CHAPTER EIGHTEEN

I turn the key in the door. The alarm trips through its four long beeps and I punch in the code on the panel by the door.

Everything is shrouded in a half-light; where Mr. Williams has pulled the blinds down, the light falls on the fractured wood like dust.

The floor of the shop looks like a grave-yard. Brittle bones of snapped necks, un-stuck shoulders, and splintered ribs are motionless on the floor. The room is silent and the atmosphere bristling with recrimination, with sorrow, with regret.

Some of the instruments are still on the racks, looming over the chaos on the floor and holding on by the barest thread of balance. I push them back into the slots and mentally catalog which ones are still standing.

A double bass has fallen — been pushed — onto its side. It lies on the floor like a tree across a path.

"I'm so sorry," I whisper.

I double lock the door behind me so that no one could get in even if they had a key. Nadia has a key and I remember with a punch that she won't be trying to get in.

I need to check the most important instrument. I can start to plan once I know what has happened to it and how desperately it has been hurt — I have hurt it. I have to start thinking in terms of responsibility; this was no casual act, this was no accident. I did this. I caused all of this horrible mess. Me, me, me.

The broken glass of the countertop glistens like frost across everything.

I pick up the double bass by its neck and right it. It has a crack through the ribs down one side and has lost the points of its bouts, otherwise it is pretty much unhurt — bar its pride. I can fix the double bass.

Hidden underneath it, as if it were trying to protect them, cluster them under its own frightened wings, are the fragments of three violins. I am fairly sure I have stomped on one, the other two are less damaged but still close to irreparable. It wasn't for me to make these decisions about the destiny of these instruments, whatever state of mind I was in. I have to make this right. Only by making it right can I begin to forgive myself.

I walk through to the workshop.

There it is.

The speed at which I can recover from this, the journey towards bringing myself back, starts with this one instrument. I have to do this first. Only when it is restored to its former glory, to more than its original self, can I start to grieve for my own lost years, my own broken heart.

I have barely given myself a chance to think about David, to examine the raw pain that exists there, but I know I am going to have to before too long. I am purposefully avoiding silence and a space to think; I reach forward to turn on the radio.

Alan's violin is still on the bench. Its neck is still attached to its body, but its ribs are in tatters. The front of the violin was already off before this happened — before I did this. I had been working on the belly. I walk across to my other bench where the front of the violin was in a box. It is still here; still in one piece. I had already started thinning out the belly, and the stripes of fresh wood I've shaved into it look like wounds now that everything else is so injured.

The ribs of the violin are staved in. They stick out like hillbilly teeth, all odd angles and dysfunction. What should run as a smooth line around the edge of the violin is a crazed and crackled roller coaster of danger and sharp points.

It's not impossible. Perhaps if fixing Alan's violin is not impossible, then I can start to climb this mountain. At the top will be a level space; a place to think.

Behind me is the Cremona cello on its stand. It has lurched slightly sideways but is still upright. It maintains its position like a martyr who has taken every unkindness, every act of spite or betrayal, but refused to buckle, refused to let go of its last dignity. The hole through its front is a monument to the last week; a testament to the tornado that has ripped through everything I am.

I will fix the Cremona cello in time. Alan's violin must come first.

I check carefully around the broken violin on the bench. I am looking for pieces of the broken ribs; if there are enough of them, I can look at patching them back together. It's the most difficult way to fix it, but it keeps the majority of the wood as Alan's work. At the same time, I have to take into account that this violin didn't really work very well, didn't have much of a voice. If I take these ribs off completely and remake a whole new set, it will give the instrument a far better chance to sing.

While I decide, I start to clear up. I'm not sure where to start so I flick on the coffee machine.

Next to it is the answerphone and the red light flashing a steady beat, a warning of waiting messages. My heart skips a beat with reality.

I know instantly that I would give anything for this message to be some kind of time lapse, a slip that will bring me out — kicking and spluttering — in a new world. In the world that was supposed to be here, on this date, in this shop and free of all the nightmares the last few days have brought.

My finger hovers over the play button. The options of what will be there run through my head. I try frantically to add consequences to all the possibility of messages. I know with certainty that there will be one from David; not a hope, not a wish, just certainty.

I don't know what I want it to say.

The coffee machine beeps and I jump.

I press the button.

"You have four messages."

I press stop. I'm not ready to hear them. David would not leave four messages; that's not his style. He will leave one crisp and clear recording, his voice deep and resonant. His words will be carefully chosen; David never panics. There will be feeling in his delivery, but I don't know what that feeling will be. I know that he will be missing me.

Once I start to defrost, to feel, I know that I will miss him too.

I wish fervently that I was the kind of person who could delete the messages without listening to them; I never will be. A flutter of hope stays inside me, a thin light of optimism that isn't ready to let me go yet. Maybe, the buoyancy tells me, David will have changed his mind, maybe the whole thing was the result of some sort of breakdown.

It would make no difference. Too much is broken. I look at the pieces of wood around me.

I press play.

His is the first message.

"Sweetheart, I've tried your mobile. I need to know that you're safe. That's all. Just text me and tell me that, even if you can't bear to talk to me properly at the moment. We'll speak soon, darling girl, sort stuff out. I'm sorry it's all so difficult right now."

And that's it. That's his whole message.

By the timbre of his voice you might think he had missed a dinner date, an opera booking. I look around at the dust, the dirt, the pandemonium of the workshop — my choice, my actions, not his. Perhaps this mess is vital in my believing what has happened. David's message is unreliable evidence. The other three messages are no more convincing: salespeople and customers talking as if the world is still the same.

I pick up a cardboard box that I had dismantled and folded, ready to put out for recycling. I reassemble it and stick tape across the join. I carry the box through to the front of the shop with me and start to pick up pieces of injured instruments.

It takes a long time to collect the poor broken pieces. On one or two instruments, I am surprised that seeing them from another angle reveals their secrets. There is a Mirecourt cello with cracked bouts; I can see now that the fault in it was down to the set of the shoulders and the neck, nothing to do with the bridge as I've thought for months. I wondered why it wouldn't sell, why no one totally believed in the sound.

I am surprised to hear myself humming. I don't immediately recognize the tune, but as it develops, I realize that it's Nadia's symphony. I hum more loudly.

A Berlin school viola has revealed a pattern of woodworm in the neck; a line of telltale dots that mean the beetles may or may not still be resident in the wood. I take the two bits of the viola — its neck has come loose from its shoulders — and put it straight in a bin bag. I scrunch the neck of the bin bag up and squirt most of a can of fly spray inside and all over the viola. I tie the bag up tightly and put it downstairs in the cellar. An outbreak of woodworm would be catastrophic; the irony embarrasses me and I feel my cheeks flush.

The phone is ringing upstairs. I take the stone steps two at a time and get there before the answerphone.

"Grace? It's Maurice Williams."

I am a little short of breath.

"You said you'd text when you got in. Are you all right, dear?"

"Oh God, sorry. I haven't plugged my phone in."

He makes a clucking sound, an approval that I haven't been looking for messages from David. I won't tell him that there was one here and, if truth be told, I have simply forgotten thus far to charge my mobile.

"Are you making progress?"

I look around. It isn't anywhere near as

bad as it looked. I have saved all the fragments of each instrument and I have started
to brush up corners of the workshop. I
resisted opening all my bottles and jars of
varnishes and pigments. I have no idea why,
but I'm very grateful. Glue, powders, and
chemicals would have made this an impossible task. They would have caused far more
damage.

"I am making progress." I haven't called
David back. This only occurs to me now
that I am speaking to another human being.
This is progress. "I'm doing well."

"Have you eaten?"

"I've had coffee." I smile as I say it and I
know he is smiling back at me on the other
end of the phone.

"Do you mind if I come down? Bring little
eats?"

"I don't mind at all," I say. "I can fix
Alan's violin, Mr. Williams. I can fix it very
easily and it will play beautifully."

"We'll talk about that."

He promises to pop down shortly with
some late lunch. I could do with it.

I concentrate on getting the shop as close
to a semblance of normality as I can. I want
Mr. Williams to be impressed with what I've
achieved and, more than anything, I don't
want him to worry about Alan's violin.

I take the end off the vacuum cleaner tube and get down on my hands and knees to get the tiniest pieces of glass out of the carpet. A couple of minuscule fragments burrow under my skin and even though I rub them they won't budge; a temporary tattooed punishment for the things I have broken.

I phone an antiques dealer I know and ask him who he thinks might repair the countertop. The glass top needs replacing and the leather, the beautifully marked leather with its tales of history and commerce, has been torn where the shards of the top went through it. He has some good ideas and, within three phone calls, I have someone who will come out tomorrow to have a look.

When Mr. Williams comes he brings a basket; not quite a picnic hamper but not far off. He has wrapped the contents in a white tea towel.

"Where can we eat, dear?" he asks as if there is nothing unusual, as if the blinds are flung up to the sun, as if the instruments are ordered and settled in their racks.

"It'll have to be my workbench, I think." I move some things around to make room and Mr. Williams puts the tablecloth down as best he can. I pick up Alan's violin to show him.

"I'm going to make new ribs. I can start them tomorrow. It'll be done in no time."

Mr. Williams is taking little plastic take-away tubs out of the basket. He has obviously been busy and intended to come here all along. There are salads and small pastry parcels, cold meats and tiny pots of home-made pickle.

"Oh wow, this looks amazing. You've worked hard."

"You need feeding up."

I look down at myself; he's not wrong. The past days have taken their toll. My jeans are loose and my T-shirt is crumpled and old; I've dressed without any regard to who might see me or what I might be doing. "I'm a bit of a tramp, aren't I?"

He nods his head slowly. "I've seen you looking better. But what do you expect? You don't eat."

"I am now." I really am. His cooking is excellent. I have filled my plate and am eating his creations with gusto. Flakes of cheesy pastry drop onto my plate and I blot them up with a finger. "Did you make this pastry?"

"I did. I haven't got much else to do these days and it's a terrific pleasure to have someone to cook for. I love cooking." His voice is wistful and I can tell he is looking into the past.

"Have you spoken to Nadia?" I ask him.

"I've exchanged a few texts with her. Not about the diary business, though."

I resist asking him what Nadia might be thinking. It's not his problem. It's a reason to charge my phone, though, and I dig it out of my bag. There is a charger already plugged into the wall.

As soon as the phone wakes, it buzzes with messages. I reach over with one hand and look at the home screen to see who they're from. There is nothing from Nadia; I hadn't really thought there would be, but I am still disappointed.

There is a text from David, just a question along the same lines as his phone message.

There are voice mail messages, too, but I flick through the numbers and none are from Nadia. One is from David, but I'm sure it will be the same untroubled voice from my work answerphone.

"I'll call her later." I hope she will answer. "And leave her text messages if she doesn't want to speak to me. All I can do is say sorry; I can't undo what's done." How I wish I could.

"Sorry can move mountains, I find." Mr.

Williams smiles sympathetically.

"And I've got a lovely strip of maple for the ribs of your violin." I reach over onto the shelf beside the workbench. The thin piece of wood is a golden color, its grain shimmers orange along its whole length like the skin of a fish. "It's beautiful, isn't it? I was going to use it for a violin I'm —"

"Grace," Mr. Williams interrupts me. "I don't want you to fix Alan's violin. Not yet."

"I have to, I'm sorry — it's not even up for discussion. It's the very least I can do."

He holds his hand up in a gesture of defiance. "No. Seriously, no. It's not what I want." His hand is perpendicular to his arm. The palm is a soft, clean pink and wrinkled. The lines across it are grooved and deep; his love line and lifeline clearly defined.

"Like I said," he continues, "sorry can move mountains. And you are sorry — anyone can see that. Alan's violin will wait. I'm an old man and" — he twinkles at me — "let's face it, my playing's not going to get any better."

"I don't know." I join in with his joke. "You might sound great on the right instrument. And that'll be the right instrument by the time I've finished it."

He shakes his head. "It's not what I want."

I shrug. I will have to hear him out at

least. I concentrate on the last of the salad, pushing the thin slices of tomatoes around my plate in a slur of vinaigrette.

"I want you to fix the Cremona cello."

We both turn and look at it. I haven't had the heart to straighten the cello, and it stares back at us as if its head is cocked to one side and it is listening.

"It's too late for that, I'm afraid." I am kind to him; it is a very sweet thought. "I could repair it to near perfection, but it couldn't win now. This cello — even if I spent months on it — will always look like someone stoved in the front and then repaired it. The only way to solve that would be to make a new front. And that would take months. Literally."

Mr. Williams doesn't drop his gaze. "When Leslie died, it was only projects like this that kept me going. Things that had a beginning and an end, things I could measure. Mending the Cremona cello is therapy."

"Therapy for me?"

"Yes. You've still got your hotel room and everything booked, haven't you?"

I nod. "I have but I can't enter the cello. It would be a huge waste of time and money even if I could fix it. It can't win." I start clearing away the lunch.

"Dear, it's not always about winning. This

is just an exercise in bouncing back, taking part. *I* want to know that you can do it. *I* want to see that you're on the mend." He stands up and looks me right in the eye. "And it's my choice. It's my violin that's suffered."

"Is that blackmail?" I'm surprised at him, surprised and touched.

"Do you know, my dear, that's exactly what it is!" He is delighted to have been found out. "I will forgive and forget — I'm actually awfully good at both — if you promise to get that cello ready for the competition. To the best of your ability."

"Even though it won't even be placed?"

"Yes." He is adamant, and I am in his debt.

"But why? Alan's violin is just as important. That could be my therapy." It's a last-ditch attempt.

"No," he says emphatically. "It has to be the cello because I want to go to Cremona with you. I haven't been to Italy in years." He puts the lid back onto one of the plastic pots with a loud snap.

CHAPTER NINETEEN

It doesn't dawn on me until Mr. Williams and I start planning logistics that I have missed the date to get the cello to Cremona by courier. The whole plan is moot before it has even got off the ground.

"It should have been picked up this week." I look at the calendar hanging on the wall of the shop. It is a violin calendar and this month's maker is Guarneri. "Two days ago."

"We can just ring another courier, surely? It might cost more."

"I've already paid for this through the blinking nose," I say. "There is only one courier they'll accept packages from. Otherwise it's hand deliveries only up to a few days before the exhibition."

"I'll deliver it." He looks so pleased with himself.

"You've been so kind. But I think there has to come a point where we cut off, give up. It's just not meant to be." I cannot imagine anything more irresponsible than sending a man in his eighties halfway across Europe on his own, carrying a cello that weighs a ton. The superstrength case I bought for this cello is really heavy. The thought crosses my mind that it's a shame the cello wasn't in the case when I kicked it.

Mr. Williams is rummaging around in the brown leather shoulder bag he always carries. When I next look over, he is concentrating on an iPad, his fingers moving at an amazing speed across the screen. "Could I have your Wi-Fi password?" he asks. "I'll have a look for flights and hotels."

He is unstoppable.

"You need a second seat for the cello." I know when I'm beaten. "It'll cost a fortune."

Mr. Williams waves one hand in a dismissive gesture. He is animated and enjoying himself.

I owe him this. "OK." I am going to give in. "But two things: first, I'm paying. For you and the cello. For everything. And there will be no discussion on that."

He bobs his head around, a smile playing on his lips. He is a handsome old man and these plans are giving him a buoyancy that lights him up. One oiled strand of his white hair falls down from his fringe and he smooths it back into place with his palm.

"And second," I say, my voice mock stern. "You have to promise me that you genuinely understand that the whole thing is futile. Even if I make a new front, if that's even possible, I'll be up against people who've spent years on their varnish and their purfling. Who've spent weeks, even, just polishing the thing. Exactly like I did," I add a little sadly. "Got that?"

"Absolutely, dear." He is triumphant. "It's not about the winning for me, anyway," he says. "It's about the Chianti and the spaghetti and the negronis. *Divertiamoci!*" He claps his hands together and giggles. "That's Italian for *Laissez les bons temps rouler,*" he says.

I know that phrase. It is one of David's favorites. I wonder who he is "letting the good times roll" with now. I think about him and Marie-Thérèse living the life I loved so much; shopping at the exquisite bakery on Avenue Victor Hugo, buying fruit from the street stand at the corner of Rue Copernic and taking it all back to the apartment, back to bed.

I imagine the white curtains and the breeze from the balcony, the long waxed floorboards and the simple elegance of it all. It feels like someone else's life already.

Mr. Williams is murmuring to himself as he looks for flights on his iPad. I can feel the excitement fizzing off him. He has earned this. It is good to have a way to give him something back.

I reach for my phone and check it for the tenth time in an hour. Still nothing from Nadia. I have done as Mr. Williams suggested and said sorry. I haven't given Nadia a cloaked *I'm sorry if you were hurt* apology; I've given her both barrels of the groveling, heartfelt pleading that I know she deserves. It hasn't moved her.

I have had a chance now to look at the damage to my cello. It reaches so far, this one stupid act of mine. This instrument is the best thing I have ever made by a mile; it had a real chance of winning, or at least of drawing some admirers from some of the markets I wanted to get into. I push the flapping pieces of the cracked front. A shard of spruce snaps off in my fingers and I press my skin against it until my fingertips hurt.

There is no other way to do this but to make a new front. I have a piece of cello wood downstairs. It'll make the cello look like a whole and entire instrument — albeit not a very good one. A repair would have made people ask questions about what had happened to it that I would not want to answer.

The wood is in the cellar and I leave Mr. Williams to his internet browsing and go and look. I know there is only one piece of cello wood; a choice of one. It is leaning against the shelving alongside at least a half-dozen viola billets and even more for violin. As soon as I take the wood out, I see the knot. It is in a corner of the wood, in a spot that — once I have split and bookended it — will be just below the bridge.

If I'm to continue, I have to use this flawed piece. I wonder about the rules of the competition; it's possible it might not even be admitted. There are lots of things I could do to disguise a knot in a cello front, tricks with fillers and varnish and smoothing, but none of them could fool the trained eyes at the competition and all of them would take time I don't have.

A billet of wood is a wedge shape, rough-hewn. The longest side of the wedge is the length of the cello back and it is exactly half the width of a cello front. I will split the wedge of wood laterally on the band saw, going clean through its middle to produce two identical pieces, half the thickness of the original. This convoluted practice makes sure that, when the two pieces are stuck together, the parallel lines that run through it will be the same on both sides of the cello front. This wood has good reed lines, they plow up and down the wedge, showing every winter that the tree endured and every summer that saw it grow.

Before I switch the band saw on I check my phone once more. Still nothing. I warn Mr. Williams about the noise before I push the screaming wood through the saw. Cello spruce is hard and the blade grinds against it as I push it. The smoke that comes off is not as pleasant as burning wood; it singes rather than catches. I'm fond of the smell, even though it's odd; an acrid vapor of resistance.

The two pieces have to be joined together down what will be the centerline of the cello. The edges must be impeccably prepared; there can't be any nicks or gaps between the two surfaces or the seam will come apart.

Mr. Williams is watching me very quietly. I can tell he wants to be an impartial observer to the magic, to watch as the new cello front begins its journey. It's quite comforting.

I take a number five plane, sharp enough to flay skin if I rubbed it across my arm or leg. I run it along the wide side of the wedge. It is too narrow by half a centimeter. I clean the curl of wood from it and put it back in its exact place, in the right order. I take a five and a half instead and it fits beautifully. I start to clean away the excess wood so that the two flat surfaces will be identical. It is a rhythmic task and hypnotic. I lose myself to it in seconds.

"You have a message." Mr. Williams holds up my phone. I hadn't heard it. It must have come in while I was using the band saw.

It is from Nadia. I offer up a tiny prayer.

i'm coming to get my book. are you there?

There is no kiss, no hope that she might let me back in. Of course she wants the diary back; I hadn't even thought about it. I let Mr. Williams clear the glass from the shelf inside the counter while I get on with clearing the bench.

come whenever you want. i'll wait. I hold my breath.

driving lesson at 3. will get dropped off at shop after.

Mr. Williams looks at me; a nonverbal question. I nod my head with relief.

I put the hide glue on the tiny stove to start melting. The smell of the softening glue is not as awful as it could be, given what it's made of. When it's warm enough, I wipe it across the two cleaned edges of the split billet and stick the two sides together. It opens the wedge out like a butterfly.

"This is called bookending," I tell Mr. Williams. "It's a bookend joint."

I start the process of fixing clamps along the length of the seam to hold the wood in place until the glue dries. I can do this mechanically and I use the empty time to think about Nadia. I am putty in her hands and will do anything I can to restore our friendship. I am utterly to blame.

I run my fingers over the small knot in the center of the wood. It isn't terrible and if it were a cello to sell or a cello for a customer, this sort of blemish would probably give the instrument an extra character, a little bit of individuality. But this is for a competition that requires anonymity, uniformness, and convention. The swirling fingerprint in the wood isn't big enough to mean the cello would be thrown out of the competition. It will still make it into the Cremona exhibition of entered instruments, but the knot is more reason, if any were needed, that it can't possibly win.

"Do you want me to go when Nadia comes?" Mr. Williams asks.

"I don't know. I suppose so." I'll be sad to see him leave.

"It's for the best. You girls need to be able

to talk freely."

I agree with him. He tidies up the last of the glass he's swept up, wraps it in newspaper, and puts it in the bin. "I've booked myself a flight in five days' time." He looks at me with a challenge. "And a seat for the cello."

We both look at the piece of wood clamped and drying on the workbench.

"Bloody hell," I say.

"I'm going to fly to Turin and take a train on to Cremona. I'm staying there for a night and then I'll drop the cello off the next morning. There's a week, then, until you arrive."

"Are you going to stay there for a week? It's a small town."

He shakes his head. "I have good friends in Venice. Friend — Paulo has expired, but Laurence is still there. Leslie and I used to stay with them whenever we could. It'll be lovely to catch up." He grins. "Laurence has already said he'll be there and glad to have me. That's all us oldsters do, you know. Sit by our email all day, hoping someone will write."

"Are the trains manageable?"

"It's how we always used to get around," he says and shrugs.

I suppose I should trust him — at his age

— to sort out a short train ride, even if it is in another country.

"I'll visit with Laurence and then come back up to join you, if I may. If you could bear to show me around?"

"Of course I can. I have two tickets for the finale concert too — one for me and one for David. We'll go together, shall we?"

Mr. Williams is thrilled at the idea. By the time he's got his iPad back out to look up the program and we've discussed the merits of listening to Italian versus German composers, it is nearly four o'clock.

He whispers good luck and blows me an expansive kiss as he leaves.

Nadia looks thin and tired. Her anger has blown through and left her hollow.

I reach down under the broken counter and pick up the sketchbook. I hand it to her instead of speaking. I have nothing left to offer her.

"Thanks," she says, but her voice holds no clues.

"How was your driving lesson?" The clumsy words spill into the shop and deserve the silence they're met with.

And then she laughs. A loud but real laugh. The sunshine side of her comes out and the cloud is gone. " 'How was your fucking driving lesson?' "

"I don't know what else to say. I assume you're bored with 'sorry' and 'what more can I do?' "

"I'll never be bored with 'what more can I do?' " She narrows her eyes. "Seriously, though, what did you read? All of it?"

"Like I said, hardly any. Some stuff about coke. Stuff about Harriet being an arsehole. Then I stopped."

"Bet you would have read more if you'd had time."

I don't answer. I don't know whether she's right or not.

"Is Mr. Williams here?"

I shake my head. "He just left five minutes ago."

"OK then, the truth. The coke thing was just a fad; everyone does it at my school. Everyone." The last word is a warning not to challenge her, not to comment. "And I stopped doing it ages ago — not because I don't like it but because I'd do it all the time and, you know, I wouldn't do anything else. And, well, I have stuff to do. Stuff more important than getting off my tits."

"Your symphony," I say, but she just shrugs.

"And other shit."

"Everyone falls out with their friends all

the time, Nad, it's part of life."

"You mean you and me?"

"No." I feel stupid now. "I meant you and Harriet, but us too if you want. But the Harriet thing, it's not a reason not to go to school."

"Who said it was?" She raises her eyebrows at me, lifts her palms to indicate that I should think of an answer, think of an answer but not bother sharing it. "Taking a year out is nothing to do with Harriet. Literally. She's not that fucking important."

"Sorry, I was trying to help."

Just when I least expect it, she softens. "I've done some stupid shit. But it's done now and it's time to move on."

I open my mouth to speak, to claim the "stupid shit" title but am struck dumb by the tide of things I have done that Nadia might term "stupid shit," by the years I have spent racking up more and more mistakes.

"Let's do it. Let's move on." I smile at her. I would love to hug her, but she just isn't that kind of girl. Her prickles are invisible, but they are real and sharp.

"Cool. I need to. And I need my job." She steps towards the counter at last, leaves her escape route behind her. "I need you a bit too, actually."

And she hugs me, pinning my arms to my sides.

I get the leftover bits of Mr. Williams's picnic out and Nadia eats them as if she hasn't eaten since we left his house.

"How are things at home?" I ask her.

"Same old, same old," she says. "There's no one there most of the time and when they are they're all about locked rooms and mobile calls. I don't give a fuck. I just play my violin, work on my music."

I think about myself when I'd first left college, locked in my room and repetitively practicing. "Are you still going to your violin lessons?"

"Violin lessons?" she asks, her mouth full of sausage roll. "Definitely. Fuck yes. That's how I know my parents are still alive; someone's still paying my teacher. I'm taking a year off the other shit, not violin."

I'm relieved to hear it.

Our chatting becomes easier, more what it was before all this. It has brought us an equality, though, this shift. Something is different. Something, oddly, is better.

I show her the cello and its terrible damage. I have put it on the bench and started to pop open the hide glue that holds the broken front to the ribs. When I have worked the front off and cleaned away all the fragments of glue and wood, I'll put my new front on and use the ribs as a template to score around. It is simple except that, at the moment, my new front is a thick chunk of wood held together by some clamps.

"Mission," says Nadia, and I have to agree.

"And then Mr. Williams is taking it to Italy? To the competition?"

"If it's humanly possible to get it done."

"What can I do? Can I do some of the sanding or something?"

"It's not sanding, that's what you do on tables, chests of drawers. Things that can take a bit of roughhousing. It's all down to me, I'm afraid."

"Can you do it?"

"If I don't sleep."

"Good." It seems to mean a lot to her, too. Perhaps it is the focus we all need.

"You know how you want to make shit up to me and all that?"

I nod. I'm picking at a curl of glue, peering closely at the Cremona cello.

"I'm coming to Italy too."

CHAPTER TWENTY

I can breathe in Italy. I suck in the warm night air and it feels like life. Exhaling is such a train of letting go that I almost start to cry.

I checked into the hotel alone. This was supposed to have been a trip with David; we had been planning it for months. The hotel is the sort he would book; elegant and expensive, of course. I fight down the angry pain that marks his absence. It presses my head like a tight band.

This is a beautiful room, but my losses ricochet around it. My sadness thunders through when I open the bathroom taps; it is everywhere. I catch sight of myself in the mirror; the fact that I am in the frame alone is compounded by the expanse of perfectly ironed white linen behind me; as if nothing has ever gone wrong in this room before.

The woman in the mirror is someone else, someone emptier. I have to start a new part of my life, but I can't seem to find the instructions. Inside this matryoshka doll is the bullet I must swallow; wrapped in the layers of the last two weeks is the stony heart betrayed by David.

We should have been here together, giggling at the funny old receptionist's bad temper, groaning at each other about the lift not working and having to drag our heavy bags up the old stone stairs, marveling at the room with its tiny balcony and the exquisite bathroom lined — floor to ceiling — with green mosaic tiles.

Instead, I threw my case on the bed, checked I had the room key, and left as fast as I could.

The place is stunning. A town map came in the welcome pack for the competition and I buried myself in it on the plane over. Everything about Cremona is magical; it is the stuff of my dreams. Stradivari's house, his birthplace, his gravestone, they're all marked on the map as if it's completely normal to be the epicenter of such creativity and invention. The city really values its history; some years ago the city elders gathered all the funding they could and bought the Vesuvius, one of Stradivari's finest violins, entrusting it to municipal ownership for the rest of time. I can only imagine the uproar if my little Kent town decided to spend its limited resources on something like that instead of dog bins or streetlights or more double yellow lines.

I'm looking for Stradivari's grave; it is in a tiny park next to the city square, clearly marked on the map. Cremona doesn't look like a city and, were it not for the reaching spire of the *duomo* visible from all the narrow streets, I would just think it was a tiny, quaint town. Unusual for a city, what it has in spades is peace.

I sit down on a park bench. The light has just gone and the evening is relying on the glow from the shops and houses behind me. I am enjoying the quiet. This feels like the first moment I've stopped in weeks; the first minutes of actual calm. I concentrate on my breathing and the soft sounds that float around this oasis.

There is a busy street behind me; I can hear the people chattering on their way past the park. The city will be full of violin makers and players. There is a huge trade fair here, timed to coincide with the competition, and it attracts people from all over the world. I will catch up with numerous old friends and acquaintances over the week; it's inevitable. I wonder what I will tell them about myself. That will depend on who I am, on who I turn out to be once the dust begins to settle.

The last few weeks have been insanely busy. I made a cello front in five days as I had set out to do. I left the knot in the wood almost bare of varnish; it had become precious to me, that simple flaw. I didn't want to hide it.

Nadia and Mr. Williams did their very best to help. Mostly it took the form of coffee — from Nadia — and hot homemade food from Mr. Williams. As much as they wanted to, there was little they could do to help me with the instrument itself.

I spent some late nights in the workshop with them; sometimes one, then the other. They tried not to leave me alone and I'm grateful. I needed those hours filled.

Nadia has been preoccupied in the run-up to Italy.

"Do you not have to go home? Not even sometimes?" I asked her when she'd spent the fourth consecutive evening watching me work.

"I haven't done for years. Did you spend your evenings at home when you were my age?"

"Wrong person to ask, Nad. I actually did."

"Loser."

I took my caliper and tested the thickness of the cello belly. It was beginning to take on its bowl shape, curving up at the sides to — literally — scoop the sound into it. I squinted to check the reading on the gauge. "Really, though? Is everything OK?" The brass stud of the gauge made a soft *tick, tick, tick* as it connected with the wood.

"It's the same as ever." She was getting the front room of the shop ready for a coat of paint. Her black hair was splattered with tiny specks that she'd rubbed off the woodwork. Her nose was powdered with the dust. "They're starting to talk about actually moving out now, though. I think they're fighting over who gets freedom and who gets me. Fuckers."

"I'm sure they're not." It was hard to tell if she was joking, but when I looked up over the curve of the cello, I realized she wasn't. "They both love you very much."

She pointed her paint scraper at me and sneered. "I'm not five. I am an adult."

You're not an adult, I thought but didn't dare say. You're a wounded girl who wishes everything at home could stay the same forever. The specter of David's nameless children flashed across my mind like a storm cloud, but I moved it swiftly away.

"Trust me, if I had anywhere else to go right now . . ."

Experience told me to be still, that she has to weather this; she has to muddle her way through the collapse of her parents' marriage as best she can. "What about going back to school to finish your A-levels? Uni would mean you could leave home far sooner than any other way."

"And my symphony?" She looked at me with such conviction, such confidence, that I had to backpedal.

"Sorry, yes. I just — you know — wondered if you could do both."

"No."

She turned and walked back into the shop with her paint scraper. Dots of dust lay in her wake.

Nadia stayed till late every evening and was back first thing in the morning. She had a brain wave when we first sat down and talked about the rescue plans. She, Mr. Williams, and I sat together, coffees and biscuits on the table in my kitchen, and made a schedule. Nadia insisted that we take the opportunity to paint the shop walls; that way, any customers who wondered why I had been closed, why the blinds were down for so long, could have a rational and plausible explanation. It was a good idea.

Mr. Williams kept slightly less demanding hours, but he must have spent a lot of time cooking when he was at home.

The cello front began to take shape. The grain didn't have the definition of the original and the pattern took on the shape of contour lines where it hit the knot. I scraped it and scraped it into a shining silver finish. The heart of the knot was as black as a burn and the thick lines around it a hearty mahogany. There was no disguising the imperfection, so I didn't try. It would have made things worse.

I let Mr. Williams put the base coat of stain on the front. It darkened the wood in stripes as he worked the brushstrokes. Here and there the stain pooled too thickly, but I bit my lip and let him carry on doing it his way. I pointed out the areas that needed a little more or a touch less as gently as I could.

"This reminds me of making treasure maps when I was a boy," said Mr. Williams. "We used to paint them with tea and then set fire to the corners for a little authenticity."

"I'm not surprised it reminds you," I said. "That is tea. Good old builders' blend. Ancient violin makers' trick."

He sniffed the tea in the jam jar. "Sometimes it's more romantic not to look behind the curtain, Grace. I shall continue in the mistaken belief I'm painting on some potion of tree roots and harmony."

The black tea leaked into the wood, more or less where I wanted it. I kept half an eye on Mr. Williams's progress while I made up the size. Size is the next part of the process; a thin solution of glue, water, and alum that keeps the varnish from soaking into the wood.

I opened my cupboard of jars and bottles and took out a small box of alum. I sprinkled the white crystals into the bowl of glue and water.

"Sugar?" Mr. Williams asked.

"Alum."

"It looks like Epsom salts." He went to poke the powder.

"I wouldn't touch it," I said. "I don't think it would be very good for you."

"What does it do?" he asked.

"It's what the old Cremonese makers used. Nothing the Renaissance craftsmen could get hold of was very fancy."

I carried on explaining. It made me feel purposeful and able; something I hadn't been in a while. "The watered-down glue and the alum, the size, makes a barrier — an isolating barrier, technically — so that if or when the varnish ever wears off, the wood stays protected. The size is the most important stage of the varnishing."

"Size matters?" Mr. Williams said in a coy voice.

I gave him a withering stare by way of an answer. "Do you want to put the size on? Or not?"

He was delighted and hummed away to himself as he completed the task. "Do you know, Grace, I would never have imagined I'd be involved in something like this. How super. I feel like I've made it myself."

I thought of the journey he had made to this humble job of washing the size onto my cello. It is a story that starts with the death of his best friend and ends with the destruction of his personal — and valuable — property, and yet here he was. He was actually grateful. I tried to put it into words. I made a bit of a hash of it, but he got my meaning.

"Isn't that the beauty of life, Grace? Those unexpected moments where a turn that feels so wrong, so awkward at the time, blossoms into an opportunity like this? I've led a life of surprises, dear, and of contrasts. I wouldn't change it for the world."

I didn't want to point out that he and Leslie were separated by circumstance during their relationship; that his partner died in the wrong house, with the wrong person, because of the hand life had dealt them.

Mr. Williams seems to have a gift for reading my mind, for guessing my thoughts. "And although things would have been easier — more open — for Leslie and me if we'd been together nowadays, so many other things would have been wrong. We were part of a great movement, a tide of change for the future." He looked up at me; his forehead wide and smooth and his slicked-back white hair still immaculately in place. "We campaigned, quietly, to reform the law and society. We only did that because we were in a compromised position, because we were persecuted, but it did help; we were part of lasting improvements."

I felt very insignificant. I put a hand on his arm. "I am slowly getting a grip, I promise."

"I think you're doing rather well." He smiled and went back to his work.

The radio was on, a Shostakovich piece that had us all working with more gusto to keep up with it. I remembered a story I'd loved as a child: "The Elves and the Shoemaker." The elves come every night and busy themselves in the shoemaker's workshop; they do all his work and make sure he becomes shoemaker to the king. I could improve on that. My elves were here, in the room beside me. They didn't appear in the dark and help behind the scenes; they were next to me, ready to — literally if need be — hold me up at any time.

It took until the final available minutes to do the sound-post adjustments on the new setup. I had slept well for the first time in weeks the night we glued the cello together and there was nothing more to be done than wait and hope the clamps did their work. I didn't have time to miss David. I didn't dream. I was so tired that my sleep was like a practice for death.

We stood around together — Nadia, Mr. Williams, and I — to undo the clamps. I left three in place and we took the screw of one each.

"Ready?"

"What if I undo mine and the top pings off?" said Nadia. "I'm nervous."

"I wouldn't risk it." My smile was genuine. I was proud of my — of our — achievement. "I've taken off all the ones on pressure points. These don't do much on their own. Watch your fingers on the top, though, the varnish is still tacky. We don't want it dotted with fingerprints."

Three turns of the screws and the clamps slid neatly off the body. The cello was whole again. It wasn't a prize-winning job, even a layman could see that, but we had known it wouldn't be. As the symbol of wholeness it had set out to be, it ticked every box. I knew then, if I hadn't before, that Mr. Williams was a very wise man.

After the fastest setup I had ever done, I put the cello, still clingy with varnish, into its case and had to drive Mr. Williams to the airport; if he had taken his own car and had to waste vital minutes parking he would have missed the plane. It was that close.

Nadia wasn't able to get on my flight; it was packed. She will arrive tomorrow, soon after Mr. Williams takes the train up from Venice. I have this one night to gather myself, to inflate and deflate my lungs and let things go as my breath pours into the night air.

There are months of work waiting for me at home, but the shelves are full again and violins hang over the double basses in their stands for all the world as if nothing ever happened. The shop is fresh and white, all the corners are cleaned and smart, all shadows and ghosts chased away. Two or three of the instruments have been rehomed, literally dead wood. They are things that I've had for years, stock that wouldn't sell and that wasn't of sufficient quality to fix.

There are empty spaces everywhere. Some empty spaces are physical; gaps on my shelves where instruments are temporarily missing, the silence on the phone that David and I use to communicate with each other. I keep my phone charged and check it often; I don't want to and I know it makes me a fool, but I can't help it. The other empty spaces are my secrets, feelings that I keep from Mr. Williams and Nadia; the deep and incomprehensible loss of David, of my balance. I begin each day, each minute, each word I speak, with a quivering fear. I have lost my understanding of the world and my place in it; my interpretation was wrong and that has sent me toppling. Mr. Williams's clever plan and Nadia's bubbling company have kept it from turning into a long, loud scream, but all the feelings are still there.

Just below the surface of my life runs a bitter seam; a desire to claw gaping holes in reality, to scratch and kick and fight my way back to what I used to think was my life. I'd give anything to return to my comfortable ignorance. This is something I can never share with the people who have tried so very hard to fix me. Every part of me — every aspect — is broken and every second, every heartbeat, feels like it might be my last.

It is turning from evening to nighttime here, the light has changed and the birds have stopped pecking around the benches. I get up to look for Stradivari's grave.

This park isn't the most auspicious of resting places; as I walk towards the back of it, it's really quite run-down. The dark corners are uninviting and there are too many bushes and trees for the streetlights to get through. At the edge of the gloomy area is a plaque in the grass. It explains, first in Italian and then in English, that Stradivari has gone to rest in the cathedral; this site is just where the original church he was buried in used to be.

Missing the first stop on the tourist trail frees me and I fold the map, slip it into my jeans pocket, and start to wander the winding streets instead. I allow myself to pause and peer in shopwindows. The shops directly behind the park are elegant and expensive. Bags and shoes, belts and coats, are artfully arranged in every shade that leather comes in and some that it hadn't before. The price tags are mind-boggling. When I look around me at the smartly dressed Italian men and the immaculate women, I can see that these shops are well patronized and sell plenty.

I am more interested in the food shops a little farther along. Cremona is famous for nougat — *torrone* — and it comes in huge, flat slabs. They are stacked on top of one another in the shopwindow, pistachio green against the soft cream of almonds, highlighted against a dark bruise of chocolate. It looks delicious.

Next door to the sweets there is a whole shop dedicated to ham and cheese. Dark pink legs hang drying in the window, the dotted black writing on their iridescent skin the same as on the cylinders of Parmesan below. Slices have been cut out of the Parmesan like a child's drawing of a cake, and I can see the salt crystals inside the cheese. It makes me hungry.

I walk around the streets looking for the right sort of bar. I want somewhere busy enough to be anonymous but not modern or garish. I want to watch other people and try and live outside of myself for a bit.

The square in front of the *duomo* is perfect. There are tables and chairs lined up along the street and it's still plenty warm enough to sit outside. The cathedral itself is stunning; each side of it seems to boast a different architecture, written in different stone. Under the portico running along the opposite side of the cathedral square, two mandolin players are busking to the evening crowds. I don't recognize the tune but it's beautiful. I sit close enough to hear them and order prosecco when the waiter comes to my table.

The drink comes with two squares of focaccia, one topped with black olive tapenade and the other with a sliver of mozzarella that leaks milky drops onto the plate. I eat them both before I'm even a quarter of the way down the glass. I need something more to eat, really, and when the waiter comes back I ask for a menu.

People are out strolling in couples and groups. I have never seen so many violin cases; not even at music college. Everyone who is anyone on the stringed instrument scene is here; the great and the good of the violin world. I see a few people I know walk past, people I have met through shows or exhibitions. I'm not ready to draw anyone's attention to me yet; I'd rather not get into any small talk. I do wonder what on earth they're going to say when they see my cello in the exhibition hall. In the week since Mr. Williams dropped it off I haven't heard anything from the organizers, so I'm assuming that it hasn't been disqualified.

The influx of people means that Nadia will have to share my hotel room when she arrives tomorrow. I don't mind; it will give me a chance to talk to her, to try and dig a little deeper into her doomed romance and her refusal to finish her A-levels. She is fragile beneath that gritty front and I will choose my moments wisely.

First, we all need a holiday. We need to relax.

I'll enjoy their company. Mr. Williams managed to rent a room from a friend of a friend. He will be just outside of the city center but an easy taxi or bus ride away from us.

I heard him on the phone making the final arrangements for his stay. Italian turns out to be in his skill set too. I hardly speak any; my Italian is strictly violin based or touristic, but his sounded pretty good.

The waiter brings my pizza. It is perfect, thin and crispy with just a light topping. I can see the dough through the cheese and know it won't drown the flavor of the sun-ripened tomatoes. I order another drink and settle into my own company.

The mandolin players move on from the portico and I walk slowly back towards the hotel after my meal. The streets are beautiful; the pavements tiny and narrow, the buildings tall and leaning in towards the road. I don't see a single supermarket between the square and my hotel, although a lot of buildings have shutters pulled down to keep out the night and the modern world may just be hidden behind them.

The shops that are still open are dazzling; one sells nothing but pasta, from tiny balls like beads to flat, soft pillows of warm orange that are the size of my hand. People are walking in and out of its door, buying their supper in what looks like cake boxes. The next shop on is full of preserved fruits, jars of spiced syrups with all the colors of autumn caught against the glass. The bakery has closed and its flat trays are left empty but for flour in every shade of brown that dusts like soft sand across the bottoms.

At the end of the road I can see the hotel. It reminds me again that I am here without David. I have gotten used to the idea that I am not here alone, at least not for long, and I'm far from sorry to be walking these streets on this beautiful evening, but I still miss him. It is inevitable.

There is a bar on my right. Outside there are six or seven tables and a gaggle of people send warm laughter floating towards the red roofs. The end table has no one on it and I sit down and take my book out of my bag.

The waiter takes my order and I open the page at my bookmark.

It begins to rain, softly and quietly. A fine, refreshing mist darkens the color of the stone pavements and dries almost as soon as it hits the ground.

A handsome gray-haired man from the group on the next table looks over and says, "Grace?"

CHAPTER TWENTY-ONE

Shota has barely changed. His hair is mostly gray, but his face is exactly the same as the last time I saw him, coming out of Catherine's bedroom down the hall from mine.

This time his smile is genuine, his surprise — although obvious — is a positive thing. Nostalgia flits across his face, leaving warmth behind it.

I have no idea how I feel about seeing him.

"Grace," he says again, and I realize I haven't moved or spoken. "I don't believe it."

"Shota." I smile and am taken aback by the involuntary movement of my face.

"Have you put an instrument in the competition? You don't live here?" I remember immediately how that same enthusiasm made me love him when I was nineteen.

"I'm a tourist," I say. "I live in Kent." And then, remembering the nomadic nature of the successful musician, I add, "In the UK."

The last time I googled Shota he was lead viola in the Iceland Symphony Orchestra in Reykjavik, the time before that the Sydney Symph.

Shota nods his head and beams at me. "I remember. I remember and I saw one of your cellos. Beautiful instrument. I looked at the label; facet *in Kent, England.* Bloody lovely cello."

My professional self should ask him whose instrument, who he knows that plays a Grace Atherton cello. Instead I just stare at him, stunned into silence.

"Grace, I'm sorry. How rude I am." He introduces me to his friends; there is a flurry of names from many different languages and cultures. "And this is my wife, Marion."

Marion stretches forward to shake my hand. "I'm so pleased to meet you. I've heard so much about you over the years." Her smile tells me that she knows who I am, that she knows what happened between her husband and me. I may be imagining that part of it even says that she's sorry, that first love is hard. I'm not imagining it; there is a kindness in her eyes.

As I shake hands with her I notice the tight round baby bump between her and the table; an imminent presence.

"When's your baby due?" is all I can think

of to say and I hope it's not too familiar. I hope she doesn't judge me by my dull conversation, my lack of sparkle.

"Seven weeks to the day. So we're hoping he or she stays put like they're supposed to and is a German baby as planned." She pats the top of the bump. "Not a surprise Italian one."

Marion is beautiful. Her red hair falls in curls and ringlets around her face. Everything about her looks totally natural and effortless. Her face is animated and her skin glows; her cheeks are rosy and round with smiling. She is immensely and immediately likeable.

I look across at her husband's square jaw and high cheekbones; this baby will be stunning.

"Congratulations," I say. I mean it.

Shota stands up. "Grace, please join us." It is an instruction, not a question. "I'll order some more drinks." He calls to the waiter in Italian that doesn't falter; no suggestion that it isn't native. "Rob, give me a hand."

The man closest to me unfolds himself from his chair. He is huge; my first thought, first stop of comparison, is that he is even taller than David. "Rob Bouvier," he says in an American accent, "sousaphone and trumpet, Hamburg Phil." I instantly envy him the coded introduction of the professional musician. I am only an artisan member of this club; I never got as far as its hallowed circle.

"Grace Atherton. I've got a cello in the competition."

"Brilliant," says Shota. "I hoped you would have. I can't wait to see it."

I bite my lip. No explanation would work here; I can't say there was an accident or an incident. I just have to let the world think that the front of my cello is a peculiar and knotted piece of wood that has been oddly varnished. I have to take it on the chin.

Rob and Shota pick up my table and move it closer to theirs. I move my chair across and their friends spread out and around to include me. I am sitting next to Marion, Shota opposite me, opposite both of us.

I was naive not to imagine bumping into Shota. He is an internationally renowned viola player; there was every chance he'd be here. I hadn't thought about it because I was supposed to have been with David. He would have been my armor against my past, against anything I didn't want to face.

"Are you looking for an instrument?" I ask Shota. That's why most players come here; the work of every top-quality maker in the world will be showcased in Cremona from tomorrow.

"No," he says, and his gray hair moves around his ears as he shakes his head. He takes a swig of beer. "Paid gig. I'm on the sound panel for viola and then I'm in the quartet that plays the winners."

I can't believe it. I can't believe I didn't check who was judging the other instruments. I had only taken note of who was judging the cellos — way back when Nadia and David first put me in for the competition. I chose the body of my cello, the outline and original model, based on the instrument that the judge played. I took care to think about the type of sound he likes, whether he likes sweet top notes or hearty bass. Back then, when I so dearly wanted to win, I employed every advantage I could. I've been so stupid. I've thrown away so much.

"And then I arranged to meet these guys here." Shota is still talking. I cobble together what he has said. He and Marion are using the trip as a last hurrah before the baby, their first, is born and they are meeting up with old colleagues from other European orchestras they've played in. "We live in Hamburg."

"Are you a musician too?" I ask Marion,

although I already know the answer will be yes. This is a close and closed society. It is hard for professional musicians to live with anyone who isn't involved in the industry. The hours and the constant touring and moving house are difficult for anyone; it helps to have a partner who understands.

"Trumpet," she says, even though she looks like she would be more suited to the harp or the flute. Her accent is American or Canadian. I can't tell which.

"I went from the Ontario Phil to the Iceland Orchestra. That's where I met Shota." I presume that answers the question about her accent. "And now we're in Hamburg. Guess I like it cold."

Most of the table are chattering about a player who has lost her violin. It has apparently been on every television news channel in every country. I think back to the last two weeks; no wonder I have missed it. A couple of Shota's friends know this woman; a principal violin player in a very important orchestra. She was at a railway station in a queue for the loo and when a complete stranger offered to hold her violin case she said yes. When she came out again the woman had vanished along with the player's £1,000,000 Guarneri. I must have had an email from the insurers; all violin shops would have. I've been so preoccupied, I've taken no notice of anything.

The bubble of happy chatter continues; the main theme, besides the woman's stupidity, is who owns the violin. These instruments are almost always bought by a hedge fund or a business; they get the tax breaks and the orchestra or the player gets to loan an instrument worthy of their talent. It makes me think about Nadia. I wonder whether she would be scatty enough to make the same mistake. I wonder whether she will finish her A-levels and get on the career path that has made these people so interesting, so cosmopolitan and adaptable.

"Are you here on your own?" Marion asks.

"No, well, yes. At the moment." I swirl the last of my prosecco around in my glass and take a deep breath. "I was coming with my partner but . . . we broke up."

It is like taking off a coat. It was a phrase I was so afraid of, a truth so barbed and vicious, but here, with these jolly people on this Italian evening, it's just a statement. It's just a fact.

I have said it out loud to a stranger, and nothing has happened. No thunderclap has split the night, no chasm has opened at my feet. Everything is the same except me.

The chatter continues. Shota asks me if

I'm here for the week; I explain that I am and that my friends are joining me tomorrow. "They're . . ." I go to describe them. I start to say that they're a funny pair, or that they're an odd little duo. Instead I find myself finishing the sentence with, "They're lovely. You'll like them."

And just like that, I am talking about the future. I am assuming that I will see Shota and Marion and Rob and their friends again. That we will all meet up when Mr. Williams and Nadia arrive.

I have avoided this confrontation for decades; I have never sought out Shota or anyone from my college days. I thought it would compound my humiliation, emphasize my failure. Now I realize it would have made me nostalgic. We are two grown adults with a brief episode of shared past; he's not a monster and I, I am not a failure. The past is mostly harmless.

Every few minutes someone walks by with an instrument case. The pavement is wide but almost entirely covered with tables and chairs from the bar. Pedestrians are forced to walk on the cobbled roadway, but no one seems to mind at all. Almost every time someone passes, one of the people at our table will know them. The group widens and shrinks again with the pulse of a living entity; everyone who drops in is immediately accepted.

Farther down the road another bar has pop music playing, it trickles down towards us and is drowned by the laughter and the shouting. A boy whizzes past on a bicycle, his girl balanced on his crossbar, her legs neatly crossed as if riding sidesaddle comes naturally to her. They pass a group of young people and call out greetings and whistles into the warm night. No one shouts from the houses along the street and tells us or the young people to be quiet; it is as if the whole city has adopted the carnival atmosphere that the competition has brought.

"I'm going to go back to the hotel soon," Marion says directly to Shota. She turns her head slightly towards me. "You guys have a good time. Don't let me down, now; anything less than the crack of dawn is for quitters."

"Shall I walk you back?" Shota asks her.

"Sure," she says and nods. "And then come back and talk to Grace, yes?"

Shota nods. "You will stay, won't you?" he asks me.

I check the time. It is half past ten; I hadn't imagined I'd still be sitting outside a bar, drinking and laughing. "I will." I am listening to a long story that the American sousaphone player is telling two women at our table. He is a good raconteur.

"Shota has wanted the chance to talk to you for a long time," Marion says, and I am certain that she knows our whole story. Why wouldn't she? She trusts this man enough to marry him and have his child; of course she knows the details of a fleeting relationship in his late teens. I'm sure she knows everything about him. "I'll see you tomorrow, I'm sure. It's been really special to meet you."

We kiss each other's cheeks and hug. I genuinely look forward to seeing her again. The exhibition will be open tomorrow and all the visiting musicians will be in there, examining the instruments. The prizewinners will have been notified, although they will still, at that stage, have to keep their successes quiet. The grand concert is tomorrow evening, the winners will be presented with their awards, and Shota's quartet will play the winning instruments. When I tried to get a ticket for Nadia, the only ones left were in a box. I've booked it for Nadia, Mr. Williams, and me; I hope they will be thrilled.

When Rob finishes his story we all hoot with laughter. The aftermath of the tall tale leaves me deep in conversation with the two women on my left. One of them is a cello player, the other a flutist; they have both worked with Shota and Marion in the past. We talk about the politics of the music business and how people choose instruments. They both know someone who has one of my violins and we chat about him for a while before moving on at tangents to other things.

Shota is back in what seems like minutes. "Anyone need a drink?" he asks, and a sea of hands goes up. "Bad timing," he jokes and calls the waiter over.

Shota sits back in his same spot and we wait for the drinks to arrive. When they come, they are accompanied by a huge plate of Parma ham and breadsticks. The women I've been sitting with show me how to wrap the ham around the breadstick in a spiral. It is a very welcome snack after the amount of prosecco I've drunk.

"Your wife is lovely," I say to Shota.

He nods. "Grace." He looks around, checks that the others are busy with their own conversations. "I just want to say I'm sorry."

"It was decades ago. A lifetime ago. We were kids."

"I've thought about it a lot over the years. Often."

I wish that I hadn't thought about it, hadn't dwelt in the past and let just a few months of my youth grow thorny and unhappy through my present. Seeing the adult version of the boy I loved puts it into such perspective; no one could accuse this man of being unkind, of being a game player.

"I got over it." I can't tell him about the months I spent at my parents' house, shut away and practicing until my fingers bled in a regime of punishment and self-destruction and that wasn't, really, his fault; just his bad timing.

"I behaved very badly and there are no excuses for what I did," and I assume he is about to roll out those excuses.

"You don't need to do this." I'm worried that the others can hear. I look across and see that they aren't listening. Some sort of card trick is being performed across the table and everyone is trying to decipher how it's done. Rob is booming his confusion into the melee; no one is looking at Shota and me.

"When I was in Japan," he says, "I was a nerdy, straight-laced viola boy. No one thought I was cool; all the boys thought I was dull and all the girls hadn't even noticed I existed. I got to music college and it was all different."

I remember that feeling. There was such a sense of relief in meeting other people who the outside world had thought odd, other kids who liked staying in and practicing. I'm sure not many people were as naive as I was, but certainly just as few were anywhere near mainstream cool.

"We all thought you were gorgeous." I smile and don't mind telling him now. History is wrapped in a blanket of nostalgia that has entirely disempowered it.

He looks down at his feet, finding it hard to take the compliment. "Anyway," he says, "you trusted me, and I behaved badly and I'm genuinely sorry. I was a shit."

I shrug and hide my face in my drink. My cheeks are red with a combination of alcohol and embarrassment. "OK, you were. It's true."

We both smile.

"But I had worse things to worry about on that day." I remember the pain of emptying my room, sliding my music books into bin bags so that I could get out as fast as possible, leave before anyone could see me.

"Have you done anything about it? About Nikolai Dernov, I mean?" Shota leans forward. He puts one hand on mine. "I'm so sorry. What happened to you was awful."

I am halted in my tracks. I have no idea

what he might mean. Everything else about this evening has been so easy, so straightforward; this is all wrong. "I got kicked out. I tried to forget it. To move on."

"Aren't you incredibly angry? As an adult, I mean?" His face is rigid, his mouth is a straight line when he stops talking.

I shrug and take another drink. "It's been hard but, you know, it's one of those things. I wasn't good enough. I had to leave."

Shota puts his drink down. He pauses as if to find words, to rearrange his thoughts. "You don't know, do you?"

There is a silence. Decades tick past in it like a flickering film. I don't speak.

"Nikolai has been charged with abuse of a position of trust. There are two women from the college standing as main witnesses, both his ex-pupils, one from our year. There are plenty more people, as everyone knows, but they haven't — or can't — come forward."

I can't speak. I squeeze the stem of my glass tightly. I am cold all over. The thoughts start to trickle across me but they make no sense. I loved Nikolai; I spent hours alone with him, being tutored. I think back to the hours of his own time he gave me, his arms around my back, moving my bow, his fingers pressing down on the ends of mine across the strings.

331

"He traded grades and lead roles for, you know . . . Everyone knew it was happening, but no one knew how to stop it. At the time, I mean." Shota's voice trails off; he is uncomfortable with these words, these memories.

I shake my head. "No." I look up at Shota, directly into his dark eyes. "I don't understand. He never did anything to me. No."

"You were the talk of the college. The girl who said no. The one who would rather leave than let Nikolai abuse his position in exchange for grades, for career advancement. The one who lost everything — at the time — by refusing him." Shota shakes his head. "Obviously as adults we know it was worse for the ones who couldn't. Didn't."

Two thoughts wrap themselves around me like hawsers. The first, smacking abruptly against me, shaking my memory and my understanding, is my last conversation with Nikolai. I remember — as if it were startling daylight, as if he and I were sitting here together — the last thing he said to me. The accusation about my playing that broke my heart. I whisper it to Shota.

"He said, 'If you really can't understand what you need to do for me, you will have to leave. You are no use to me or anyone else.' And he told me to get my stuff, told me to go."

Shota closes his eyes, his head is shaking from side to side. I cannot tell if his overwhelming emotion is sadness or anger, but I know he is completely on my side. He leans forward and puts his arms around me.

As I lay my head on Shota's shoulder, accept his friendship, his support, the second thought catches me like a cloud. It engulfs me and surprises me; it stops me in my tracks and lifts me up. It was my parents. It was my crazy cotton-wool-wrapped childhood; their intense and stupefying adoration of me that saved me from Nikolai. They allowed me to be a child so wholly and for so long, that I didn't even understand his veiled threats. I couldn't read between the lines of his innuendo. The palace of childhood that they built for me and the pedestal I lived on in their eyes, were a sanctuary.

I wish they were alive for me to tell them. I wish I could tell them that they made all the right decisions.

"I thought I was a rubbish player," I say quietly into the night. "I thought he threw me out because I couldn't play well enough."

"Grace," says Shota, "you were the best cellist in our year. Probably in the whole college. I've rarely met anyone as gifted as you."

CHAPTER TWENTY-TWO

It was a late night. I wake with a splitting headache but an immense feeling of calm. Shota and I stayed out till the small hours. In the busy bits of conversation, where everyone was laughing and no one particularly listening to what we said, he filled me in on more details about Nikolai. I thought that Marion would worry about Shota being so late but he explained, gently, that she already knew all the things I didn't, that she understood that we had a lot of talking to do.

I've missed my alarm — I have no idea how — and Nadia is due at the bus station in less than twenty minutes. I don't even know where the bus station is yet. We argued, Nadia and I, about her ability to get to Italy on her own, let alone to get from the airport to Cremona. She petulantly held out and insisted she could manage; it turns out I wouldn't have made it to the airport at all. She would have been catastrophically triumphant.

"You're having a good time, then?" she asks as soon as she sees me.

"I think I am — no, I really am. Why?"

"Because you look like shit." She beams at me. "But in a good way."

"Is that a compliment?" I ask her.

"Yeah, sort of," she says, and grabs her bag from the hold of the bus. I go to help her with it but it weighs a ton.

"What on earth have you got in there?"

"Clothes. Bit of makeup." She shrugs and a cloud crosses her face. "I'm on fucking holiday."

I squeeze her tight. "You are; we are. We're going to have fun. I've made a bunch of new friends and you'll love them. They're all musicians."

She brightens as swiftly as she had previously darkened; I love how she can do this. I wish I could wipe away this headache as quickly.

"How about we eat," I say, "and then I tell you everything I've done so far. Which is mostly get pissed, if I'm honest . . ."

We are late to breakfast and most places are bustling to get their lunch menus out. We find a restaurant in the lea of the looming cathedral and sit outside sucking in the atmosphere and the Italian sunshine.

I have ordered a frittata, yellow with egg and speckled with pink ham. Nadia has a long bread roll, dripping with mozzarella and vivid tomatoes. Even the orange juice we've ordered seems brighter, more real. I wonder if I have been living in a dream.

"So this old perv . . ." Nadia speaks with her mouth full. "This old perv blackmailed girls at the college for years?"

"Decades."

She nods. "I've heard about him, and a couple of other disgusting old men, at the national youth orchestra. People tell you who to avoid. How come you never knew?"

"Because I didn't stay in touch with anyone. If I were still friends with Catherine, with any of them, I'd have known about it. I wasn't, and I made sure I never talked about being kicked out of college with my customers, so I just never heard any of the rumors."

"Why didn't you stay in touch with Catherine? I thought she was your best friend." Nadia has almost finished her bread. With her spare hand she holds the menu, looking for pudding while she talks.

"Because she slept with my . . . you know." I remember as I speak that teenagers make terrible mistakes; that they don't think about the things they do.

"Oh, fucking hell, that old chestnut," says Nadia and puts her head in her hands. She's not angry; she seems more amused than anything.

I move the conversation swiftly forward. "We need to get a move on. Mr. Williams will be in Cremona by now. He's going to text when he's had a rest. He does all right for eighty, doesn't he?"

"He's not eighty," says Nadia.

"Really?"

"We were looking at passports, just before he left for Venice. He's eighty-six."

"I don't believe it." I am genuinely shocked.

"I asked him why he says he's eighty and he said it's because he's vain." She shrugs her shoulders as if to emphasize the obviousness of this fact. "Bless his little heart."

Around us, Italy goes about its business. The town is busy with visitors and the market is bustling. In the time that we've sat here, almost all the tables nearby have been filled; genteel women sip prosecco and their well-groomed husbands knock back red wine with a midmorning biscuit. Like anywhere, the people with the time to watch the world go by are all older but, unlike most places I know, that doesn't seem to mean that they can let themselves go. From the back, most of these women look like they're in their twenties. On more than one occasion I point out a wrinkly old man, well turned out but definitely ancient, sitting with a remarkably young woman. When we peer closer, look at her face instead of the back of her solid-set blond hair, we realize that the women are almost certainly their wives, and have been for a very long time.

By the time Mr. Williams texts, Nadia and I have been back to the hotel and dropped off her things. Nadia will share my room for the next few nights; I can't believe she doesn't object. Maybe the sunshine is mellowing her.

We arrange to meet Mr. Williams in the warm afternoon, near the exhibition of instruments. We will be among the first people into the hall, provided there is no queue.

I almost don't recognize him as he ambles towards the bar where we are waiting. Venice seems to have invigorated him; his skin is tanned and glowing, his hair whiter than ever.

"You look fabulous." I kiss him on both cheeks.

"Thank you, dear, I certainly feel it. It's

the Mediterranean diet, isn't it? And the sunshine."

"I'm not sure," I say, "but I want some, whatever it is." I hope I don't still look as hungover as I did this morning.

The exhibition of instruments is extraordinary. All three of us gasp out loud as we walk through the ornate double doors.

In an exercise in alchemy, a dusty old hall has been transformed into a maze of stringed instruments, a labyrinth of wood and satin varnish. Hundreds of instruments hang, hovering in midair, tethered by fine nylon wires that are invisible to the imaginative eye.

It is the hall of mirrors from a dream.

"Well, I'll be," says Mr. Williams. "I've never seen anything like it."

I am so glad that the three of us share this, that we all love violins, violas, and cellos with just the same passion. Involuntarily, I reach out to either side of me and take their hands.

"It's absolutely beautiful," says Nadia.

All we can see is this forest of wood, turned and polished and shaped into large or small versions of the same thing. It's like magic.

The legions of violins are first, all facing

forward, angled to the door but with enough space for visitors to walk around and wonder at the smooth backs, the standard of the carpentry, and the delicate layers of varnish. By each instrument is a small white label, hanging on a see-through thread of its own, that gives the name of the maker and their country. Behind the violins hang the violas, and behind them the cellos. The double basses are arranged on a wide plinth, too heavy to be suspended from the ceiling.

The idea that my little cello is in this room, is part of this enchantment, is indescribable. I am so proud. I stare past the violins and through the violas to look for it, but there are simply too many instruments to see clearly.

At the very end of the room are five instruments; a violin, a viola, two cellos, and a double bass. The way they are separated off means that they are — without doubt — the winners, and I can't wait to see them in all their splendor. Just to be included in this company is accolade enough for me; the level of skill is breathtaking.

Most people in here are like us. They are players or makers. The general public will, I'm sure, pick up the scent of this extraordinary exhibition over the next few days, but for now it is the participants and those look-ing for a scoop — a bargain — who make up the majority of the human souls in the room. These are people who can pick out the minuscule knife marks around the f-holes, see the tiny traces of tools in the shoulders; they know the pattern of the blockwork inside the instrument without having to open it for proof. This is the epicenter of my work world, and the people in here are the major movers and shakers.

I wander around the wildwood of violins, each scroll level with my chin, each neck curling like mine as I bend to look at the details on the label. I recognize many of the names. Some are people I trained with, some were even tutors at my violin-making school. There are instruments here from all over the world.

The three of us have separated slightly, strung out as we pause at different points or stop to look at different things. I will eventu-ally come back and look again at these instruments, inspect them in more detail. There is a lot to learn from other modern makers, just as much as from the old mas-ters. The etiquette of the competition means that I have to find the maker and ask permission to touch their instrument. They will watch me as a ritual begins. We violin makers know how to hold instruments, how to turn them in our hands and see all sides, all angles. We are looking for different things from players and we stand out in a crowd, we are quite obvious. All this is for tomorrow.

Already I have made a mental note of three instruments that I must know more about. There is one stunning little Amati model violin that I want to examine at close quarters, and two violas that look Cremonese, although I can't quite attribute the shape and style of them to any one maker.

If this is the standard of the entries, I'm more thrilled than ever to have been included. It makes me happy to know that this is going on all over the world; people are gouging and shaping and varnishing by hand, there is still no better way to do it.

"Awesome." Nadia is beside me. "I'm really glad I've seen it. Lost in a sea of violins."

"It's beautiful, isn't it? Just the sheer number."

"It makes me want to write music for all of them, all of them at once like a giant orchestra." Nadia is bewitched, her voice is a whisper.

We wander through into the violas, the scent of spirit varnish is stronger here and it makes me smile to know that I wasn't the only person to put an instrument in its case when it was only just dry. All this wood is yet to stretch and wake. Each one of these instruments will improve over the years to come and the thought dwarfs me that some of them will still be played hundreds of years from now. I feel part of something amazing.

The cellos are perfect. They are too perfect at the moment, test pieces of the makers' skill. The beauty of the instrument will appear with every dint and mark that history will leave on the smooth belly and the tiny scratches of dirt that will work their way into the back. Time is the missing ingredient in these liquid-skinned masterpieces.

There are makers from America, Korea, and Finland, from China and Japan and Italy. When I look in more detail at the people whose work I don't know, have never heard of, I see simple mistakes that I made myself once upon a time. These are the best of a new generation of makers, in a profession that can only teach through trial and error, and it is wonderful that they can exhibit here alongside the leaders in the field.

"I can't find the cello, Grace. Your cello." Mr. Williams is concerned. His glasses are propped on the very end of his nose and he looks around him as if my cello might jump out at him at any time. "I thought I'd recognize it anywhere."

As he speaks, I am staring at the five instruments standing alone on the plinth at the end. One of the cellos, the one on the edge, slightly apart from the others, has a dark mark just to the right of the bridge. I daren't hope.

I walk towards the end of the room as if my feet are stuck in treacle. This is the fairy-tale ending, the delicious dream sequence, it cannot be real life. I slow down as I move. It is my cello. I know those shoulders, that waist, those fat round bouts, that replacement front and all its history.

The closer I get, and I am only feet away from it now, the more obvious it becomes that the cello is on its own, that the winning instruments are in one group. A terrified child inside me is suddenly petrified of a dunce's hat, of a worst-in-show prize.

Nadia strides past. She is animated and bold; she isn't frightened of the caption in front of my cello. She isn't remotely worried what the little card says.

"Holy fucking shit," she says, and the words echo around the hallowed space.

I lean down towards my frozen feet. There

it is; the truth. Words that I will never be able to pretend I didn't read.

"What the fuck is the tone prize?" asks Nadia, taking the words straight out of my mouth.

"Oh, Grace; oh, my dear." Mr. Williams is lost for words.

The front of the cello shines under the lights, unapologetic, not even the smallest bit ashamed of its knot. It is strong and glossy and vigorous.

Our little trio of wilting old man, breathless maker, and swearing teenager has attracted attention. An official hurries towards us, his ID card swinging from a lanyard around his neck.

"Can I help you?" he asks. He is bald and swarthy. The hair he once had must have been as dark as his shiny suit. He needs a curly mustache to complete his look.

"I'm Grace Atherton. This is my cello."

"How do you do, Ms. Atherton?" He bows as gracefully as his suit allows. "Many, many congratulations."

My mouth opens and closes but I have no idea what to say.

"Is this the instrument with the best tone

346

in the competition?" Mr. Williams asks. "Is that what the prize is for?"

"*Sì*, of course." The man shrugs his shoulders as if it couldn't possibly be anything else.

"I thought the winners already knew." Even as I say it I'm checking for my phone in my bag. "I thought you let them know before the exhibition."

"We have left messages for you on your phone and at your hotel, Ms. Atherton. All day."

The red circle on my phone has a number six inside it. Six missed calls, six messages.

"I was out," I say, as if everyone should already know.

I turned the ringer off on my phone straight after Mr. Williams texted me. I didn't want my time with Nadia interrupted and I really wasn't expecting any other calls. I have spent eight years with my phone on, ready to leave any situation to talk to David. It feels like a relief now to turn it off.

"Six missed calls," I tell Nadia, Mr. Williams, and the man. "Six missed calls."

"At least six," the man says, a little put out. "But now you are here and now you know. We have a bit of paperwork to do and some photographs and so on." His accent is thick, although I'm not sure it's Italian.

"And the knot doesn't matter?" I ask. "The funny front?" I look at my cello like it's human; what I did to it was unforgiveable and yet it has come back from the ashes, stronger and bolder than it ever was. I want to tell it that I'm proud.

The man clicks his tongue. "You are the winner of the tone prize. Our judges were most insistent." He shakes my hand, pumps it up and down. "This cello is worth a lot of money now. The city of Cremona will buy it for the prize money. Your instrument is now valued at thirty thousand euros."

A knowledge comes up from inside me; I didn't see it arrive and I had no idea it was there. It takes control of my face, my mouth, my heart.

"I'm terribly sorry," I say. "This cello isn't for sale."

There is a sudden throng of people, of congratulations and questions, of handshakes and back pats. Mr. Williams and Nadia choose to go and sit at the café in the cool courtyard of the municipal building. I wonder if this is all a bit too much for them. They must be tired.

I can't even think straight. I am walking on air.

I pinch the skin on the back of my hand;

a white mark appears then dissipates as suddenly as it came. I am awake. This stuff of dreams is in my real life.

I almost cry; I think I will and then I realize on the next breath that I'm not going to. I realize that if I had a choice, I'd go outside and I'd shout and shout. I'd scream out with joy, with newfound freedom, with openness and honesty and all my fresh voice. The scream stays inside me but the smile is wrapped tight around my face. I can't believe it.

The official, whose name turns out to be Renato and who is as Italian as Guarneri and as Cremonese as Stradivari himself, shows me around the building, introducing me to all the people I suddenly need to meet.

There is an older lady who explains that she will sort out my seating for tonight's concert, that I will no longer be in my box with Nadia and Mr. Williams but on the front row with the other winners. I meet the mayor of the town and she kisses me on both cheeks, babbles at me in incomprehensible Italian. I beam back at her, convinced by now that everything she's saying is nice. There is a man from the local television channel.

Renato explains that the television man is

bubbling over with excitement that a maker who is also a player has won a prize. "It is in your CV that you went to the Northern conservatoire at the same time as Shota Kinoshita," he says, the words tumbling out. "And that you studied the cello."

The lady from the concert interrupts to say that the television man also thinks I'm perfect television material and rather pretty for a violin maker. I thank him for what I assume is a compliment, at the same time as I desperately try to tell them that they're wrong. That I can't do this.

Before I know it, I am being pampered by a makeup artist. She appears from nowhere with hairspray and a powder puff and begins to dab at me. We are in Renato's office near the main doors and I look around frantically for Nadia. I'm sure she will be able to convince them; she could play instead.

"So you are happy to play? What will you choose?"

It dawns on me slowly that I have somehow agreed to play my cello live on Italian television. I feel faint. The sweaty pricking in the palms of my hands is as familiar as a tattoo. I keep my mouth closed to stop my heart from bursting out of it.

We go out into the square outside the building. The front of the hall is a columned portico with wide steps running up to it. The steps are wide enough to take a chair, a cellist, and an instrument. The crew buzz about with lights and angles, holding little meters up against my face and the cello's spotted front.

Nadia and Mr. Williams have joined me in the square. They both think it's perfect that I should play, right here and now. I'm not as certain.

"What have you got to lose?" asks Nadia. "This lot aren't going to let you get away without. You'll make a bigger fool of yourself if you fuck off right now." She gestures to the cameraman and the man who originally started talking about the idea.

"Thanks for your support," I say, and the makeup woman steps in between us and cocks her head at me like a sparrow. She wipes a little something under my left eye.

"And you look good." Nadia changes tack.

"You look ruddy marvelous," says Mr. Williams. "Absolutely glowing."

"What are you going to play?" Nadia asks, and I realize with horror that — in my panic — I haven't given it a moment's thought.

"La Follia" is my favorite piece in all the world, Corelli's version, the one that David and I saw that terrible night in Paris. It seems like a lifetime ago now, but I still know the slides and the stops, the swoops and the segues as well as I know my own hands.

The cameraman moves me, three or four times after I've sat down, to get the angle of the light just right. I look down at my legs; I'm wearing jeans and suede ballet flats for my television debut. My feet are dusty from the streets and the market.

The little square around the building is typical of the town. There are houses on two sides and the third, opposite the hall itself, is a gateway; an arched bridge wide enough for a car to go under. The building above it is derelict and pigeons peek from the broken windows.

In the center of the square is a green and leafy patch of ground. There is a bench among the shrubs and an old man sits on it, his flat cap keeping the sun off his head, his shirt unbuttoned almost to his waist. He pays no attention whatsoever to the kerfuffle in front of the exhibition hall. A thin road runs around all four sides of the tiny garden.

I have had to borrow a bow from someone inside the exhibition. I bounce it against the strings a few times, making sure I understand its weight, getting used to the feel of the grip against my fingers.

There is a sizable crowd around the steps

now and I look around for an exit, a route out past the people. Nadia stands in the only space I could leave through, reminding me to stay.

"Nadia, have you got any water?" My lips are dry, my tongue thick against my teeth.

She passes me her bottle and I sip, trying not to smudge the lipstick that the makeup lady has carefully applied. "You can do it, Grace," Nadia whispers.

Someone is waving at me from the edge of the crowd. It is Marion, grinning madly. Beside her, Shota raises both his arms, giving me a double thumbs-up. He looks like a boy again.

"Are you ready?" Renato asks, and I nod. It is now or never.

I squint my eyes against the sun and it occurs to me, at that second, that Nikolai Durnov might see this broadcast. Nikolai might watch this and know that he didn't defeat me. I will play for the other girls, the ones who weren't as lucky.

I put the bow to the strings, my fingers in position for the first singing C of "La Follia."

It is wrong. This is not my song anymore. This is not the tune this cello deserves. The madness is all behind us.

I curl down and strike out the first wild notes of the "Libertango." Nadia whoops as she realizes what I'm playing and I look up at Mr. Williams's face, full of joy. This is our tune, our team song.

I close my eyes and play like I have never played before. As I reach the very end of the fingerboard, my fingers pulsing with the pressure to stay on the strings, the friction of the sliding note buzzing in my arm, I look up and out at the people who are watching. I forget the cameras, I forget the pressure.

This is what I was born for.

I skim across the faces as they listen, see how much people are enjoying the music. My heart is flying.

I look from one side of the line to the other, right across the tiny gardens.

There, standing underneath the archway on the other side of the square, unmistakable and as beautiful as ever, is David.

Chapter Twenty-Three

My bow slows down across the strings; it is as gradual as it is involuntary.

I am struggling, through a net strung across my mind, to remember the next phrase. David is wearing a cream-colored suit. I cannot find the strength to put enough pressure on the strings. His hair is slightly wild, which suits him. I can hear the music pouring away. His face is soft; there is sorrow in it. I almost miss a note; instead I play it weakly and at quarter speed. He smiles at me, a half smile, tentative. I hold my bow in position, perpendicular to the string but no sound comes. His palms are open, his arms extended slightly towards me at his sides. I stop playing altogether. A pigeon flies from one of the windows above the archway and David looks up. The flapping of the pigeon's wings is the only sound in the square.

My mouth forms a silent shape. It is his name.

My heart pounds in my ears.

It takes a second to realize that there is another noise, that music is flying into the air beside me. I notice David take his eyes from me and look to my left. I turn my head to follow his gaze.

Nadia is standing beside me like a warrior. In her left hand is a violin, her chin juts out in defiance over the instrument. In her right arm, like a sword, is a bow. She is playing the "Libertango" without me, above me, instead of me.

She is playing it for me.

I take a deep breath, press my bow back onto the strings. As I count myself back in, identify the refrain that Nadia is playing and where it comes in the piece, she and I lock eyes. When I strike the note, tear through it like paper with my bowing arm, we are one.

Nadia has started from where I left off — close to the end of the tango — and we go straight into a second run.

I look up at David. His arms are slack now. He has put his sunglasses on and his expression is difficult to read. Part of me wants to shout, *Please don't go!* I could never face Nadia again if I did, but I don't know if that will stop me.

Another line of melody joins Nadia. Mr. Williams, stooped over like the old man he is, has somehow found a violin. He is playing the steady rhythmic line he played in my dining room, back in another world. I don't know where his violin came from but I smile at him and he raises his head to nod back at me.

The three of us are looking at David.

In front of me, Shota is undoing his viola case. Beside him, Marion is signaling to other people. They are all quietly turning fine tuners, tightening bows.

The sound is awesome. There are about fifteen people standing a few feet below our stage on the steps, curling music into the warm afternoon.

"Again," Nadia shouts to me as we approach the final eight. I smile and nod vigorously.

We play it again, but faster.

People are whooping and shouting, clapping and stamping.

This is what the "Libertango" was written for.

For defiance.

For the hot air, the vivid sun.

For lost lovers returning.

The TV crew are absolutely delighted with

what they have. Our raggle-taggle band included some of the world's finest strings players, people who regularly play Carnegie Hall or the Vienna Musikverein. Mr. Williams is beside himself to have played with Shota Kinoshita, one of his favorite viola players of all time.

It takes a few minutes to get my bearings, to work my way out of the crowd and through the well-wishers. When I look across to the other side of the square, David has gone. For a while, even the idea of him melts away into the city. Other makers want to show me their instruments. People want to know why I chose a cello front with such a large knot on it. There are questions and introductions and meetings.

"I'm going back to my digs for a sit-down, Grace," says Mr. Williams. His eyes are shining but he looks tired. "I shall have a nap and be right as ninepence for the concert."

I'd forgotten about the concert. More important, I've forgotten that I shall be sitting on the winners' rostrum, collecting my award in jeans and dirty suede flats unless I find something more appropriate to wear.

"Nadia." I pull on her shirtsleeve. "I have about an hour in which to find an outfit for tonight."

"And shoes," she says, looking at my feet and raising her eyebrows.

"Will you help me?"

"Definitely. I'm your girl."

We say our goodbyes, explaining that we'll be at the concert tonight, that we'll be at the after-party and happy to chat.

Shota is leaning with one arm on his viola case, the other arm around Marion's shoulders. "I like your friends," he says. "Neat little trio. I take it you've played that before."

"We have," I say. "Nadia, this is Shota Kinoshita and this is his wife, Marion."

Nadia blushes a little; she has seen Shota in concert and is a fan.

"You're an amazing player," Shota says to Nadia. "You've really got something." He hands her his card. "Drop me a line, would you? I'd really like to stay in touch."

I nudge Nadia with my elbow, grin at her.

"She reminds me of you at that age," says Shota. He points at me. "That's how good she is."

Later Nadia tells me she was dying to add, "I'm so much better than her," but felt the situation deserved more gravitas.

"What an opportunity, though," I say to her as we shuffle through rails of clothing, all impossibly small, even for me. I wonder if David thought I looked different; I have not been at all careful about food since I last saw him. I have enjoyed every single thing that has passed my lips.

There is no word from David. I have checked my phone a few times. I am cool about it because he knows where I am. He knows which hotel we booked and he knows that the concert — and the awards ceremony — is tonight. I wonder if he knows that I won.

"Anyway," says Nadia, pulling a long blue dress from the rack and holding it out in front of her. "I can't go off and be a musician until I've finished my symphony."

"Or gone back to school."

"What if I don't go back to school? What if I go straight to work? Learn on the job?" She holds the dress out towards me.

"Ask Shota about that. We'll see them later. Make the most of his experience and his advice." I touch the fabric of the dress. It is the blue of a duck's egg, delicate but strong. "Do you think? It's a bit pale."

"It's beautiful," says Nadia. "I'll ask him, but he has to understand my commitment to the symphony."

She says this with calmness, with a played-down determination. When she talks about this project I have no doubt that she will see it through to its very end. I wonder what made her do it, what made her stop her frenetic teenaged life and let this thing take hold in the way it has. I wonder if she even knows.

In the changing room, I zip the dress up at the side. I would never have picked this color or probably even this style. I favor things that are short and bold. This is long, grown-up, and absolutely perfect. There is no need to hitch it down at the sides or tug the straps to stop them falling off my shoulders. It is beautifully tailored. When I look in the mirror, I see my mother. I am now the age she was when I was born and, in this dress, I look just like her. And then I realize why: this is the modern — sophisticated — version of the dress my mum bought to watch me play in Nikolai's showcase, the dress she never got to wear. It is the exact same shade of blue. It's like a message from her and I know I will buy it, whatever it costs.

"What do you think?" I open the curtain and show Nadia what the dress looks like on.

She gasps. "It's like something from Hollywood. Fuck the violin makers; you could go to the Oscars in that."

"Shh," I say to her and tell her to stop swearing.

"No one here speaks fucking English. Or hadn't you noticed?" She raises her penciled-in eyebrows, challenges me to continue. "Hurry up and buy it. We've got to get shoes and I'm starving."

I hadn't even thought about food. In the changing room, I sit on the small stool — back in my jeans — and get my phone out to text Mr. Williams about supper. We need to eat before the concert.

There is one message; it is from David.

you were amazing.

I lock the phone and put it back in my bag. I don't delete the message and I feel like I am betraying my friends for that. "Come on, I still need shoes," I say, but it is not what I'm thinking about and I feel like a liar.

The shoes are as easy to find as the dress was, as if I am being helped by fortune and the fates.

We have left late to eat and I have arranged to meet Mr. Williams at the little bar near our hotel. They do pizzas and pasta. We can eat properly after the concert.

When we get there, he is already in his seat outside the restaurant. He leans casually back in the chair, his legs crossed and his beige suit barely crumpled. He looks fantastic; his cream Panama hat leaves just the sideburns of his white hair sticking out. He takes it off when he sees us and jumps to his feet.

I have a box with my dress in; it is wrapped with ribbon and the box alone looks like it's worth every penny I spent on the dress. I put it beside my chair with the shoe box.

"What a day," he says. "I slept like a baby. Too much excitement." He winks at me. "It was wonderful."

"If he turns up again, he's not sleeping in my bed." Nadia doesn't look up from the menu as she says it. We all know exactly who she means.

"He can share with me," says Mr. Williams, and grins.

"Your bed, as you call it," I say to Nadia, "is actually my bed." We stop talking for a moment to order drinks and food. The heels on my new shoes are small, but I still avoid alcohol so I won't trip on the stage later on. "I know the beast and, actually, I'm pretty sure he will have gone again."

"Really?" asks Mr. Williams. "Paris to northern Italy just to see you from afar."

I nod and shrug. "I wouldn't put it past him. And he won't have been able to get a hotel room anywhere nearby."

"That's true. The closest I found was

Milan," Mr. Williams says.

"So let's not worry about it," I say with a nonchalance I don't feel.

"Especially when we could worry about what a cock you're going to make of yourself tripping over the hem of your dress tonight." Nadia takes a huge glug of the orange juice the waiter has brought and looks very pleased with herself. "I'm only kidding; I've never seen anyone I actually know look so amazing."

"I can't wait to see it," says Mr. Williams. "I'm so utterly proud of you."

"Thank you for making me do it," I say, and I nearly cry but manage to hold it together. I'm sure tonight will be an entirely different matter.

I don't look like me once I'm dressed. I look like a sophisticated and able woman. The way the dress hangs makes me look like someone with a figure I would envy and a bank balance I would covet. I don't look like me, but I do look like the woman I would rather be when I have to stand up in front of all those people in an hour's time. I definitely look like the person I want to be in the *Strad* magazine and all the promo pictures I'll splash all over my website to take full advantage of this prize.

I shout through the closed bathroom door, "Nad?"

"Yes?" she answers from the bedroom.

"Are you ready to go?"

"Yep."

"Do you want to go down to the foyer, then, and wait with Mr. W.?"

I can hear her wandering about in the room. "Are you going to make a grand entrance?"

"Exactly that. And I don't want you to see me first."

"I'm out of here," she calls back, and the room door slams.

When I come out, I sit quietly on the bed for a few moments. This room is lovely, the floor-to-ceiling windows open onto a tiled terrace and the sunlight floods in. I treasure the silence. It is lovely to be still.

I check my phone one last time before I leave it on the bedside table. There is nothing more from David, although emails from dealers are queuing up; all asking to meet me before I leave Cremona.

I need to avoid the dealers until later, even though they will be teeming around the city. I already know from a glance at the emails that the value of the stock in my shop has shot up — however arbitrarily — overnight. It will have even paid for the dress.

In the corridor outside our room, I practice walking like someone who would wear this dress. I see my knees through the fabric and try to concentrate on making my gait slightly less enthusiastic.

I choose the stairs over the lift, thinking it'll be good practice for getting up onto the stage. The stairs open onto the reception area, the lifts are farther over by the bar, near Nadia and Mr. Williams.

"Ah, Ms. Atherton." The receptionist calls me over. "A gentleman left this for you."

My lips flick an involuntary twitch of a smile. David's style is so classic. I know without having to ask that it will be from him. When I see my name spelled out in his black fountain pen, in his looped and cursive handwriting, it is no surprise.

The box is about the size of a paperback book. I know the livery; it is from a jeweler in Paris who David and I have known for several years. I have had earrings, necklaces, all kinds of gifts delivered in this same sort of box, midnight blue with a pale gold ribbon. On the top it says, *Grace Atherton, luthier.*

"I haven't time to open it, I'm afraid," I say to the receptionist. "Do you think someone could leave it in the safe until I come back tonight?" I know what this jeweler's prices are like. "Can I collect it then?"

She says it's fine and calls someone to take the box.

I walk through to the bar. I don't know who looks best out of the three of us. Nadia has curled her hair and pinned most of it up, the rest falling like tendrils around her face and her long thin neck. She is wearing a plain black top and a vintage circular skirt; she looks adorable. She has washed and scrubbed my suede flats and, with her outfit and her long legs, they look fabulous.

Mr. Williams looks like the gentleman he is. Some people are born to black tie, can carry it off with the nonchalance of a bathrobe. Mr. Williams is one of them.

"Ladies," he says, and bows low before offering us each an arm. "May I escort you to our carriage?"

We get out of the taxi outside the Theatre Ponchielli; we are not overdressed at all. We mill around with the other concertgoers. There are all sorts here; music students in their squeaky new tuxes and gowns, violin-making students in jeans and T-shirts, people dressed for the theatre, people suited and booted for business. There are Italians and Brits and Koreans and Kiwis. It is a hive of networking.

Marion and the big sousaphone player are in the foyer.

"You look incredible," she says and kisses my cheeks. "All of you." She greets Nadia and Mr. Williams the same way.

"Would I be inappropriate in saying that I think so too," says the big guy, and I remember that his name is Rob.

I mumble a thank-you.

"Where are you sitting?" I ask them.

"We're not sure yet," Marion says. "We just assumed we could hover backstage, but so far we can't seem to get any sense out of anyone."

"I have seen calmer foyers," says Mr. Williams. He's not wrong. There are people everywhere. Ladies with furs draped over their arms call out to men they have sent to queue at the box office or in the bar. It is a crush.

"We've got a box," I say, "and I can't sit in it, so there's one spare seat. Maybe we could drag another chair in."

"Or the person who didn't arrange the tickets for his best friend's gig could stand up for the whole thing?" says Marion, and raises her eyebrows at Rob.

"I can do that," says Rob, and grins.

The door of the box is covered by a heavy red velvet curtain, its hem frayed and its folds dusty. The narrow door behind it seems to be made entirely of cardboard and old carpet.

"Er, not quite what I'd imagined," says Nadia in a loud whisper.

I push open the door and she peers past me.

"Holy shit," says Nadia, and we all crane our necks to see.

The inside of the theatre looks like an illustration from a child's storybook. There is a theme of red and gold through the entire cavernous space. Gold leaf streaks up and down across the carved columns and red banners hang like Christmas swags along the hundreds of boxes. The boxes are like the cells of a beehive; edge to edge around three sides of the theatre and stacked four deep on top of one another.

The outside of this theatre looked like every other small-town cinema or local music hall; the inside is a staggering exercise in neoclassical opulence.

"Gotta love the Italians," says Marion.

At one end of the theatre, directly opposite the stage, the royal box splits the symmetrical arrangement. A vast curtain of scarlet hangs over it from a classical arch, twice the height of the other boxes and molded in gold that points towards the ceiling.

There are two chairs and, behind them, two high stools.

Nadia leans over the edge of the box. "How many of these boxes are there?" she asks. "This is flippin' amazing."

"There're thirteen on each side, I think," says Mr. Williams. "Jolly rough count, though."

"And four deep," says Rob. "Where are we, third layer?"

"So just looking from here, there're over a hundred individual boxes and they've all got four people inside," says Nadia. She points downwards. "And all the people in the flat seats."

"The stalls," I say. "They're called the stalls."

"Whatever they're called," says Nadia with a huge grin, "they're all going to be watching you."

"Go, Grace," says Marion in that transatlantic way, and Mr. Williams applauds gently, each clap the rhythm of British reserve.

The houselights, bold lamps sticking out like horns on each column between the boxes, begin to dim and the judges start to arrange themselves behind a long table just below the edge of the stage.

"Shit, I'd better go." I scatter out of the box and leave their shouts of good luck behind me. I find my front-row seat just as the houselights turn off and thousands of tiny bulbs, like a night sky, switch on above me. I turn and introduce myself to the other winners; I don't recognize any of them.

There are five of us: one maker each of violin, viola, and double bass; and two for the cellos — the tone prize and the overall prize. There are silver and bronze medalists dotted around us, but we stay together; just five.

There are speeches, in Italian and then in a translation so heavily accented it may as well have been Italian. The other four winners and I grin at one another. The viola winner is Italian; he leans towards me and whispers, "It was boring, anyway."

We go up, one by one, and receive our medals. I have never been so overtaken by nerves in all my life. Up in the boxes, I swear I can hear four voices screaming congratulations, and whooping, definitely whooping.

I manage to walk up, squinting in the stage lights, shake hands and mutter my thanks, and walk back; all without tripping or fainting. I am so relieved to sit back down.

After the presentation, the concert begins. The quartet are playing the instruments of the winners around me. One by one, they come onto the stage. There are two violinists, a cellist, and, of course, Shota on viola. They are joined by a bass player, and she stands slightly to one side of them.

The quartet leader explains that the second violin being played belongs to the silver medalist. Apparently the tone prize has always gone to a violin and traditionally that has been the instrument played as second violin in the quartet. This is the first year it has ever been won by a cello and that has somewhat thrown the program. He adds that they will be playing a special piece, not listed, to show the capabilities of the winning cello at the end. I blush to the roots of my hair as the yells of my support team echo around the building.

I hide my embarrassment by studying the program in my lap. The quartet will play Ravel, Mozart, Brahms, and Bartók; pieces specially chosen to accent each instrument and then show off its talents as part of a group.

Shota has grown into the viola player I always knew he would be. I've seen him play on television, but I've not seen him live since we were at college. He is amazing. The quartet plays to a hushed hall and two thousand people hang on their every note.

Finally it is time for my little spotted cello to take the center stage. I know the cellist; Mathieu Scharf. I have admired his work for a long time; last time I saw him play was when David took me to Salzburg for one of his concerts. I cannot believe that Scharf is holding my cello in his hand, talking the audience through the reasons it was chosen, explaining the qualities that made it the winner. I can barely look.

He sits and starts to play. Bach's Adagio in G Minor from the Sonata for Viola da Gamba and Harpsichord soars through the room. I couldn't have picked anything more perfect if I'd been asked to choose myself. The notes dance around my head and fall like snow onto all of us. The silences between the notes quiver through the auditorium and I have never heard anything as profound in all my life.

Finally, I allow myself to cry. These are warm, happy tears.

The after-party is a triumph. If I were to sell my cello, I could have done so thirty times over. I seem to have the card of every violin dealer in Europe and a good clutch of Asia and the Americas too.

The bar of the theatre has been cordoned off and we are all behind the ropes with the great and the good. It is like a dream.

Mr. Williams is flagging. He is sitting in a red leather chair and his head is dropping forward. He has beads of perspiration on his forehead and he is fanning himself with a paper napkin.

"Are you all right?" I ask him, dropping into the chair next to his, suddenly feeling the weight of the day like lead in my legs.

"Grace, dear, I am utterly overwhelmed. What a wonderful time I've had."

"I'm exhausted. I can't imagine how you must feel."

He closes his eyes and leans back in the chair. "I'm going to call it a night, I think. Discretion is still the better part of valor and all that."

Shota and Marion are deep in conversation with Nadia. I try to catch her eye. She mistakes my gesture and all three of them come over to join us.

"We're all going back to our hotel to watch the VT from this afternoon." Nadia is bubbling but I cannot tell whether it's alcohol or excitement.

"The 'VT'?" I have no idea what she's talking about.

She rolls her eyes at me as if she's been a professional musician for years, not just talking to two for half an hour. "The video-tape. Of us three this afternoon. Fancy it?"

"Yes." It's the perfect solution. "Mr. Williams and I will go first, get the first free cab. And I'll meet you guys in the bar. Yes?"

This time it's Mr. Williams who takes my arm. His age is showing this many miles from home and after such a crazy day.

We call the first cab we see and it pulls in. Mr. Williams opens the door for me and I give the name of the village he's staying in to the driver.

Mr. Williams does up his seat belt and leans against the headrest. He gives a big sigh.

"Are you OK? Really?"

"I'm fine," he says, "I am." He puts his hand on my arm. "But there is something I need to tell you. I'm not going to be around, when you go back to England."

CHAPTER TWENTY-FOUR

I can't breathe. I can't ask him to explain because I don't want to hear what he has to say. I am not ready to let him go: the space he would leave in my heart would be an inconsolable grief.

And then I think of Nadia; it would be worse for her. She is in the middle of her worst year, a year where everything is crashing around her and every stability, every firm ground, is threatened.

The pulse in my ears is so loud that I do not hear what he has to say. I block it out.

"Grace?" he is asking me a question. "What do you say, dear?"

He has the wrong expression on his face; he isn't panicked or sad. He isn't worried.

"Do I have your blessing?"

"Mr. Williams, I'm sorry." It sounds so stupid. "I wasn't listening."

"It's been a long night, dear," says Mr. Williams, and turns to watch the buildings rush past us behind the cab windows.

"No, I need to hear it now. I'm listening now." I realize that I'm pawing at him and take my hand off his arm. "Sorry."

There are trees lining the road we're driving down and people outside every café, every restaurant. It is still summer here.

"Laurence and I. We're going to give it a go."

" 'Laurence'?"

"My friend, in Venice. I'd just been staying with him for a week."

Mr. Williams has a boyfriend. I look at the taxi driver; he is impervious. If he spoke English he might have turned around and mentioned Mr. Williams's advanced years, congratulated him even.

"We had a thing a long time ago." He is holding on to his seat belt with one hand, keeping it away from his chest. "Before Leslie, before his Paulo. We were in the army together." There is a smile playing around his mouth. "But things were very different then. I came home, met Leslie. Laurence stayed on in the army and eventually retired to Italy, to Paulo. We were good friends, the four of us." He clears his throat.

I don't know if I'm required to contribute or not, but I can't get my thoughts into any order.

"The army wasn't for me, got out as soon as I could; but Laurence adored it and, frankly, it adored him. He retired as a major."

I manage a stock response but I'm still processing. "I'm really pleased for you, really pleased." It doesn't seem enough after all his kindness.

"So, I'm going from here back to Venice. Probably tomorrow, I'm afraid."

"Is that a bit soon, I mean to be moving in together?" It's out before I can catch it. "That was stupid," I say. "You're a grown man."

"Dear, I'm eighty."

I don't say anything.

"Who knows how long I've got. The only thing I'm certain of is that it isn't the length of a conventional lifetime."

I shrug, he has a fair point.

"You have to grasp life by the balls, Grace," he says, "and don't bloody let go until you have to."

We are out on the open road now; churches stand alone in wheat fields, no discernible parish around them. Factories push up against the roadside and intermingle with farmhouses. There seems to be no order to the architecture and yet it looks so right, nothing feels out of place.

"What will you do with your house if you stay in Venice?"

"Ah, now, I wondered — and tell me if this is silly — I wondered if Nadia might take it for a while. Is that inappropriate?" He turns to face me. "I know she's awfully unhappy at home and I just thought it might help. It would help me; I don't want anything for it."

"I don't know," I admit. "I don't know anything about teenagers. Sometimes I think I don't know anything about her in particular."

"She adores you. Worships you."

"I adore her too." And I realize how very much I do. I realize how valuable it has been to watch that little girl grow and blossom. I acknowledge how proud I am of her for coming through everything this year has thrown at her. "You'd — we'd — have to run it past her parents. And that's assuming she wants to. I honestly can't see them saying no, not with everything they have on their plates."

"It sounds to me like they won't even realize she's gone," says Mr. Williams, and then we pause; the thought crosses both our minds that we don't have children and can't be certain we wouldn't be doing the same in their shoes. "There's a piano there, she can write, and no neighbors to irritate. Perhaps the space will do them all good."

We are both silent for a moment while we digest the plans.

"And I don't intend to die any time soon." He smiles at me. "Or, for that matter, come back from Venice for more than the odd holiday."

"Good for you."

We are in the village where Mr. Williams is staying. He promises to take the bus in first thing tomorrow so we can discuss his plans with Nadia.

"I'll try not to be too early, dear," he says, and kisses me on the cheek. "Thank you so much for all of this."

"No," I say and hug him. "Thank you."

By the time I get back the party is in full swing. There are musicians everywhere and something close to a ceilidh is threatening to take place.

"Where've you been?" Nadia says. "I'm dying to watch the film. Shota and Marion said we had to wait for you."

A large television screen has materialized at one end of the bar; I'm sure it wasn't there before. These musicians look like people who know their way around hotel life and who are used to getting what they want.

"OK, OK," yells Rob above the din. "Grace's here. Let's get this show on the road."

The VT has been queued up to the right place and everyone settles onto banquettes and bar stools to watch. Shota passes me a huge glass of red wine and I drink it too fast.

I'm dreading this; I don't want to see my face when I realize that David is there. I really don't want to hear my wishy-washy playing when I see him.

It doesn't look so bad. No one even asks me what I'm looking at. In the video — and perhaps it's been very cleverly spliced — Nadia steps in only a couple of seconds after I stop. Watching this, it looks almost as if we meant it to happen this way, as if it were all planned.

I look at Nadia on the screen, her beautiful defiant face, her warrior nature. There is something in the way she carries herself, in how she stands. The frightened angry child has gone. I have been privileged to watch this whole evolution, from girl to woman; it happened right under my nose and I missed most of it.

Her spirit shines out in the video and her

playing is incredible. For most of the rest of the clip, the cameraman is enchanted by this dark-haired girl and the way she makes her violin sing, the way she dances as she plays, the way her eyes light up. He focuses almost exclusively on Nadia, just the odd shot panning out to the crowd supporting us.

"Oh God, how embarrassing," she says under her breath. "I knew he was a perv."

"You look amazing, just incredible," I say back to her. "You look possessed."

Later in our bedroom, once the lights are out, the peace affords me time to think. Something has been bothering me since I watched the video; something different, something changed. The realization comes quietly, gently. It is made up of instinct and observation in equal parts. I finally see the link between the furious girl of Nadia's diary and the bold, fearless woman of today. In the precious anonymity of darkness, I turn to her.

"You're pregnant, aren't you, Nadia?"

It is a conversation that we can't carry on in the dark. After her initial mumbled and, to her credit, straightforward yes, there are too many questions to ask, too many plans and promises to undertake; it needs light to take away the fear. I click the bedside lamp on with my thumb.

Questions tumble through my mind; I'm not sure which should be the first. I go for the obvious.

"How pregnant? How many weeks?"

She just shrugs. She's sitting on the bed, wearing tartan pajama shorts and a pink vest with hearts on it. She doesn't look like a round picture of pregnancy, but there is just a thickening, a convex band around her midriff. She could still zip up a pair of very small jeans.

I'm making us a cup of tea, trying to balance the kettle and the cups on the awkwardly sized tray that the hotel has provided to keep everything off the polished wood.

"How long do you think?" I don't want to have to spell it out; I have no desire to ask her graphic questions about when and with whom.

"It was snowing. I was at a party and I walked there in my boots because I'd get wet feet." She doesn't look at me, instead she swings her long legs back onto the duvet and lies down facing the ceiling.

I stir the tea, pretend to be busy. Instinctively I know she does not want eye contact for this conversation.

"Nad, it can't have snowed since . . . when? March?"

I look back at her. What I used to think of as her angry face is set firm. I know now that it is her most hurt face, the mask she uses to cover her vulnerability. A single tear rolls down across her cheek and into her hair. "Yes, it snowed in March," she says, and knits her fingers together over her face. "On March fourteenth."

I'm trying to do the math. It is the end of September. Tomorrow is officially October. I sit down hard on the end of the bed. "Are you sure?"

"My friend Laura's party." She turns onto her front, her face in the pillow. "I remember it well."

"Have you seen a doctor?"

"No." Her voice is muffled as she presses her face into the pillow. "I'm trying not to think about it. It's worked so far."

I reach behind me and close my fingers gently around her ankle. It is small and bony, the leg of a child. "I think that gives you about two months to go."

She doesn't answer.

"And then there'll be a whole other person on the planet. A new human." I don't know if I'm helping her, it's just what I think. "What a wonder."

"I thought you'd be angry."

"Why?"

"I thought everyone would be angry."

I'm surprised, shocked. I'm a little scared for her. I'm scared for myself when I think about getting her home. Then I remember that she got here on her own; she was very nearly as pregnant then as she is now.

"Does anyone know?"

She sits up again. "No."

"Not even Harriet?"

"Definitely not Harriet," she says, and I remember the diary, remember Charlie. Now is not the time to bring it up.

"What about school?"

"I don't go to school, remember?"

Maybe Nadia is not as unprepared as I think she is. "What about your symphony?"

"This is my symphony," she says. And I believe her.

It is three o'clock in the morning when I wander down to the reception. I ask them if the bar is open and the man behind the desk says that, yes, of course, he can open it. I thank him and order a red wine.

I sink into a huge armchair in the bar. The skin is tight across my forehead and I am wired with thoughts. I ask myself briefly whether all of life is like this and I simply haven't seen it through the filter of David. It can't be. Perhaps David and being with him protected me from this frenetic activity. Perhaps when you open your life to other people this is the chaos that overwhelms it.

I have come down here to open the box that David has left. The bar is silent. The receptionist has gone to get it from the safe for me; he has not even questioned the situation. He must deal with craziness all the time.

When he comes back with the box, I have drunk more than half the wine and eaten all of the small fish-shaped crackers he brought with it. I ask him for another glass and he goes to fetch it without comment.

The box is on the table in front of me. The neat, blue box brings back so many memories. It means holidays and celebrations, it means secrets and surprises. Once or twice, in ideas that wash across my mind like waves of a winter sea, it means Christmases alone with my phone faceup on the table, watching its screen for a flash or waiting for a call.

I pull one corner of the ribbon. The waiter comes back with my wine and a small plate of bruschetta. I'm grateful for the bread; I am hungry. I eat the three pieces of bruschetta before I pull the rest of the ribbon; it gives the man time to go back behind his desk. Whatever is in this box is private, that's why I'm sitting here alone in the middle of the night.

I lift the lid of the box.

Inside there is a smaller box, squat and square, and two envelopes. Both envelopes have *Grace* written on them in those suave, sloping black letters, the calm of his handwriting, the familiarity of his habits.

The top envelope, the smaller of the two, has *2* written neatly in the top right-hand corner. I shuffle through. The other envelope says *1.* The ring box, and it is — without doubt — a ring box, no matter what might turn out to be in it, says *3.*

The first envelope contains a single first-class train ticket from Ashford to Paris. It is dated for next Friday. The 7 of October. I am being summoned to Paris.

I have missed Paris.

In the corner of the thick velum envelope is a pair of keys; I have to shake them out. They are the keys to David's apartment, one to the outside door and one to the intimacy of the apartment itself. In eight years, I never had a set of these keys.

I take another drink before I open the second envelope.

The letter is handwritten, elegantly set

out, as if David has counted the number of words that will fit on a page and made sure it starts at the top and ends at the bottom. I knew from the moment the box arrived that I would read this. The rational parts of me say that I am reading this because I want him to say sorry. I want him to apologize for all the years that he gambled with my future, to take back all the pain and the twisting.

The other parts of me, the parts that pull — physically and without negotiation — they want him to plead with me, to need me, to beg for me.

Dear Grace,

There are no words to unravel the terrible mess I've made. I have lost the thing I valued most in the world. And Grace, over the last months, I have lost a lot. There is one thing that burns, one thing that keeps me awake at night. I have lost you.

I didn't imagine that life without you would feel like this. I was a fool.

I can't begin to tell you how horrible it's been and I don't want to. You know everything I've done. There's no need to write the things that torture me during the day and haunt me at night. You know what I did, and there are no excuses. It is all over. I have learnt the humblest of lessons in the hardest way.

I have told my children about every mistake I have made. I have, for the first time in my life, been honest with everyone. I have been seeing a counselor and he has helped me take responsibility for the way I behave and the way I've treated everyone I love — not just you.

Please, Gracie, if you can bear it, come to Paris. My children will arrive on Saturday, 8 October, for the night. I would love you to meet them. I would love to introduce you to them and to our future.

I am so, so sorry. Please find it in your heart to forgive me.

I love you, Grace. Just you. I always have, I always will.

David

I open the second box, just as I was always going to from the second I saw the dark-blue wrapping and the palest gold ribbon, from the moment I knew he was back.

Inside the box is a ring. It is, unequivocally, an engagement ring. It is a white-gold band with a single round diamond fixed to it with the tiniest of clawed clasps. The front of the diamond is cut so beautifully that even the dim lights of the bar bounce off it at every angle.

I stretch out the third finger of my left hand and ease the ring on. It settles between the bony joints of my finger, bright against my tanned skin.

It is a perfect fit.

CHAPTER TWENTY-FIVE

Paris is, as my late father used to say, where I left it. The city doesn't know that anything has changed. In the same way it always has, this city accepts me just the way I am. In return, I love it back.

This week has brought the first cooler breeze of autumn. It is my favorite season. I love the elegance of it, the falling leaves, the signs that everything will be bare and ready for a fresh start. Autumn convinces me that there will be new growth, that there will be spring. It reaffirms my faith in time and order.

I walk the short distance from Gare du Nord to Gare de l'Est. It is enough to remind me that I am here, that Paris is different from my home. This city sings and buzzes and is alive. I listen to the voices as I pass people in the street and try to process the impenetrable chatter.

I wonder how long I would have to live in

Paris before I could talk like them, until I could swap casual stories like a native. It would take a lifetime; I am not a natural linguist. I wonder, not for the first time, whether David's children's English is accented.

At Gare de l'Est I run down the steps into the Metro. I know the underground system of Paris just as well as I know the Tube in London, possibly a little better.

The train is not busy. My favorite journeys are always those where someone gets on with an accordion or starts a singsong with a prerecorded backing track. I have never lost the touristy pleasure in carriage buskers. Those things, to me, are quintessentially Paris.

Some things have become homogenous over the years; the smell of candied peanuts that once used to pinpoint my location exactly, is something I've found in recent years in London, in New York: the tendrils of this city curling out to grow in other hearts.

I get out of the Metro at École Militaire. No other city has this depth of architecture, this history so plain to see, so obvious on every street corner. This place exists in the imagination of the world, in films and books, in poems and songs. It does that for good reason.

I love this walk, everything about it. I love the gritty sand surface of the paths through the Champ de Mars, I love the Peace Memorial and its etched glass panels; most of all, I love the way the Eiffel Tower looms over everything, reducing us all to the specks of dust we are, making us as tiny and uniform as ants. There's no avoiding the history of Paris; nothing disguises or hides it and nothing tries to. Behind me, the walls of the École Militaire are peppered with bullet holes from wars, from practices, from executions, and yet now, in our relative peacetime, it seems so calm and innocuous. Napoleon studied in that building as a boy soldier. He walked in long black boots along the same paths that I'm scuffing my feet upon now. It never fails to amaze me or to put me in my place.

When I told Mr. Williams about Nadia, he didn't flinch. His exact words were, "Well, she'll have to paint up the guest room; it's a little dull for a baby."

"Aren't you worried about her being in your house? On her own with a baby?" I had asked him. We were sitting outside the railway station at Cremona. Mr. Williams was on his way to his new life. He had one single leather suitcase beside him.

"Girls with far less about them than that one have done it, dear."

I nodded. "Humans, we're a rum lot. I just hope she manages."

He smiled at me. "You worry too much. She's done very well so far, all by herself."

"Her parents are going to be livid." I was thinking out loud.

"Not for too long, in my experience." He leant back on the bench and let the sunshine light up his face. "What is the phrase? *Babies bring their own love.* I'm sure it's so, dear."

Shota was even calmer, more bemused than anything else. "I don't know where these girls put them," he said.

I'd asked him to meet for a drink before I went. We were sitting outside the bar I'd first seen him at.

"Marion had a trumpet pupil couple of years ago; same thing. Only she didn't give eight weeks' notice."

"Really?"

"Seriously. Skinny as a bone . . ."

"A *rake,* Shota." I remember that, at college, one of the first things I loved about him was the way he said "coming down in cats and dogs" when it rained.

"Still haven't got it." He grins and runs his hand through his hair. "Anyway, upshot is — one day she's having a trumpet lesson, next day she's having a baby on the bathroom floor."

"Bloody hell," I said. "What happened to her?"

"First trumpet in Reykjavik Phil. Just carried on. Plenty of support; Mum helps out, I think."

I wondered about Nadia, worry about how much support she would have. And then, like a light, like a birth of my own, I remembered that she has me. She supported me when I needed it and I am more than ready to do the same for her. It would be an honor to be part of her little miracle.

"She'll only be around the corner from me," I said as if it was the most natural thing in the world.

"There you are, then," said Shota. He pushed a business card across the table. "I've asked her to keep in touch with me; she's a phenomenal player. I said I'd do some master classes with her when I'm next in the UK. Maybe even more important now."

I picked the card up but didn't recognize the name.

"It's Rob's," Shota says. "He's joining the BBC Phil in January and doesn't know anyone. He wondered if you'd show him a bit of London. One good turn and all that?"

"Meaning?"

"I'll give Nadia some help, contacts and so on, if you can look after Rob a bit; introduce him to some people, take him out."

I said that of course I would. I said, and found I really meant, that any friend of Shota's was a friend of mine.

"And if you want to know more about the Nikolai thing, all that stuff" — he leant in, his face full of sympathy, and he bit his lip a little — "I can put you in touch with some people who know more about it." He put his hand over mine. "And the rest of it? Catherine and all that, I just want you to know that I'm so sorry. I'd do anything to change it, put the clock back."

Shota is a good man and I really felt for him; it was only fair to let him lose this ghost, put it to rest. "Shota, you were a kid. We both were. And kids make mistakes. And you stuck your neck out for me with Nikolai. That still means a lot." I stood up and kissed him goodbye. "Don't think about the shit stuff anymore. And I won't either, OK?"

He hugged me tight. "Fresh start."

The crowds aren't thick at all under the Eiffel Tower. There is the usual queue at the South Pier, but it is nothing like as crowded as it usually is. I'm sure as the day wears on it will start to get busy, but I will be long gone by then, safe across the river.

I walk north towards the Trocadéro and its fountains. I look briefly at my watch to see if I have time to wait for the parade of water, for the sequence to run through. David and I used to watch these fountains in summer when the fine drizzle of spray misted our faces under the parched air. There isn't time to wait for the fountains, not even for old times' sake. I'm due at the apartment in a few minutes.

Passy Cemetery is on my left. I think about going in, but instead I follow the brick wall along the edge of the road and let myself into David's building. He knows what time train he booked for me, so he has a rough idea of when I will arrive. We have both resisted the temptation to text or speak.

I have not seen him since he appeared in Cremona. I have not spoken to him since his words shattered my heart in Paris.

The brass lock of his front door is from the 1920s; it is as old as the apartment and its frame has been polished gold by hundreds of knuckles as they turn the key.

The French windows at the end of the apartment are open. I can feel the breeze play around my ankles. It is warm in the hallway and music laps gently at the side of my mind. It is Bach, the Cello Suites.

Maybe, I think, heaven looks and feels a little like this.

And then David steps forward from the kitchen doorway. He is wearing a deep-green shirt — the top button open — and wool-cashmere trousers. His feet are bare. He looks as handsome as he ever has; maybe slightly taller, wider. I have imagined him as less, and the picture I keep in my mind's eye has diminished. Now that I am back, close, beside him, my eyes refresh and correct my memory. He is solid and tall.

He lifts his hands, so slowly, and takes mine in his. He is frightened, I can see, and he trembles slightly.

My lips are dry. I swallow hard and look up at him, at that jaw, his high cheekbones, his perfectly groomed eyebrows.

He turns my hands over in his palms, lifts them to his mouth and softly kisses the backs; one, then the other.

I can smell him, a mix of soap and after-shave, clean smells underplayed with the scent of his skin. I know the smell of him as well as I know myself. I breathe deeply, inhale him. I have missed him like air.

He bends his head and brushes my lips

softly with his. "You're so beautiful," he whispers.

I cannot trust myself to speak. I squeeze his hands.

He looks down at my fingers. "You're not wearing the ring."

I shake my head.

"Did it fit?" he asks.

"It fit perfectly. Thank you." I drop his hands and reach into my handbag. I take the ring, still in its box, and put it on the side table. "It was a beautiful choice. Perfect."

The table I've put the ring on is antique oak; a reflection of the framed photograph on it shines up at me. I look at the photograph; it is of me. I look around. I am everywhere. There are as many pictures of me as there are of David's children. We look like a family. The only picture missing is one of us all together.

"But you're here." He doesn't understand why I'm not wearing the ring, why I've given it back. David holds me tight, folds me into him and I can feel the muscles in his arm, the strength of his chest. "You've come back to me, to us."

"I'm not staying." I whisper the words, almost as if I don't want them to be true. But I do.

"Grace, darling, please. Tomorrow, the children . . ."

"I can't stay."

"I've told them all about you. They're coming all this way to meet you."

"It's too late, David." These aren't my children; they're not even my children's siblings. They are David's responsibility, as is their disappointment, their confusion.

"Gracie, please. I'm so fucking sorry. I'll do anything."

He means it, I can tell. David has finally become the person I wanted him to be. He has changed, I can feel it in the way he holds me, I can sense it — almost smell it — from every fiber of him. His longing is real.

But I am not the same person.

"I'll never stop loving you," I say. "You're very special."

"No. Please." His voice is cracking. "Please don't leave me. I need you."

I run my finger along the line of his chin, trace the smoothness of his cheek. "We had such good times," I say, and I try to smile even though tears are overwhelming me. It would be wrong to speak about the terrible times; dark days of doubts and failings.

David is crying now, without the drama that I've heard him add in the past. This is real; regret and loss and longing. These are sounds I recognize.

"Please. I'll do anything. I'm seeing a counselor, facing up to myself; I'll get better." He holds me a little way away from him, looks right in my eyes. "Why did you come here if you don't want me?"

I say the words and I am desperately sorry; truly surprised that I am walking away from him.

"David," I say. "I came to say goodbye to Paris."

I know I can't go back to Paris. Maybe one day, in another life, but not for a very long time. Until then, I hope Paris can forgive me; I know it will. Paris, more than any other city in the world, knows about love.

My tiny, chocolate-box town is rife with rumor. I'm surprised by how many of my local clients turn out to know Mr. Williams. I am bemused by the number of small repair jobs people have suddenly asked me to do on their instruments, just so they can take the opportunity to find out what I know. Apparently an eighty-six-year-old man they'd assumed was a bachelor, going off to live with his boyfriend in Venice, is even bigger news than the local violin maker appearing in all the national papers.

I only tell them what I know — that Mr. Williams is very, very happy and that, almost more than anyone else I can think of, he deserves it.

I have promised some sheets and towels to Nadia. Getting them out of the airing cupboard has, as these things do, turned into a longer job; an afternoon of discovering shoe boxes and receipts, throwing away nonsense that I kept last time I tidied.

I reach into the back of the car to drag out the bin bags; I am running out of time. I have a date this afternoon; an unbreakable appointment with a dear friend. My hair is spot-on and a little spiky. I'm wearing my favorite lipstick; one that manages to look like I have no makeup on at all — just fabulous lips.

Nadia's house is very neat. She rearranges furniture and straightens curtains all day long. I don't believe it's a nesting instinct, I think it's an extension of a game; she has found herself in a giant dollhouse and she intends to make it perfect.

"Where do you want these?" I dump the two sacks on the kitchen floor.

"They'll be fine there, thanks," says Nadia. "I'll go through them and take out what I want. But can you take the rest back with you, drop it off at the charity shop?" She hates clutter.

She bends down and starts to unfold and fold the duvet sets and the towels. She puts them into two perfect piles that already make the way I packed the bags look slovenly.

She bends easily. Her bump began to show within days of her big reveal, but although she is obviously pregnant, it is hard to believe she is going to have a baby in a few weeks' time.

"It's the last prenatal class tomorrow," she says and looks up at me. "You won't miss it, will you?"

"Why would I?"

"Just checking. That's all."

I'm sure everyone at the classes thinks I am her mother and that's fine. I am thrilled that I will see this baby born, less enthusiastic about being Nadia's sounding post. She has embraced every holistic and natural birth idea going. She has an app on her phone that will measure contractions and time events. When it does happen, I am sure it will be a tide that even Nadia can't control and what will be, will be. Shota and Marion's baby is a week late; refusing to budge. I am convinced they will be born on the same day.

"How's the writing?" I ask her.

"Good. Really good. It's easy to think here." The pile of stuff she doesn't want is huge. She puts the one duvet set and one towel that she is happy with on the kitchen work surface. "I emailed a new bit to Shota last night; he loves it."

Shota is staggered by Nadia's symphony and has every faith in it being her key to fame and fortune.

"And the last bit? Is it finished?" I ask her.

"For fuck's sake, Grace, how many times?" She pats her small bump. "I have to meet this crazy little person first."

I have three minutes to spare when I unlock the shop door. I rush through to the back, past the double basses upright in their rows, past the cellos, straight and polished. There is nothing in here to fix now; all the instruments have been repaired and a peace has settled over everything. It looks as magical as it ever did.

In the window, on the music stand, I have left the score of Elgar's "Nimrod" open. It is almost November and, in so many ways, everything is about remembering, about listening to the lessons we have learnt.

There is one more cello in the rack than there was. The cello David bought me many years ago is now shop stock. I still love it dearly and it is a beautiful instrument, but I will never part with my beautiful spotted Cremona cello and I can't play two.

The violins proudly hang from their shelf, the violas as backup behind them. They all face towards the door, the outside world, and the whole shop looks ready to meet the future.

In the workshop, my iPad begins to buzz. It is three o'clock.

Mr. Williams beams at me when the connection is made. He is tanned and happy, the air obviously suits him. We wave at each other frantically for the first ten seconds, even though we have the option of speech.

"You look fabulous, dear," he says, "very glamorous."

"I didn't want to let you down. This is the highlight of my week. Thought I'd better dress up for it."

"I'm assuming there's no baby news," he says.

"Nothing yet. But your house is so tidy."

"Has she told you what she's going to call him?" He is grinning from ear to ear.

I nod vigorously. Nadia's baby is a boy; she found out at the scan as soon as we got back to England. She asked me what Mr. Williams's first name was and I told her

405

that, unfortunately, it was Maurice.

"Little Mo," she said straightaway. And that seems to be it; Little Mo he is.

"Her father's father is Mohammed," Mr. Williams says from the screen. "So it works all ways round. Little Mo." He shakes his head as if he can't quite believe it.

"How's Laurence?" I ask although I don't need to. I can see from Mr. Williams's face that everything is wonderful. I have "met" Laurence through the magic of the internet and he is not at all what I expected. He is larger than Mr. Williams and hearty. His voice booms around the shop from the screen and he laughs at the end of almost every sentence.

Rather than looking like someone who has lived in Venice for thirty years, Laurence looks like he's just jumped off his tractor. He needs a frenetic spaniel beside him, and to be marching off across the fields with a cocked gun in the crook of his arm. There is no denying that he and Mr. Williams are in clover.

"You must come, dear, Venice is so perfect at this time of year."

"There's not going to be much traveling for me for a bit. And my first trip is going to be to Hamburg to see Shota's new baby when it arrives. I might take Nadia and

Little Mo."

"You know where we are, Grace, when you need some R and R."

The purpose of this call is to check every detail of Laurence's address. We check the post codes and building number and I write them on the brown paper package in front of me with a fat marker pen. This parcel will be picked up by courier tomorrow and, the very next day, will be in Mr. Williams's hands in Venice.

Inside the parcel is Alan's violin. It is completely restored; it is ten times the violin it was before. Because of the terrible damage I inflicted on that poor instrument, I had to look long and hard at the construction. The wood of the neck — once it was cracked and I could see the inside of it — was unseasoned; it hadn't had the three years it needed after harvest to stop growing and to lose its suppleness.

The job was, for all Alan's skill as an amateur, a bodged one and the violin would never have been strong enough to survive a few journeys to orchestra in its case, never mind the next couple of hundred years in various players' hands.

Although I will never tell Mr. Williams, and he will never find out, the violin has little left of Alan's original work. On the outside it looks just like Alan made it, just as it always did, but inside it has been completely rebuilt by — I am reliably told — one of the best violin makers in the world. It is robust and firm, and it will hold for a long time. As a result of everything that happened to it, it is an instrument Mr. Williams can trust.

"I've put loads of clippings in there too for you. *Telegraph, Guardian, Times.* There's a ton of glossies as well, but they won't come out till next month." I have been interviewed by — it seems like — every journalist in Britain. It has been a long time since a Brit won a prize at Cremona, and everyone wants to talk about it.

"And the Revelation Strings? Have you signed up yet?"

"I actually have. Honestly. I'm going tonight." Revelation Strings is one of the orchestras Mr. Williams played in — now short one violin player. They're amateurs but the entry standard is high and most of the musicians are retired professionals or parents on a career break.

I have been to many of the Revelation Strings' concerts and the shop has sponsored their programs for years, but I didn't tell any of them that I played. Even just thinking about playing in an orchestra again feels like swimming, fast, to the surface of a sunlit pool. I will explode through the water into the daylight and my lungs will fill with air.

Behind Mr. Williams, Laurence shouts that it's *apéro* time and Mr. Williams signs off with a pretend air of irritation at the deep joy of being needed.

I have just days to finish my project. It is almost done.

When I came back from Paris, the first thing I did was to move the dusty cardboard boxes in the workshop. Behind them, hidden and almost cowering, were the tiny pieces of a cello that was never built.

I took the miniature ribs, the perfect scroll, and carried them gently to my bench. I blew the dust away from them with lips shaped like a moon, and a tear fell onto the wood as I kissed those missing babies goodbye. The salt tear softened the dust and the flame in the wood did its best to shine through the years of being tucked away.

The tiny, hollowed-out belly of this cello is the perfect shape; I am impressed at the job I did so long ago, at the craftsmanship. This wood will withstand being played with, explored; learnt on and leant on.

I have glued all these pieces together now.

The tiny cello, smaller even than a violin, is complete. I have varnished and smoothed, I have polished and tuned. The bridge and sound post are in place, and today I shall make the final adjustments to the sound.

This cello will be a companion to Nadia's baby until he outgrows it, and perhaps, one day, another baby will need it.

For now, his soft fingers will curl around the wood, will explore, will learn. It will be a wonder to watch.

There will be music again.

ACKNOWLEDGMENTS

Top spot goes equally to Phil McIntyre, who gave Grace her stake, and Jacqueline Ward, for her unparalleled ~~nagging and bullying~~ support and encouragement. Enormous debt to each of you.

Thanks to my family: To Colin for all the years of support (financial and otherwise), and to Joe, Ella, Lucy, Georgina, Mike, Lizzy, Charlie, Ruby, and Alba.

My team has been amazing — huge gratitude to all of you, in every territory, but especially to Tara Parsons, Isabella Betita, Isabel, Abby, Cherlynne, and everyone at Touchstone for all their fabulous work. The faith they had in this book, and the work they did to get Grace and her friends out into the world, has been invaluable. Enormous thanks to Jenny Bent in the US, Bastian Schlueck and Aylin Salzmann in Germany, and everyone else involved in my foreign sales. Thanks too to my editor in the

UK, Jo Dickinson, and the rest of her brilliant colleagues. There are so many worldwide cheerleaders for Grace and her friends and I'm grateful to all of you.

Most of all, thanks to the BEST AGENT IN ALL THE WORLD, Sarah Manning: Never have the words "without you none of this would be possible" been more apposite. Fact.

ABOUT THE AUTHOR

Anstey Harris teaches creative writing for Canterbury Christ Church University and in the community with her own company, Writing Matters. She was the winner of the HG Wells Short Story Competition in 2015 and was recently short-listed in the National Gallery short story competition. Her short stories have been widely published in anthologies and online. Anstey lives in Kent, England, and is the mother of singer-songwriter Lucy Spraggan. *Goodbye, Paris* is her first novel.

The employees of Thorndike Press hope you have enjoyed this Large Print book. All our Thorndike, Wheeler, and Kennebec Large Print titles are designed for easy reading, and all our books are made to last. Other Thorndike Press Large Print books are available at your library, through selected bookstores, or directly from us.

For information about titles, please call:
  (800) 223-1244

or visit our website at:
  gale.com/thorndike

To share your comments, please write:
Publisher
Thorndike Press
10 Water St., Suite 310
Waterville, ME 04901